TRUE BLUE

Connie Bailey

Dreamspinner Press

Published by
Dreamspinner Press
4760 Preston Road
Suite 244-149
Frisco, TX 75034
http://www.dreamspinnerpress.com/

True Blue
Copyright © 2008 by Connie Bailey

Cover Art by Connie Bailey
Cover Design by Mara McKennen

ISBN: 978-1-935192-25-1

Printed in the United States of America
First Edition
November, 2008

eBook edition available
eBook ISBN: 978-1-935192-26-8

Dedicated to John Hughes for directing "Pretty in Pink"

 **CHAPTER 1**

THE small placard to the right of the dorm room door read "Barclay, B." Heydn was in the right place; this was the room assigned to him, and the summer campus was almost empty, but he knocked anyway because that's how he'd been raised. After a count of ten, he knocked again. After another few seconds, the door opened with a jerk that telegraphed the occupant's irritation as clearly as the scowling face.

"What do you want?"

Heydn smiled broadly, his default response. "Hey. I'm Heydn Case. I'm supposed to be stayin' here." Heydn held up a piece of paper that was ignored. "Maybe I'm in the wrong place?"

It certainly seemed possible. Though the sign on this handsome brownstone building marked it as the senior boys' dormitory, the slight figure in the doorway was not so easily labeled. Long lank hair clung like black seaweed, partially obscuring androgynous features, and the baggy dark clothes gave precious few clues as to what was underneath.

Heydn's nervousness grew and his smile widened to a grin that he feared made him look like the bumpkin he was. "You're Barclay, right?"

"School hasn't started yet and anyway I'm not supposed to have a roommate."

"Well, I don't know about that, but this is where they told me to go at the office."

"And you always go where you're told to?"

"If I say yes, are you gonna tell me to go to hell?"

"As it so happens…yeah. Those would have been my next words. Shit! They told me I wouldn't have to room with anyone, those frelling 'nads."

"What do you suggest we do about this?"

"I'll have to…" Blue paused. "None of your business, but I guess I can't leave you in the hall until tomorrow morning. Well, what are you waiting for? Drag your crap in here."

Heydn snatched up his bags and hurried in, kicking the door closed behind him. "Where do I sleep?" he asked.

"If it isn't immediately obvious which bed is mine, you take the one on the left side…for tonight."

"Plannin' on switchin' bunks?"

"Is that what passes for humor where you're from? I meant that you'll only be here for one night."

"That would sure explain why you haven't bothered to introduce yourself."

The grouch finally looked Heydn in the face; his eyes were as dark as the kohl that outlined them. "My name's Brooke Barclay," he said. "If you ever call me that, I'll curse you and I mean it. If you have to call me anything, you can call me Blue."

"As in blue balls?"

"Yeah, that's right," Blue sighed. "Next time I'll be sure and give you a frame of reference that you can relate to. Now I'm going back to what I was doing before I was interrupted."

"Whoa. I didn't expect the welcome wagon, but I didn't expect the welcome tank, either."

"Expectation is the bitch mother of disappointment."

Heydn blinked. "I'm startin' to see your point. Why would I want a room with anybody that looks like a sixteen-year-old girl and talks like a snooty professor?"

"Is that a rhetorical question?"

"Am I bein' graded?"

"Every day of your life." Blue turned to the desk beside the right-hand bed and sat down in front of his laptop.

Heydn watched the other young man for a few seconds before he carried his bags to his bunk and pulled out a few items. "Bathroom?" he inquired.

Blue didn't look away from the screen. "It's the only door at this end of the hall. We share with this side of the floor. That's six other guys once school starts."

"Uh-huh. So what's the man-to-toilet ratio?"

Ignored, Heydn took his towel and toothbrush down the hall. The bathroom was large, with four stalls, four sinks, four showers, and one long urinal. It smelled of damp overlaid with the cloying perfume of scented piss cakes. Oddly comforting, it was the odor of every communal bathroom he'd ever been in. Even the mirrors over the sinks were the same, unframed and flecked with tiny specks of shaving cream, toothpaste, and God knows what else. Despite a recent haircut, Heydn himself looked just the same as he always had as he grimaced at his reflection: ordinary dark blond hair, standard blue eyes, the kind of features people generally meant when they used the term "all-American boy." He was nothing special in his estimation and so far, it seemed like the world agreed with him—especially his new roommate.

Heydn always hoped it would be different when his mom's job took the two of them somewhere new, but it never was. He was always roundly ignored by the popular kids at school who could smell his lack of money, and he wasn't quite weird enough for the outsiders, or geeky enough for the nerds, and he wasn't a stoner; he just didn't quite fit in anywhere. Resolving to go to sleep as soon as he got back to the room, Heydn finished up and turned off the lights.

Blue didn't acknowledge Heydn's return, but Heydn was caught by the glimpse he got of Blue's monitor. "Hey! That's 'Demon Armageddon'!"

"Yes, it is. My, what a big grasp of the obvious you have."

"Man, I love that movie. Have you seen it before?"

Blue deigned to shoot a withering glance over his shoulder.

"Dumb question, I reckon," Heydn said. "Oh, hey, I love this part comin' up."

"Of course you do. Everyone loves wing-burst." Blue referred to the scene where the Demon of the Red Desert revealed his true nature and enormous bat wings sprouted from his back in a sequence both gory and majestic.

"It's an amazin' blend of computer graphics, models, and prosthetic makeup. Still holds up after almost seven years."

"Are you some kind of techno-geek?"

"It's just an opinion. Forget I said anything."

"What did you think of 'Demon Resurrection'?" Blue asked as Heydn walked to the other side of the room.

"The title is 'Demon Regeneration'," Heydn replied. "Did I pass your little test?"

Blue snorted. "You've barely finished writing your name at the top."

"But I *can* write my name. That must count for somethin'."

Blue fought it, but he couldn't keep his sneer from dissolving into a grudging smile. "So you're not a troglodyte like ninety-nine percent of the inmates. I must have a medal around somewhere."

"That's okay. I'll settle for you treatin' me civil. I got nothin' against Goths, but I'd appreciate it if you'd cut me some slack with the attitude."

"I'm not a Goth, and I'd *appreciate* it if you'd stop categorizing me."

"Dude, you're dressed in black. Your hair is black, and you're wearin' some kind a vampire makeup. If you don't want people to think you're a Goth, you might wanna change one of those things."

"As if I care what people think."

"Okay. I get it. You are what you are, and if folks don't like it, that's their problem."

"Wow," Blue said in a monotone. "You really do understand me. I'm going to try harder to make friends, and I'm going to stop and smell the roses. How can I ever thank you for showing me the world from a different perspective?"

Heydn chuckled. "What a wiseass; I'm impressed."

"Yeah? Welcome to the world's smallest fan club."

Heydn's gaze went to the monitor. "Hey, check it out. Blood Maelstrom's first appearance on screen."

Both young men gave their attention to the screen and the next half-hour passed in near silence as they shared a common passion for the Amer-Asian blend of the sword-and-sorcery genre. Heydn's admiration was more for the artistic achievement, while Blue's had a strong streak of wish fulfillment running through it. However, both agreed that the "Rising Demon" series was killer and most definitely the best of the breed. When they discovered that they both loathed the anime series "Princess Demon Rose-Pink," there was no denying that a bond was forming. Blue resisted, trying to maintain his lone-wolf pose, but he couldn't deny how nice the camaraderie felt. Heydn was just happy to be making a friend so quickly.

Blue and Heydn spent most of the next day holed up in their room watching videos. Heydn was duly impressed with Blue's collection and shared his own small but distinguished library, brought back from his mom's frequent trips to Asia. They found they had more in common than they would have thought at first. At one in the morning, they were still awake, watching a compilation and polishing off the pizza they'd ordered for dinner several hours earlier. Though Blue rarely touched alcohol, he accepted the beer Heydn offered—his fourth, if anyone was counting. Both young men were very relaxed, leaning back on pillows piled against the side of Blue's bed, legs stretched out toward the laptop on the floor in front of them, enjoying the classic scenes strung seamlessly together and set to kick-ass music.

"Uh, hang on a second," Blue slurred as one sequence ended and another began. "You might not want to see this one. The guy that put it together is kind of...out there, you know? I only know him from the 'Net. He's a wizard with graphics and noise, but I don't interact with him anymore. Like I said; he's out there."

"Hold on! What is this? Hentai porn?"

"Um, sort of. Are you familiar with the term yaoi?"

"Yowie? Is that the boy-love one? I might've heard of it."

"Spare me the sarcastic tone. I'll skip ahead."

"That's okay; let it run. I'm not scared."

"You sure? It starts with the big-boob Hentai chicks, but that's supposed to be ironic, or something. It switches from cheesy nudes to..." Blue paused as a close-up of a very well-drawn cartoon penis penetrating a very well-drawn cartoon anus appeared on screen. "To some rather hard-core man-on-man action."

"You like this stuff?"

"I told you; someone sent me this."

"Relax. It's well-done, and I'm not afraid it'll turn me gay or anything."

Blue rolled his eyes. "So you do speak Neanderthal."

"Grow up."

"You grow up. I'm not the homophobe here."

"Would a homophobe watch this?" Heydn pointed to the monitor, which was now showing a pretty, pink-cheeked youth with cat ears and tail being ravished by a much taller male with luxuriant silver locks that floated weightlessly and twined around both figures. "What series is this from?"

"I don't know. Weird, huh?"

"I like weird," Heydn took a long drink of his beer. "And it's probably not very long, right?"

"Right," Blue agreed as he settled back. He was very aware of the sloppiness of his speech, the loss of motor control, and how close his left leg was to Heydn's right leg. He was convinced he could feel the body heat radiating from the other young man and did his best to ignore it, but his unaccustomed drunkenness had weakened his barriers. The best thing he could do at this point was scurry off to the bathroom, hope it was empty, and jerk off in one of the stalls.

"I don't care if you're gay or straight," Heydn said, gesturing toward the screen. "That's hot."

Blue concentrated on the images of an exquisitely beautiful man with long candy-colored hair sweeping an equally beautiful man into his arms in a passionate embrace. It was a stock yaoi image: the long-haired dominant seme was much taller than his lover and impishly forceful; the shorter, slighter uke, or catcher, had an expression approaching panic on his blushing face, but his body language was submissive. Blue had seen this played out many times, and it always affected him the same way.

"I gotta take a piss," he said, as he started to get up. The back of his hand brushed the seam of Heydn's jeans, and he quickly turned to apologize. The swift motion made his head spin and he sat back down with a thump.

"Whoa there," Heydn said softly. "You okay, Blue?"

Blue focused on Heydn's face, and then his gaze dropped along with his jaw.

Heydn grinned nervously, but didn't stop what he was doing. "Caught me with my hand in my pants," he said, giving his crotch a healthy squeeze.

"You're really…not self-conscious at all, are you?"

"I probably would be, if I wasn't so drunk. Don't tell me you never stroke it while you're watchin' porn."

"That would make me a liar. I hate liars."

"You're pretty drunk yourself," Heydn said. "Wouldn't bother me at all if you wanted to…"

"With you here? I don't think so."

"You never whacked off with a buddy?"

"I don't have…buddies."

"Not even when you first started jerkin' off?"

"Do we have to talk about this?"

"No, but I'd sure like to." Heydn paused, his fingers going still beneath the denim. "Unless you're too much of a homophobe."

"Are you actually daring me?"

"I could cluck like a chicken, but that seems a little childish."

"Look, if I wanted to, I would. I just don't want to right now." Blue's hard-on pulsed, mocking him.

"You sure?" Heydn stared at the crotch of Blue's jeans. 'Cause I thought that's what you were runnin' off to the bathroom to do. I was just lettin' you know that I don't care. Stay in the comfort of your own room if you want."

Instead of wilting under scrutiny, Blue's cock grew so taut that it ached like an empty stomach. He wanted to grab it and stroke it until he popped, but.... He'd never spoken this candidly with anyone about sex, much less masturbated in front of them.

"C'mon," Heydn lowered his voice, the deeper timbre vibrating along Blue's nerves. "We're just a couple a guys beatin' meat. Doesn't mean we're queer or nothin'. Happens all the time."

"Not to me."

"It does now."

Blue stared, hardly daring to breathe, as Heydn opened his pants. He couldn't take his eyes off Heydn's fingers, shuttling up and down the length of Heydn's cock. The curved shaft was a deep dusky rose and a bead of salty honey welled at the tip. The need to taste that bar of hard candy swelled in Blue like a rising bubble about to burst. Afraid of what he might do if his hands were free, Blue thrust one under his waistband and took hold of his dick.

"Feels good, huh?" Heydn said, running his thumb along the drooling head of his cock.

"Duh." Blue couldn't quite summon the daring to expose his hardness, but he spread his legs wider and kept his eyes on Heydn's crotch as he fondled himself. The sight of the other young man's busy hands was bringing Blue to the brink at an unprecedented speed.

Heydn watched the screen with heavy-lidded eyes, giving Blue the illusion of privacy. Pumpin' pink iron, as it had been called at summer camp, was something Heydn had learned from an older boy during his first stay away from home, and he still derived the most enjoyment from the act if he had an audience. Over the intervening years, he'd learned that lots of guys will whip it out and yank it if they think no one will find out, and he'd become adept at recognizing the most likely ones.

Blue wasn't anything like those guys. Blue wanted what Heydn wanted, even if Blue pretended to despise it: acceptance, approval, nothing less than unconditional love. Heydn knew how unlikely it was that either of them would get what they needed, but there was a lot to be said for a good climax shared with someone simpatico. He was also smart enough and self-aware enough to know that most eighteen-year-olds hadn't had this insight yet, and he kept it to himself. Being taken for a rube was bad enough; being taken for a cracker barrel philosopher would be worse. When people heard the twang in his voice, they automatically estimated his IQ as somewhere south of normal. If he said something intelligent, it surprised and confused them, and those people rarely react well if they feel you've tricked them. Sometimes, it was better to let folks believe what they wanted.

A sharp intake of breath drew Heydn's attention to his roommate. Blue was propped on one elbow, his head lolling back, the long hair falling away from a face caught on the cusp of longing and fulfillment. Heydn's hand moved faster on his shaft as Blue's eyes opened and fastened on his.

"Oh man!" Heydn groaned as a powerful jolt of pleasure lit up his spine like a carnival midway and blew fuses along all his neural pathways. "I'm cumming!"

Blue's mouth fell open as he gasped for air, wet pink tongue circling dry lips, dark eyes locked on Heydn's spurting cock. A soft groan shivered up from his chest as the muscles of his lower belly clenched in anticipation and then he was lifted up and held fast in the silken fist of his orgasm. He froze, a cry of ecstasy stuck in his throat, fingertips digging into the cushion as the galvanic grip eased and a warm wave flooded his every cell. Cradling his dribbling rod in a sticky fist, he sagged to the floor on his back, enervated and throbbing in time with the echoes of his best climax ever.

"Damn," Heydn breathed. "That sure was somethin' else. Got anymore a that yowie stuff?"

Blue didn't reply. He couldn't be bothered stringing words together just now.

"You can thank me later," Heydn continued. A snore answered him and he leaned over to look into the other young man's face. "Lightweight," he said, his tone affectionate.

Blue didn't wake when Heydn lifted him to his bed. Heydn closed the laptop and went to his side of the room. He used his underwear to clean up with and tossed them in a ball at the end of the bed. Sleep was not far off, but he had time to enjoy the hope that it might be different here after all.

FOR the remaining eight days of summer break, Heydn and Blue were nearly inseparable around the deserted campus of the Acton-Pierce Academy and Audley Cove, the nearby small New England town. They made forays for supplies, but spent most of their time in the dorm watching videos and gorging on snack food. Neither mentioned it, but both knew that at some point late in the evening, they'd be hauling out their dicks and whacking off. Blue's spit would dry up as he clicked the yaoi video file and settled back with studied indifference, not daring to look at Heydn until he was sure his new friend was engrossed. Only then would Blue slide a hand under his waistband and take hold of his hard cock. And he was hard more often than not these days.

He and the shy guy from Texas were a pack of two and the world was a lot less scary, a little smaller, and much, much brighter with a friend. Little by little, Blue lowered the shields of apathy and disdain he carried to show those who rejected him that he didn't want their approval in the first place. The first time Heydn reached over and covered Blue's hand with his, Blue had climaxed and managed to laugh at himself along with Heydn. After that, they weren't shy about giving each other a helping hand, in Heydn's tacky words. Emboldened, Blue leaned over one night in post-orgasmic bliss and touched his lips to Heydn's cheek, sliding sideways until he found his mouth. Heydn didn't even flinch. He grabbed Blue by the back of the neck and returned the kiss with enthusiasm. Blue didn't know for sure if he was gay or not, but given the way that kiss made him feel, it seemed like a safe bet. No matter what it was called, he was certain that he loved Heydn Case.

Each day deepened their friendship, and each night was filled with new wonders of sensual pleasure. And then fall fell on them. The venerable stone quadrangles of the campus with their neat squares of carefully tended grass around ancient oaks rang to the shouts of returning students greeting friends they hadn't seen all summer. The raftered halls echoed with the shuffling and scraping of baggage being dragged along the 150-year-old wooden floors. To Blue, it was the equivalent of an inimical alien invasion, a very real war of the worlds, but this year, he wouldn't face it alone.

CHAPTER 2

"WHO'S the lame?" Peyton Crane asked in his supremely bored drawl.

Blue sat one row down from Peyton and twisted in his seat to face the other young man. The auditorium was empty except for the drama teacher and one of his familiars fussing around with the curtain. "I still haven't developed psychic powers, Peyn," he said. "Which lame are you referring to? This school abounds in Abercrombie zombies. It makes me glad we wear uniforms most of the time."

Peyton, who fancied himself the Oscar Wilde of Acton-Pierce, tilted his chin up and regarded Blue down his aristocratic nose. "A pink polo shirt and a popped collar and you're suitably attired for anything from touch football at the clambake to a wedding reception at the yacht club. This fashion tip endorsed by Astor Q. Aldrich, Prince of Preppies."

"You should use that in your column."

"Is the school paper ready for such a controversial subject? I know Mr. Carmichael would approve it, but Drexel Ewing is editor this year."

"Gah! Drexel J. Crewing? How will you stand it?"

"I cleaned out my step-mom's medicine cabinet before I left home."

"Anything interesting?"

Peyton shook his head, his dyed red hair brushing the collar of his Anarchy Angels T-shirt. "She's into being a vegan now that she's playing hide the salami with her yoga instructor, and she's on this total health kick. Too dreary for words, and I had such hope for her when she married the gangster. But don't change the subject; who's the lame?"

Blue raised his eyebrows inquiringly.

"The slice of white bread I saw you walking out of the dorm with this ay em," Peyton elaborated.

"Heydn?"

"Great googly Gawd! His name's Hayseed? That's perfect."

"Hey...din."

"Is that supposed to be an improvement?"

"Shut up, Peyn. He's my roommate."

"How do you stand it?" Peyton said archly.

"He's all right."

Peyton leaned forward, looking into Blue's eyes in the scant light. "He's all...right?"

"That's what I said."

"Correct me if I'm wrong, but was he not wearing a pearl snap shirt...with short sleeves?"

"He makes it work."

"Oh, of course. It was obviously *meant* to go with those stone-washed jeans."

"Now you're exaggerating. His jeans are a little faded but..."

"They're *jeans*," Peyton said, as though jeans were synonymous with herpes.

"Whatever." Blue stood. "I'm going to have a smoke. If Mr. McIntyre ever decides to get started, tell him where I am."

"Behind the gym pulling a train for the swim team?"

"You wish."

"Do I ever," Peyton sighed.

Blue paused. "Does it ever bother you, I mean really bother you, that people think you're a homo?"

"I am a homo."

"Forget I asked."

Blue walked away and Peyton silently cursed his clumsiness. If Peyton had taken a moment's thought before replying, he and Blue might be in the middle of a deep and meaningful conversation right now. For nearly two entire years, Peyton had been gathering his courage to let Blue know how he felt, but somehow the time was never right. He wanted the moment to be absolutely perfect so that there would be no possibility of Blue rejecting him. Somehow, he had to make it happen before the end of the school year. After that, they'd be off to different colleges and the chances that they'd hook up would be slim to none. Peyton cursed himself again for blowing an opportunity to talk frankly about sex with Blue. "Real subtle, asswipe," he said in a harsh whisper.

BLUE leaned his shoulders against the mellow red-gold bricks of the auditorium's back wall and pulled his smokes from his backpack. Smoking was strictly forbidden on school grounds and that was all the reason Blue needed to light up. He drew in a lungful of smoke and blew it out slowly, watching the silvery blue wisps coil and twine as they slid up a bar of sunlight, his mind devoid of thought for a moment as his eyes followed the diaphanous dance. It was amazing how beautiful everything was, how serene he felt. He could contemplate the day that lay ahead of him without dread or utter disinterest. Even the descent of the preppie hordes was a mere nuisance now. He had a real friend, someone who understood him without trying, accepted him as he was. Life was good, and Blue knew it would only get better after they graduated and were considered adults.

Loud laughter jarred Blue out of a daydream and he peered around the corner of the building. The half-smoked cigarette fell from his fingers as he stared at the trio swaggering across the south quad. Allerton King and Logan Newcombe were two of the most popular guys at Acton, only Astor Aldrich had bluer blood. They were the stars of the track team and held positions in student government, but more importantly, their fathers and grandfathers and so on had attended Acton. They were politely snotty, card-carrying country club brats with the bland handsomeness of a pair of catalog models and the self-assured demeanor of young men who know the world is their oyster bar. They were everything Blue hated about Acton, and they were flanking Heydn, laughing and flipping their floppy blond bangs out of their blue eyes as they floated by on a cloud of privilege.

Blue's fingers curled, forming fists, fingernails digging into his palms. This wasn't right. How could Heydn talk to a couple of drones who probably never even heard of Demon Rising, much less Cub Love QT? It was unnatural, like a gazelle strolling with a couple of hyenas. The sight actually hurt his eyes, to judge by the stinging.

"Blue!" Peyton hissed. "Didn't you hear me calling you?"

Blue spun around and hurried toward the other young man. "Thanks," he said as he passed Peyton.

Peyton fell into step. "You looked like you were in some kind of trance."

"It's certainly possible."

"Whatever." Peyton let it drop. "Mr. McIntyre's in rare form after a whole summer to think up new and exciting ways to desecrate the classics."

"What did he rewrite this time?"

"One of Shakespeare's comedies, *As You Like It*. I anticipate a complete butchering of the bard's sublime verse, but I'll do my best to save it."

"You hate Shakespeare."

"No I don't; I just think he's been overdone."

"Remind me again why you're in the Drama Club?"

"I live for drama," Peyton said as he held open the auditorium door for Blue.

Mr. McIntyre spotted the two young men and hailed them effusively. They came down the aisle to join the group sitting in a semicircle around the man on the stage and the next hour should have passed quickly for Blue. Despite the drama teacher's stereotypical flamboyance and the self-absorbed nature of the actors, Drama Club was Blue's oasis at Acton. He had a flair for drawing, the way Peyton was good with words, and he had carved a niche for himself painting scenery. However, as Mr. McIntyre talked, Blue wasn't imagining how he would depict the Forest of Arden on backdrops. He wasn't listening to the teacher; he couldn't stop thinking about Heydn and the Gold Dust Twins. The mental image of the three of them striding along like trust-fund triplets would not leave his head as he plodded through the rest of his schedule. Orientation had officially become the longest day of his life. By the time it was over, all he wanted to do was get to the dorm and have a private talk with Heydn.

Blue groaned when he saw Peyton waiting for him outside the building. "What's up?" he asked.

"Orientation is over. It's time to get wasted."

"I'm not feeling it. Give my regards to the damned."

Peyton bugged his eyes discreetly. "This is a tradition. You can't blow it off."

"Doing something twice doesn't make it tradition."

"I don't want to argue semantics, or whatever. Go change into something inappropriate and meet me at the bus stop."

"I'm not going, Peyn."

"I'm not listening. If you don't go, I'll be on that bus by myself."

"What about Rolly?"

"Well of course Rolly's going. What's your point?"

"I don't want to argue either. Go away, okay?"

"It's your loss." Peyton feigned nonchalance. "If you'd rather be stuck in your room with Hayseed, that's..." He paused. "That's exactly what you're going to do, isn't it?"

"What?"

"Hang out with that meat puppet."

"So what?"

"I can't believe my ears. Okay, Blue. I'm going. Have fun playing Monopoly, or raiding a corporate slush fund or whatever it is those guys do for kicks."

"I'll go next time," Blue promised. "I just have something I have to do tonight."

"No big deal," Peyton lied.

"See you tomorrow then." Blue brushed past Peyton and hurried into the dorm. For some reason, it was important that he be there when Heydn arrived. This was a situation entirely unknown to Blue and he was operating on sheer instinct. He needn't have rushed. Heydn didn't show up for another hour, giving him plenty of time to think about what he was going to say. However, when Heydn walked in, or more accurately, bounced in, grinning breezily, all of Blue's carefully chosen words evaporated like dew in sunshine.

"You look like you had a good experience with Orientation," he said, instead of demanding to know where Heydn had been.

"It was good," Heydn confirmed. "This school isn't so bad. I have a best friend already. My teachers seem decent. And the track coach practically begged me to be on the team. I still have to try out with everybody else, but he more or less guaranteed me a spot."

"The track team. Really."

Some of Heydn's effervescence bubbled away. "Yeah. I was running to the gym and the coach saw me. It's just about the first time I've been picked for anything in my life."

"Didn't know you were into that stuff."

"Sports? Well, I'm not going to sit around watching the Super Bowl, but I like getting a little exercise now and then."

"Fine. It makes no sense, but whatever."

"Want me to order a pizza?" Heydn asked.

What Blue wanted was to reproach Heydn with his betrayal. What he hoped for was Heydn's ardent assurance that he was just goofing on the preppies.   What he feared was Heydn's immediate rejection following any confession of love Blue might make. "Pie sounds killer," he said. His next words were among the bravest he ever spoke. "So you going back out or you want to watch some vids?"

Heydn waggled his eyebrows. "Got any a that yowie stuff?"

That night, things progressed in a quantum leap when Heydn slid down and put his mouth on Blue's cock. Blue froze for a moment in surprise and then the sheer intensity of the sensation kept him immobile for several seconds more.

"You okay?" Heydn looked up.

"Hell yeah," Blue breathed. "Please don't stop."

"Don't worry." Heydn wrapped his lips around the head of Blue's cock again and slid down the full length. Sucking lightly, he raised his head and bobbed it again, repeating the motion with variations as he fondled Blue's tight balls. "How's that treatin' ya?" he asked, as he relinquished Blue's dick to give his sack a few licks.

"I can't believe how good it feels."

"How about this?"   As Heydn resumed sucking, he rubbed a fingertip against the sensitive skin around Blue's hole. The crinkled opening flexed and Heydn pressed firmly with his thumb.

"Shit!" Blue gasped as his cock squirted a powerful stream against the back of Heydn's throat.

Heydn smiled as he swallowed, and let Blue's shiny rod slide from between his lips. "That was fast," he said, leaning his elbows on Blue's knees. "Aw, don't pout. When I got my first blowjob, I shot off in the dude's eye on the first lick. So, you feel better now?"

Blue nodded lazily. "I want to suck you too," he managed to say.

"I don't know, rookie," Heydn teased. "Promise not to bite me?"

"Promise." Blue smiled, too content to take offense.

"Then how can I refuse?" Heydn stood and unzipped his worn jeans. Moving closer, he straddled Blue's thighs and put his crotch in Blue's face.

Reveling in the freedom he was granted, Blue satisfied his curiosity about the taste of cock, balls, and everything in the vicinity. His touch was inept but eager and adoring and he soon had Heydn trembling on the same precipice he'd so recently occupied. Heydn's thigh muscles shivered as his whole body strained toward release. He interleaved his fingers with Blue's thick shaggy hair, pulsing his fingertips against the other young man's scalp, gently guiding his rhythm. Blue took the hint, bobbing his head faster and shuttling his hand up and down the hard shaft. Heydn made a choked noise and thrust once, shoving his cock deeper as his climax roared and his seed erupted. Blue swallowed tentatively then gagged and sputtered, spraying Heydn with cum.

"Sorry," he said, dragging his sleeve across his mouth.

"Don't worry about it. Sex is supposed to be messy."

"I'm wiped."

"You really are a lightweight," Heydn said, as he pushed his jeans all the way off. "Is there anymore pizza?"

Blue toed the takeout box in Heydn's direction. "It's all yours," he said as he lifted his feet onto his bed and stretched out.

"Are we okay?" Heydn asked as he shut the laptop down.

"I'm fantastic," Blue drawled. "You?"

"Feelin' purty good."

"Goodnight then."

Heydn let it drop, said goodnight, and wolfed down two slices with half a bottle of lukewarm beer. It felt like everything had settled back in the right places, but it was hard to tell. Sometimes things developed hairline cracks and shattered later when you weren't expecting it. Tossing the empty box in the trash, Heydn went down the hall to piss before he went to sleep. Things would be all right. Blue was smart and respected the rights of others. Everything was fine. With these comforting thoughts, Heydn fell asleep.

CHAPTER 3

"THANK you. I'm really counting on you, Brooke."

The sound of his real name got Blue's attention and he looked up from his painting. Mr. McIntyre was smiling at him in a way that set off alarm bells. "Sorry, sir. My mind wandered for a minute."

"No need to apologize. I'm a right-brainer myself, you know. We creative types tend to get absorbed in our art."

Blue had no ready reply and continued to stare at the collar of Mr. McIntyre's sweater.

"I'll let you get back to work," the drama teacher said. "Thanks again. You're a trouper."

"God, I hope not," Blue said under his breath as Mr. McIntyre left the backstage area.

"Have you gone completely mental?" Peyton asked, as he emerged from behind a plywood tree.

"Years ago. Are you just noticing?"

"Do you have any idea what you just agreed to?"

"What?" Blue added a line of bright white to the edges of some leaves, trying to ignore the sinking feeling in the pit of his stomach.

"You just sat there nodding your head. You have no idea what McIntyre said, do you?"

"I was hoping that if I acted like I was really concentrating on my work, he'd get the hint and go away. The fact that you were hiding in the corner and I could still smell the blunt you were smoking might have distracted me."

"Thanks for reminding me." Peyton reached into the pocket of his uniform jacket. "Want a swat?"

Blue put his brush in a jar of water and stood up. "No. I'm quitting. Let's take that outside."

"Quitting? Painting, or smoking?" Peyton asked as they stepped out the rear door.

"Smoking."

Peyton looked around before he took a drag off the joint. "Why?"

"It bores me." Blue shrugged.

"A lot of things you used to like bore you now."

"I guess."

"Do you know how many times you've hung out with me and Rolly since school started?"

"Enlighten me."

"Twice in over three weeks. We used to smoke and shoot the shit down by the lake almost every night last year."

"I remember."

"So…what's up?"

Blue wished he could take a hit of the strong-smelling weed Peyton was inhaling, but he'd made a vow to himself. Smoking was one of the sacrifices he was making on the altar of love because Heydn didn't like the way his mouth tasted when he smoked. "I thought you were going to tell me what McIntyre said," he stalled.

"Oh, yeah! Let me tell you how thrilled I am that you'll be playing Rosalind in our little production of *As You Like It*." Peyton paused. "The look on your face is priceless."

"Ha ha, now tell me what he really said."

"I'm serious. Foster Keene dropped out of the Drama Club and you know he was McIntyre's go-to boy for all the female roles."

"So?"

"So...Drama Club needs a Juliet, and you're the prettiest."

"I thought her name was Rosalind."

"Just a figure of speech. This will suit your sense of irony. You'll be playing a girl playing a boy trying to talk another boy out of being in love with her."

"No, I won't. I'm going to McIntyre and telling him I'm not doing it."

"You mean you're not a trouper?" Peyton pretended shock.

"I'm not getting up on stage in front of an audience."

"I think you should."

"You're high."

"Yeah, but never high enough." Peyton pinched the coal off the end of the joint and dropped it into an inside pocket. "Seriously, though, you should at least give it a try for my sake."

"For your sake?"

"Well, I *am* the student director."

"I'll think about it, but I doubt I'll have time."

"Since when?" Peyton caught up as Blue began walking away from the theater. "No, wait; I remember. Since you contracted a mad crush on your cowboy roommate."

"Shut up," Blue mumbled, turning right on the walkway that led to the senior boys' dorm.

"Why so defensive? It's me, Peyton. You can admit you want his hot bod. He really does have a hot bod, damn it."

"Drop it."

"I just don't see what all the fuss is. Everyone gets impossible crushes. Just because you'll never..."

"Never what?" Blue stopped before he reached the hedge that bordered the quad. "Never kiss him? Never make out until it feels like my balls will pop? Never suck his dick? Which has a very nice flavor, by the way."

Peyton Crane looked genuinely surprised for the first time since Blue had met him. "Are you kidding me? You…and a meathead jock?"

Blue instantly regretted saying anything. "Look, it's personal, okay? And I don't want to talk about it right now."

"Wait! This is bad. If you were thinking clearly, you'd see how bad it is. You can't be with a jock; you just can't. It shakes my faith in an ordered universe."

"You always talk such shit, Peyn."

"I'm talking shit? Jocks don't fall in love with freaks, Blue. You know that."

"Heydn isn't like Allerton or Aldrich or any of those jerks."

"He's using you," Peyton said. "It's the only thing that makes sense."

"That's a really shitty thing to say."

"I know, but it's true. Look, man, I just don't want you to get hurt."

"Thanks, but you're wrong about Heydn. He's not a clone."

"No one ever listens to me."

Blue straightened the black-edged lapels of Peyton's charcoal gray school jacket. "That's because you're always talking shit."

Peyton dropped his eyes, focusing on the spiky ends of Blue's hair brushing the white collar of the Oxford shirt until Blue stepped back. The question of Blue's sexuality was answered, but he had tragically fallen prey to an interloper from the west with a tanned, gorgeous body. It wasn't fair. "He'll hurt you," Peyton said.

"Fine. You've proved you're a good friend. Now, please, just drop it."

"Whatever." Peyton yanked on Blue's loosened tie. "I'll see you around."

"Hey, Peyn? Don't mention this to anyone else, okay?"

Peyton mimed zipping his lips. "As long as you'll be in the play."

Blue sighed. "I'll try," he said, as Peyton sauntered away. Wondering how he was going to get out of appearing on stage, Blue went to his room and dragged a couple of plastic grocery sacks from the closet. A half-hour later, he was ready for Friday night with Heydn. A bottle of cheap red wine waited beside two plastic cups on the nightstand. Two folded blankets and some newly purchased pillows formed a nest on the floor. The laptop was programmed with the evening's entertainment and Blue was showered, deodorized, and hard. He was beginning to think he was going to have to jerk off at least once when his phone rang.

"Hey, Blue!" Heydn said. "Coach made it official today! I'm in! I'm runnin' in the meet next weekend!"

"That's…great. I'm really happy for you."

"Yeah, I can tell you're doin' cartwheels. I know this stuff doesn't ring your bell, but I wanted to share it with you."

"You could be doing that here. I've got…"

"Sorry," Heydn interrupted. "It's really hard to hear you over the racket."

"What is that noise anyway? It sounds like fireworks or something."

"Yeah, isn't that a hoot? Coach invited everyone to a barbecue and he's got a skeet range behind his house. I used to hunt quail with my dad back in Texas before the divorce."

"You killed birds?"

"Not very often," Heydn chuckled. "I was just a kid. I could barely hold up the shotgun."

"Well, this is fascinating, but I've got a bottle of wine to get through. Am I going to have help?"

"Oh...I don't think so. It looks like I'll be here for a while. Coach just put the steaks on and some of the guys are talkin' about gettin' in the pool."

Blue gritted his teeth a little harder each time Heydn used the word coach as if it were a name. "The guys?" he repeated.

"You know, the guys on the team. You sound kinda funny."

"I don't feel funny. Quite the opposite, in fact."

"I like you a lot, but I don't always get you."

"You've got that backward, too."

"You know, you sound kinda bitchy, like a jealous girlfriend."

"I don't have a frame of reference for that."

"Well, I just wanted to let you know that I made the starting team."

"Duly noted. Anything else?"

"I guess not. See you later."

Blue disconnected without saying goodbye. How could Heydn blow off Friday night? With track practice before and after school, Heydn and Blue both looked forward to Friday when they could stay up late and stretch things out. Blue wrapped his hand around the neck of the wine bottle; his need for Heydn was a fierce ache in his chest and behind his pubic bone. He didn't bother with a glass, but drank directly from the bottle, brooding and pretending to watch *Faust's Planet*. Neither the film nor the alcohol took his mind from his misery, but they did eventually lull him to sleep.

"Hey, Blue?"

Blue sat up suddenly and nearly knocked foreheads with Heydn. "What the hell?"

"Sorry. I couldn't tell if you were sleepin' or not."

"What time is it?"

"It's just a little before two. You are such a lightweight. "

"So you've mentioned. Why'd you wake me up?"

"I'm horny and I thought you might be too. Or am I too late?"

"You ditched me to hang with a bunch of muscle heads."

"Just for a few hours. If you don't feel like doing anything right now, that's cool."

"I'm drunk and half-asleep."

Heydn leaned in and Blue fell back against his pillow. "Let me wake you all the way up," he said, as he covered Blue's mouth with his in a long, tender kiss.

Blue was pressed into the mattress as Heydn threw a leg over his hip and rested some weight on him. Eagerly, Blue responded, wrapping his arms around Heydn and molding their bodies together. Nothing in his life had ever felt as good as being this close to Heydn, feeling his warmth and breathing in the smell of his hair. Then the closeness bred its predictable results and the kisses became deeper and wetter. They moved more insistently against one another as they squeezed and stroked the skin under their hands. Heydn grabbed Blue's hips and aligned their crotches so that their hard cocks rubbed together. Getting his other knee onto the bed, Heydn pumped his hips, dragging his dick across Blue's.

"Shit," Blue gasped. "Can we do this without the pants?"

"Right away," Heydn said, yanking his track pants down and kicking them off. He unbuttoned Blue's black gabardine uniform trousers and peeled them down. Tossing the soft pants over his shoulder, Heydn dove onto Blue, kissing his way along one shoulder and up Blue's neck until he found his lips. Slowly, Heydn flexed the muscles of his ass, rubbing his hard-on up and down Blue's cock and balls and the crack of his ass. Blue moaned and lifted his pelvis as Heydn rocked against him. "Hey," Heydn whispered against Blue's lips. "Any chance I could get in…just a little?"

Blue caught his breath as Heydn's hard dick slid the length of his cleft. "I guess we could try it."

"I'll just put the tip in," Heydn said, his voice thicker. "If you don't like it, I'll take it right back out. Promise."

"It's okay. I want to know what it feels like."

Heydn looked into Blue's dark eyes. "You're still drunk, huh?"

"Not that drunk. I'm loose, but that's probably a good thing, right?"

"Yeah, that's good. Now we just need something to use for grease." Heydn went to his side of the room and rummaged in the suitcase under his bed. "Sweet!" he said, holding up a short strip of lubricated condoms. He bounced the bed as he returned, moving between Blue's thighs and rolling a glistening condom down over his cock. Pinning one of Blue's knees to the sheets, Heydn leaned in to take his mouth again in an ardent kiss. When he pulled away, he pressed two fingers to Blue's lips until Blue sucked them into his mouth. With a moan, he drew his fingers from the warm wetness and trailed them up Blue's crack. Blue shivered as a fingertip prodded his hole and pushed in, but Heydn chose that moment to pinch his nipple through his T-shirt, distracting him. "You okay?" Heydn asked, wiggling the end of his finger.

"Uh-huh," Blue answered in a strained voice.

"I'm just gonna go a little deeper. Still good?"

"Well…" Blue took a deep breath and let it out again. "It's not thrilling me so far."

Heydn chuckled softly and Blue's groin pulsed with need. "It gets better. I'm looking for your prostate. You've heard of it, right?"

Blue shuddered and made a funny little strangled noise.

"Am I there?"

"Feels…good," Blue groaned.

Heydn grinned as he continued to rub the springy little bump. "Think you can handle another finger?"

"Go for it."

As Heydn worked another finger into Blue's opening, he bent his head and nuzzled Blue's cock. Sucking and licking, he made his way up and down the hard column of flesh as he corkscrewed his fingers in and out of the tight passage. Blue's toes curled and he clutched at the sheets as wave after wave of nearly overwhelming sensations washed through him, pain and pleasure inextricably mingled in a rising spiral.

"Oh yeah, you're ready," Heydn said, tasting pre-cum on the back of his tongue. Gently, he pulled his fingers from Blue's sheath and pulled Blue's ass up onto his thighs. "Man, my hands are shakin'," he said, as he took hold of his hard-on. Blue fidgeted as Heydn worked the tip in and Heydn put a palm on his trembling inner thigh. "It's okay," he soothed. "I'm stoppin'."

"No," Blue said, his eyes bright with tears. "Keep going 'til it feels good again."

Heydn gazed at the spot where his dick disappeared into Blue and a jolt of pure erotic energy sizzled along his nerve endings. Cupping a hand around Blue's sack, Heydn drew it up out of the way and eased in a scant two inches. Another bone-deep shudder wracked Blue's frame and he whimpered as Heydn pulled out. "Hang on, babe," Heydn whispered feverishly, pushing back in at a new angle. Blue flinched as the blunt head of Heydn's curved cock dragged across his prostate and a long moan purled out of his throat. His chest swelling with pride, Heydn took hold of Blue's hips and thrust delicately, withdrawing almost completely on each stroke, steadily increasing his speed, but never penetrating deeper than three inches as he worked Blue's prostate. When he let go of Blue's hip to stroke his dick, Blue came spectacularly, shooting cum as high as his rucked-up T-shirt.

"Oh God…oh God…oh God," Blue panted as Heydn seesawed lazily, squishing in and out of his clenching opening.

"Mind if I finish?" Heydn asked, and Blue shook his head, black hair lashing the white pillow. Heydn placed his hands on the backs of Blue's thighs and pushed until his full length was sheathed. His eyelids fluttered with pleasure as Blue's interior muscles tightened around his shaft, blindly trying to expel it. "So good," Heydn groaned and Blue clamped down intentionally, hugging the hard rod as it slowly churned. "So sweet."

A pleased little smile curved Blue's lips despite the discomfort of stretched tissues as Heydn began to thrust harder and faster. Heydn's loss of control was proof of how much he liked doing this with Blue, and

Blue urged him on in every way he could think of. Less than a dozen erratic strokes later, Heydn dug his fingertips into Blue's hips, buried his cock in Blue's sheath, and his seed spooled out in a joyful eruption. Shaking and gasping for breath, Heydn grasped Blue's cock and held it, squeezing lightly as the tremors of his climax began to subside. Blue felt as though he might burst at the seams, but the way Heydn's eyes were shining was worth the minor pain.

"That was incredible," Blue said.

"I thought I was going to explode," Heydn panted. "Fuck, you're amazing."

"You really think so?"

"Are you kiddin' me? Look at you. Look at those lips. I gotta kiss 'em."

Blue grunted as Heydn leaned in, bending him double to bring their mouths together. He didn't care how undignified it might have looked; he parted his lips and welcomed Heydn's tongue, wallowing in the aggressive affection. "I love the way you kiss," he said. "Can we lay here for a while and just be like this?"

"Sure, just a second."

Blue groaned as Heydn withdrew and the vague ache of emptiness replaced the too-full feeling. "You rock," he said, as Heydn found a way for both of them to fit on the single bed. With a long sigh, he settled against Heydn's smooth chest with Heydn's heartbeat in one ear and the early morning silence in the other.

"We fit good together," Heydn said against Blue's forehead. "Thanks for…you know…for letting me put my cock in you."

"It was my pleasure, believe me."

"It's not like I've got a lot of experience, but that's the first time a guy ever came while I was inside him. I knew it was possible, but you're my first."

"I don't have to tell you that you're my first, do I?"

Heydn's soft chuckle rubbed against Blue's ears. "Not mad at me anymore?"

Blue snuggled closer. "Not at the moment."

They fell asleep that night in the same bed and though Heydn was up and gone before Blue stirred, Blue took it as a very good omen. Peyton was wrong. Heydn truly cared about him. Moreover, Blue was no longer a virgin. He had undergone a rite of passage and come through unscathed.

CHAPTER 4

"THAT look on your face has become intensely annoying," Peyton said.

Blue looked up from the lines he was trying to memorize. "I didn't know I had any particular look on my face."

"You look like a cow that's eaten too many magic mushrooms."

"Nice."

"I wish I had a mirror. Oh wait, I do." Peyton took his fingers from the keyboard and reached into his pocket, producing a compact.

"Just describe it to me."

"I just did, but I'll elaborate. You look smug and complacent and higher than the cost of gas."

"I think I'm insulted."

"I think you're penis-whipped."

"Shut up, Peyn."

"Why is your sex life off limits as a topic?"

"It's private."

"We're guys...ostensibly. Let's act like guys. Let's swear, and spit, and brag about our sexual conquests while we see who can piss the farthest."

"I thought you were supposed to help me get into character. I doubt Rosalind is a spitter."

"That's funny. I can't wait to see you in a dress."

"I spend half the play as Ganymede, a dude."

Peyton smiled. "Shakespeare for stoners. Far out."

Blue smiled back. "How's the reporter gig going?"

"I take it you're not reading the paper. Well, I just had a little item vetoed. The article addressed the rampant sexual harassment on this campus."

"What? How much did you smoke before you wrote it?"

"I'm serious. I'm sick and tired of being singled out for abuse because of my sexual orientation."

Blue put his head down. "You didn't."

"Of course, I did. You know what it's like to be singled out because you're different. I thought you'd understand."

"I understand, but I don't think a school newspaper is the place to talk about it."

"What would you do?"

"If I truly felt harassed, I'd go to one of the deans."

"That's very easy to say, but some of these guys have very heavy daddies."

"I know you don't want to hear this, but I think it's a good thing the piece was pulled. All it would have done was brought you more grief."

"Man, what happened to you? You used to be a rebel."

"I just choose my battles a little more carefully now, that's all."

"Oh come on, Blue. We both know when you changed. The second that jock started slipping you the salami, you…"

"Peyton," Blue interrupted, "I like to think of us as friends, but if you keep talking, I don't think I'll be able to…think that. That didn't come out right, but you know what I mean."

"Okay, I'll shut up. It's your business. My business is to turn you into a Shakespearean heroine."

"Thanks, Peyn."

"Don't thank me. The costume will make or break you."

"Do I get to have big boobs?"

"I'm surrounded by sexists."

"Yeah, I know. Can I take these pages with me? We've been at it for a while and I've got other stuff to study."

"Don't you mean you need to bone up? Sorry. I'll try harder."

"You know, that one was actually funny. I'll see you tomorrow."

"You'll stop and see Buckles for a fitting on your way out, yes?"

"Okay," Blue sighed, picking up his backpack.

"I'd go with you, but I don't want to peek until it's finished."

"You're truly strange." Blue smiled over his shoulder. "I admire that."

Blue found Buckley Caldwell, who represented half of the wardrobe department, and held his arms up while a gown was slipped over his head. When he was covered, he dropped his uniform trousers and let Buckley pin up the high waist of the Empire-style dress. Peyton had persuaded Mr. McIntyre to move the setting of the play to the Napoleonic era, mainly to spare Peyton the sight of anyone he knew wearing tights. Blue didn't care. He was in a dress either way. Mr. McIntyre could call it a costume all he wanted, but it was a dress, and as liberated and unusual as Blue thought he was, he was still glad when he could take it off. There were too many people walking around backstage, and he wasn't in character. As soon as Buckley pulled the gown back off, Blue headed for the dorm. Heydn should be through with practice by now.

THE scrawled note on Blue's pillow read "Meet me at The Monks." Blue didn't take the time to change clothes. He dropped his backpack on his bed, stripped off his tie, and shoved the sleeves of his button-down shirt above his elbows. Not once on his way across campus to the lake did he feel the ground beneath the soles of his shoes. His imagination had preceded him to the clump of shoreline boulders everyone referred to as The Monks. He could already feel the warmth of Heydn's arms around him and his stomach jitterbugged at a mental image of Heydn pushing into him, filling him, taking him along on a ride to the stars. They'd done it two more times since the first one and it was better each time. In between, they'd found it hard to stay away from each other and started meeting in out-of-the-way places to steal a few melting kisses and roughhouse gropes, separating reluctantly, breathless and as hard as marble, counting the minutes until they could be alone in their room. As soon as the door was closed and locked, they leapt at each other as though bent on kissing, licking, or stroking every centimeter of flesh as quickly as possible. Neither could get enough. Even when sprawling sated in the afterglow of climax, it took no more than a meeting of their eyes to reignite the perpetual smolder. Blue wasn't surprised that Peyton thought he looked stoned. He felt high all the time.

"Hey!" he called, smiling as Heydn straightened from his slouch against one of the big rocks.

Heydn grinned and gestured for Blue to follow him around the group of boulders to the tiny cove on the other side. Bounding up the rocks of the miniature promontory, Heydn led the way to the sheltered inlet. They went a little farther along the pebble beach until they reached a line of trees that screened them from view. Heydn flopped down on his back and held up his arms to Blue. Blue settled atop Heydn, thrilled to find the other young man as hard as he was. Slowly, looking into Heydn's blue-gray eyes, Blue pulsed his hips, rubbing his cock against Heydn's.

"Oh, man," Heydn's groan turned into a chuckle. "It's like one of your yaoi vids where the hero is compelled by a curse to have hot sex with one of those ridiculously good-looking boy creatures. I just haven't figured out where you're hiding your ears and tail. Hey!" Heydn grinned as he got hold of Blue's cock. "I think I found your tail after all."

"I love the way you touch me," Blue said in Heydn's ear, as the other young man stroked his shaft through the layers of his trousers and briefs. "Like I belong to you."

"I'm just after your lucky charms."

Blue laughed and ducked his head to kiss Heydn. He knew they didn't have the time or supplies to do everything he wanted to, but he wasn't leaving here with an aching hard-on again, and neither was Heydn. With a little maneuvering and a lot of snickering, they managed to get their mouths on each other's cocks and a feverish contest began, both doing their utmost to make the other cum first. The competition ended in a dead heat with Blue climaxing as soon as he tasted the first drop of Heydn's seed. They lay for several long moments, faces buried in damp crotches, mid-afternoon sun warm on their bare skin as the water of the lake lapped against the rocks in a ceaseless lullaby.

"Crap," Blue said as he yawned. "I can't fall asleep."

Heydn sat up and fastened Blue's pants for him. Blue returned the favor and then they were rolling entwined over the grass, laughing and wrestling. Heydn landed atop Blue and pinned the other young man's wrists to the ground above his head. Panting and grinning, they gazed into each other's eyes for a moment suspended outside time, and then Heydn rolled off Blue.

"We really gotta go," he said, as he got to his feet.

"Right. I got carried away. Again. I swear I lose my mind when we're doing it."

"Yeah, me too." Heydn stared across the lake as if lost in the thought.

"I'd like to stay here all day, but I guess we should go," Blue said hesitantly.

"Yeah." Heydn picked up his jacket and followed Blue back along the shoreline. He still appeared to be deep in thought and didn't speak again until they could see the chapel spire above the trees. "Hey, I might be late tonight. After my meetin' with Coach, the team is supposed to watch some video about motivation or some such shit."

"Thanks for letting me know. I'll start without you."

"Asshole."

"Definitely one of my finer features." Blue smiled impishly. "Shall we go?"

"I was kinda waitin' for you to go first."

"Right." Blue leaned toward Heydn for a kiss, but the other young man recoiled.

"What are you doin'? We're too close to campus."

"Sorry. Don't freak out; no one saw us."

"But they could've. Damn it, Blue; I like messin' around with you, but if anybody found out...it wouldn't be good, you know?"

"I know." Blue sighed. "Why are people such asshats?"

"I don't know, but I wanted to ask you something."

"Go ahead."

"Somebody told me they saw you wearin' a dress."

"Yeah. It's for the play. Can you believe McIntyre and Crane talked me into it?"

"You told me you were goin' to be in the play, but you didn't say you were goin' to wear a dress."

"I know; it's so humiliating, but it's just a costume."

"So you're goin' to do it?"

"Well...yeah. I said I would and it'd be kind of hard to find someone else now. What's wrong?"

"I just can't believe you're goin' to go out in public dressed like a girl. It makes my skin crawl."

Blue frowned. "Are you fucking with me?"

"Flamers creep me out," Heydn said. "I don't care if somebody's gay or not, as long as they keep it to themselves. It's the ones that parade around in wigs and makeup that gross me out."

"I'm not doing it because I like it."

"Then don't do it."

It was a few seconds before Blue answered. "You want me to quit the play?"

"I just don't want to be humiliated."

"What's it got to do with you?"

"You're my friend. If you start sashayin' around in high heels, people are gonna draw conclusions."

"You're kidding, right? I doubt most people on campus would even suspect we're friends. It's not like they see us hanging out or anything."

"Our schedules are different and anyway I've never seen you at a track meet."

"Why would I go to a track meet? To watch a bunch of jocks trying to prove they have the biggest dick? Not my idea of a good time."

"No, you'd rather be doin' a drag show."

"That's not fair."

"Sorry, but that's how I feel. Look, I don't want to get into a big nasty fight. Let's just go and meet up later."

Blue nodded. "If that's what you want, but we're going to have to talk about this again."

"Later, okay? I'll see you tonight."

"Okay." It took all of Blue's willpower not to touch Heydn, but he let him go without another word or gesture. When they were together again in their sanctuary, they'd settle this, but only after slaking their hunger for each other again. Blue's smile came back as he began daydreaming about the night to come.

"GAWD! There it is again," Peyton said. "I'm really starting to hate that smug smile of yours, Barclay. Now stop spacing out and say your next line."

"What a flake," groaned Rhodes Vaughn, the young man playing Orlando.

"Do we need a break?" Peyton asked loudly, looking around at the other members of the Drama Club.

"I could use one," Blue sighed.

"All right." Peyton waved his hands in a shooing gesture. "Take five, people."

Rhodes rolled his eyes. "Whatever princess wants, princess gets."

"Jealous?" Blue asked.

"I'm righteously pissed," Rhodes shot back. "I'm at rehearsal on time every day with my lines memorized and I'm tired of you disrespecting me and the rest of the cast. If you're committed to this production then get your head out of your ass and start working with the rest of us."

"You practiced that speech, didn't you?"

"I knew I'd get some smartass answer." Rhodes turned to Peyton. "You piss me off too, Crane. Why should the rest of us suffer so your boyfriend can be a star?"

"I was going to ask Mr. McIntyre the same thing about you," Peyton replied.

"Go suck donkey dong."

Peyton exchanged a glance with Blue. "Did you tell Rhodes about my trip to Mexico?"

Blue cracked up, drawing a furious glance from Rhodes. "Lighten up, Vaughn. Peyn didn't insult you and it was funny."

"Just because I like the theater doesn't mean I'm a fag like the two of you. From now on, keep your homo humor to yourselves."

"I'm not the one that brought up donkey dongs," Peyton drawled, arching his eyebrows.

"You can both go to hell," Rhodes said as he turned away.

"We don't have time to visit your mom right now," Peyton called after him. "We've got a play to put on. Be back here in five minutes."

Rhodes shot him an over-the-shoulder bird as he hurried off.

"What a dick," Blue said.

"Yeah, but he's right. I know you aren't thrilled to be doing this, but could you try a little harder?"

"Am I that bad?"

"Mostly you're distracted, but today you're somewhere else entirely."

"Sorry, Peyn. I've got stuff on my mind."

"I'd ask, but as we know, I'm not allowed to talk about Saint Heydn."

"Why is everything so damned complicated?"

"That's just the way the world is. I know that's not a good answer, but…"

"I wish I was older," Blue interrupted. "I wish I could live somewhere with Heydn where no one knows us, somewhere where no one cares if we want to kiss in public."

Peyton took a deep breath and let it out, trying to ease the sharp pain in his chest. "I hear San Francisco's nice."

Blue laughed as Peyton hoped he would. "Now all I have to do is convince Heydn."

"What? He won't jump for joy at the idea of running off to Queer City with you?"

"Like I said, it's complicated."

Peyton made a frustrated noise. "This is killing me. I don't know why you can't see what's going on. You used to be so sharp and now you're just…" He made the noise again. "And the worst part is that you won't even let me talk about it."

"I won't listen to you talk trash about Heydn."

"Can I say just one thing?"

"If you want to take that chance, then go for it."

"I have to." Peyton paused. "I care about you, Blue. I'm not some jock who'll let you suck him off ten times a day and not speak to you in public."

"Heydn talks to me. We just have different…"

"I wasn't finished," Peyton interrupted. "I was going to make a prediction. As soon as Heydn thinks there's a possibility of his new friends finding out he likes dick, he'll drop you cold."

There was a short silence while Blue pulled Rosalind's gown over his head and draped it carefully over a chair back. When he turned to face Peyton again, his face was devoid of expression. "I know you don't like Heydn," he said softly. "I understand that, but if you really cared about me as much as you say, you wouldn't hurt me like this."

"What am I supposed to do?"

"Be happy for me."

"It won't last."

"Then be happy for me for as long as it lasts."

"I can't. I know he's going to hurt you a million times worse and it's driving me mental that you can't see it. You're not a tough guy, Blue. When he dumps you, you'll be…"

"I don't want to hear anymore. If you can't stand to be around me, don't force yourself, but we still have to do this play together."

"Don't do this," Peyton said. "I'm still your friend."

"Are you? I'm beginning to wonder about that."

"Don't. I'm probably the only person on this campus that truly cares about you."

"Gee, thanks."

Peyton started to speak again, but Rhodes and the others returned and rehearsal resumed. There was a marked difference in Blue's performance. He spoke his lines *to* Rhodes instead of at him and, by the end of practice, the atmosphere backstage had undergone a subtle change. The unspoken resistance to Blue's presence thawed and over the next few nights, he was gradually accepted as a bona fide member of the club. No one invited him over for tea, but he was taken seriously and suddenly the bickering bunch of actors was a cast.

Blue decided not to raise the issue with Heydn, preferring to deal with it when, or if, it came up again. It was so much nicer to spend his time with Heydn goofing on the computer or fooling around on the bed, or the desk, or the floor. The sex was always spectacular no matter where they did it and it always left Blue with a warm glow that lasted for hours. In this light, it was easy to believe that things would sort themselves out, that Heydn would see what phonies his jock pals were, that the play would go unattended by a single student, that he'd wake up in a world where no one cared who you chose to love.

Heydn put in more time on the track as he won more races. The coach was impressed by his speed and his lack of attitude and began grooming him for a slot on a good college team. Other students began referring to Heydn as a track star. Kids he didn't even know smiled and said hello to him in the hallways. He was invited to parties and trips to the shore. He still felt a bit like an imposter, but he was getting better at simulating the bored insouciance of his teammates. Allerton King had more or less taken Heydn under his wing and Heydn was grateful. He was enough of a realist to see that Allerton was probably just trying to keep his iron control over the track team, but that was motivation that Heydn could understand and cope with. In return for being a team player, Heydn got the admiration of the student body and the feeling that he finally belonged somewhere.

So Blue and Heydn were both happy, each in his own way, as a round and golden October rolled to an end. Cross-country season began and Heydn trained for hours and miles, collapsing at night, but somehow finding the energy to respond when Blue went down on him. Blue had started on his costume for Halloween and the project easily filled the time between the end of rehearsal and Heydn's arrival at the dorm. If either was bothered by small changes in the other, neither was willing to risk rocking the boat for something trivial.

Peyton, the only other person that knew about the relationship, watched both young men from a distance, waiting for the inevitable wreck and hoping there would be enough of Blue left to salvage. That's why Peyton was waiting for the track team to come out of the locker room after practice the day before Halloween. He intended to follow Heydn, but he was spotted first by two junior members of the team.

"Crane!" Sloan Spalding exclaimed. "What's a cock-jockey like you doing so close to the gym?"

"Cock-jockey," Copeland Graham hooted. "That's a good one, Skip."

"Yes, very clever, Skip," Peyton drawled. "And I'm here in my capacity as a journalist."

"Yeah, that sounds a lot better than 'I was trying to cop a look at some wang.'"

"If I was trying to get a look at your wang, I would've brought my microscope and tweezers."

Copeland laughed again and Sloan glared at him. "Sorry, Skip. It was funny," Copeland said.

"Really, pencil dick?"

Copeland subsided, his overbite disappearing in a sullen pout. Sloan returned his attention to Peyton.

"I don't care what you're doing here, dicklick. If I catch you outside the locker room again, I'll kick your ass all the way to the bus stop. This ain't the Village, Tinkerbelle."

"I can go anywhere on campus that I want to."

"And I can kick your ass if I want to." Sloan moved closer, shoving Peyton back into a shrub.

From the corner of his eye, Peyton saw Allerton King exit the locker room followed by Logan Newcombe and Heydn Case. "If you hit me again, I'll go to one of the deans," he said loudly.

"Your word against mine."

"There are witnesses," Peyton said, glancing to his right. Heydn's gaze brushed his and then traveled on to Allerton who was in the middle of telling a joke that required humping motions.

"I don't see any witnesses. Do you see any witnesses, Cope?"

Copeland shook his head. "I was never here."

"Now I'm going to have to repeat myself," Sloan told Peyton. "I hate repeating myself.

Peyton had an answer to that, but Sloan's fingers around his neck cut off his air. He was propelled backward through the hedge and slammed against the wall.

"If I ever see you here again, you'll get more of the same," Sloan said and let go of Peyton.

Peyton slid down the wall, gasping for breath. It had happened so brutally fast that his head was reeling. Putting his hands on his knees, he fought the urge to retch.

"Come on, Cope," Sloan said. "I think he got the message."

"Fuckin' A, Skip!" Copeland slapped the other young man on the shoulder and they sauntered off.

When Peyton's stomach stopped shaking, he came out of the bushes. Sloan and Copeland were just turning the corner of the building, headed in the direction of the cafeteria. Across the athletics quad, he could see Allerton, Logan, and Heydn ambling along. "Assholes," Peyton whispered fiercely. He blinked furiously at the tears that scalded his eyelids, refusing to let them fall. A silver-spoon thug called Skip should not be able to make him cry. Maybe he didn't have the muscle mass to retaliate in kind, but he ought to be able to think of a way to strike back.

CHAPTER 5

HEYDN surveyed Blue's sleek frame decked out in the handmade Halloween costume and shook his head. "That is seriously sexy, but you're not actually goin' to wear it outside this room, are you?"

"I spent way too much time on it not to show it off. Don't get all torqued though; nobody from school will see me."

"Where are you going trick-or-treatin'?"

"There's this club in Eastburn, the next town over from Audley. They have this annual costume contest. Me and Peyton had a blast last year."

"And you think you'll win wearin' that?"

"I don't expect anyone to even recognize who I am. I don't care. I'm doing this because it's fun."

"I recognize you," Heydn smirked. "You're Kat Kaoru, the hero's fox demon sidekick from *Goblin Market Patrol*."

"How do they come up with those names?" Blue rolled his eyes.

Heydn smiled and shook his head again. "Okay, the ears really are cute, but are you wearin' a black sport bra?"

"Also known as a uni-boob," Blue answered. "It was the closest thing I could find to Kaoru's top."

"Well, I can see your stomach all the way down to the top of your bush and every time you raise your arms your nipples show."

"And?" Blue said coyly.

"I want to jump on you and fuck you through the mattress."

"What's taking so long?"

"I'm makin' a point. Is this club you're going to like a gay bar?"

"Yeah. It's fun."

"Look, if I feel the overwhelmin' urge to pounce on you, I'll bet a room full of horny old homos will feel the same way."

"It's not that kind of place."

"Sure it isn't," Heydn scoffed. "Old queers prey on the kids just comin' out, if you didn't already know."

"Who told you that?"

"Nobody had to tell me anything, okay? Let's get back to your costume."

"I'm not sure the costume is the issue."

"Oh no," Heydn said melodramatically. "Do we have issues?"

"It sounds like it."

"All I'm sayin' is that I don't like the idea of you walkin' around in public in a pair of black tights."

"They're leggings and I'm wearing a jock strap."

"Yeah, but it's on the outside and it's painted silver."

"Pretty good, huh? I cut up different brands of soda cans and hot-glued the colored pieces on to make the dragon skin."

"Yeah, it's really good, but it's just a tad too much."

"Too much for what?"

"Well, when did you turn into such an exhibitionist? When I met you, you seemed like the kind of guy that spent all his time at the keyboard. Now you're in the play and wearin' a dress, makin' out with Rhodes Vaughn, and goin' to bars lookin' like a slut."

"You take that back. Kat Kaoru is not a slut. He's a fox demon."

"Who'll have sex anytime, anywhere. He's a slut."

"I'm sorry to hear you say that since you inspired the costume. That day by the lake, I thought you were comparing us to Kaoru and Hiro."

"What day by the lake?"

It was a moment before Blue answered. "I guess that doesn't matter. I thought you liked Kaoru and that's why I made this costume."

"Well, I told you how much I like it. Wear it all you want in the room."

"I'm wearing it to Giddie's tomorrow night."

"Why are you bein' so stubborn? You know how I feel about stuff like that."

"What stuff?"

"You know, gay stuff."

"I am gay, Heydn. Everything I do is gay stuff."

"No. We're just messin' around because there aren't any girls here. When we graduate, we'll be adults and we'll stop doin' kid stuff like this."

"Where is this coming from? I've never heard you say anything like that before."

"We never really talked about it." Heydn shrugged. "I figured you felt the same way."

"Liar." Blue felt like he was choking and barely got the word out.

"I can see you're gettin' a little emotional. Maybe we should stop talkin' and do what we do best."

Blue was chagrined by the wave of heat that melted his groin. "I don't want to," he heard himself say, his voice hollow and distant.

"Bullshit." Heydn grinned as he hooked a finger in the waistband of Blue's leggings and pulled him closer. "You always want it."

"No, I really don't."

Heydn's mouth covered Blue's, his tongue sliding between Blue's lips. Blue whimpered as Heydn squeezed his ass cheeks, pulling them apart. There was no disguising how hard Blue's cock was as Heydn pressed him against the closet door.

"See, you want it as much as I do."

"Maybe, but that doesn't mean I'm going to do it right now."

"You're the one that got me hot with this costume."

"Seriously, Heydn. Get off me."

Heydn stepped back, holding up his hands. "Okay. Settle down. I'm not gonna rape you."

"That's not remotely funny."

"You're damn right it isn't. What would you have done if it wasn't me pawin' at you? What if I was some nasty-ass child molester? You look about twelve in those ears."

"So now your excuse for being a dick is that you're afraid I'll get raped?"

"This is useless," Heydn sighed. "It's like talkin' to Mom when she's on the rag. Nothin' I say is right."

"You're hanging out with those preppie jerks so much that you're starting to think like them."

"Hey, the track team is my shot at a good college. Not everybody has an education handed to them on a silver platter, you know. I can't afford to turn up my nose at an opportunity."

"You would sell your soul to be part of the country-club set? What a hypocrite."

"Look who's talkin'. You hate bigots, but you are one. You're prejudiced against rich people."

"I'm prejudiced against a system that perpetuates a privileged lifestyle for a bunch of snobs that consider themselves anointed by God. I can't believe you'd buy into that."

"It's easy to reject somethin' when you've had it all your life. You grew up with nannies and ponies and skiing in Switzerland. So I don't think you have the right to judge me."

"I'm not..." Blue paused. "All right, maybe I am judging you a little."

"Maybe a little," Heydn snorted. "Look, I don't want to lose what we have, but I have to know that you won't screw up my chances by flouncin' around in a dress, or whatever. What do you say?"

"How can I promise something like that? I have to keep my word to do the play, and any one of a million things could ruin your chances at a scholarship. You're not being fair."

"Blue, I know you know that life isn't fair. I don't want to make this decision, but I can't risk losin' my spot on the team. And believe me; if Coach thought I was gettin' it on with a dude, he'd kick me off so fast I'd be dizzy for a week."

"You're better than this."

"No, I'm not. This is who I am. If I'm not good enough for you..."

"I love you," Blue blurted out.

Heydn's shoulders slumped. "I was afraid of that, but it makes this a little easier, since I'm doin' it for your good too. I'll grab my gym bag and sleep on Allie and Logan's floor tonight. Tomorrow, I'll ask to be moved."

Blue remembered vividly the day he'd opened the door to find Heydn standing there. He recalled how annoyed he'd been that he wasn't going to have a private room. "You don't have to do that."

"Yeah, I do. I can't stay here with you knowin' how you feel. That'd just be mean." Heydn stuffed a sweatshirt into his bag and zipped it up. "Well...I guess I'll see you around.

The door opened and closed before Blue's paralysis broke. He ran into the hall as Heydn started down the stairs. Heydn's name rose to his lips, but he heard voices downstairs and didn't call out. He watched as Heydn descended until the other young man was out of his sight, a stray beam of light glinting off his dark blond hair as he disappeared. Numbly, Blue went back to the room.

The room looked completely normal. There was no sign at all of the tragedy that had just occurred. If Blue sat down on the bed, he could pretend that Heydn hadn't come home yet. He could do it over and somehow keep Heydn from leaving this time. Pulling the headband with attached ears from his head, he turned it in his hands as he replayed the argument repeatedly trying to figure out how things had gone so wrong, so fast.

ALLERTON KING swung open the door of his dorm room. "Case," he said. "What are you doing here? Wow, that was rude. Come on in and tell me what brings you to my den of iniquity."

Heydn held up his gym bag. "I was hoping you and Logan would let me crash here tonight."

"Logan's not here. Bennington Kaplan's staying at her dad's place and he called her up. She drove down and he sneaked out to meet her at the highway. I figure right about now, Bennie's playing a solo on Logan's skin flute. So why do you need a place to stay?"

"I don't really want to get into it."

"Hey, no prob. Anyway, I think I have a pretty good idea why."

Heydn swallowed. "You do?"

"It's Barclay, right? The little fag tried to grab your package or something."

"Um, something like that."

"Gross! Did you wake up and find him sucking your dick?"

"No!"

"Chill, bro. You don't need to say anything more. I'm just glad you got out of there. Listen, Logan won't be back before morning so you can take his bed tonight."

"Thanks, Allie," Heydn said, as he stretched out on top of the covers.

"No sweat. Fey little fags like Barclay make me want to puke. Why the hell would anyone dye their hair jet black and wear eyeliner at this school? You know what I think? I think queers like him want to get beat down. Why else would they advertise what they are?"

"I don't know."

"I'm no prude. I know things happen when you pen up a bunch of horny young guys. I've got nothing against whacking off with a best bud while you're watching a little tasty porn, but guys like Barclay like that shit. They get off on sucking dick. I bet Barclay would take it up the ass and beg for more dick." Allerton chuckled as he turned off the light. "Maybe we should pull a double shift on him before you move your things out. Bet he'd love to have a dick in his ass and one in his mouth."

"I'm really tired," Heydn said.

"I'll let you get to sleep then, but I have to ask one question just to satisfy my mind. You let him blow you, didn't you?"

"Why would you think that?"

"He's got those sweet dick-sucking lips. I bet they look really good wrapped around a fat cock. Hell, I might even let him blow me if he was blindfolded."

"Blindfolded?"

"Well, I don't want him getting a good look at my junk."

Heydn smiled into the darkness. "Go to sleep, Allie."

"I'll try, but now I've got a hard-on from talking about blow jobs."

"Then get Logan to take care of it when he gets back."

"Fuck you." Allerton threw a sneaker across the room.

FEELING like a complete coward, Heydn waited until he knew Blue was at rehearsal before he went to collect his things from the room. He moved in with a junior named Judson Lenoir who was on the second-string track team. Jud idolized Heydn and the rest of the starters so when Allerton told him to give Heydn his privacy, Jud spent as much time as he could away from the room. It was easy for Heydn to avoid Blue, to keep his head down over his books and his eyes on the finish line. It was harder to keep thoughts of Blue from creeping into his head. He often had to put a hand down his pants and beat off just to relieve the pressure. His body missed Blue's the way grass misses rain. That's all it was, he told himself. He was having some kind of withdrawal. That's what made his guts ache like he'd been scooped hollow with a giant melon baller. He'd never had sex that good in his life and naturally, he missed it and craved it, but he wasn't going to give in to it. His mom couldn't support him forever. He was eighteen and it was time he started taking care of himself. It would be a proud moment when he could look her in the face and tell her she didn't have to worry about his college tuition. As he headed for track practice, he reminded himself to call her that evening when it would be morning in Tokyo.

Heydn jogged to the gym, meeting Allerton and Logan out front before continuing on the eleven-mile run around the lake. They returned to their starting point and went inside to get some water. Across from the water fountains, a group of art students was painting banners for the weekend meet. Among them, Heydn saw Blue's shaggy head and he quickly looked away. Logan noticed and nudged Allerton surreptitiously. Allerton spotted Blue and made a point of strolling past the painters on the way out.

"Great work, guys," Allerton said. "Thanks for showing your school spirit."

"Yeah, this is really pretty," Logan added. "You used lots of colors."

Heydn looked straight ahead as they passed by, flinching when Allerton touched his elbow.

"Barclay's really talented. That's why we let homos enroll at Acton. Some things just need a woman's touch, you know?" Allerton said loudly enough for everyone to overhear.

Logan laughed loudly and hurried to catch up with the other two. Heydn pretended he hadn't heard and walked faster, almost jogging by the time he reached the door.

"Hey, what are you running away from?" Allerton asked as he followed Heydn outside.

"You. That was really rude. Those kids painted that banner for us and you spit in their faces."

"Wow, did it really come across like that?"

Heydn turned to stare at Allerton's boyishly handsome face, dropping his gaze from the vivid blue-green eyes to the saddle of freckles across the bridge of his nose. "Don't play innocent. You know what you did."

"Oh, so what. So I cracked on a couple of art geeks. They practically invite that kind of thing."

"What's up your butt, Case?" Logan asked as he joined them.

"He's afraid we hurt the delicate feelings of the art club."

Logan laughed. "Maybe he still has feelings for his old boyfriend."

Allerton chuckled. "Is Logan right? Are you mad at me for talkin' trash 'bout your woman?"

Heydn tried a smile, hoping it didn't look as false as it felt. "Yeah, that's right," he said. "Don't make me bust a cap in ya."

Logan and Allerton cracked up, and the three of them walked away together. The tense moment passed, but the roiling in Heydn's stomach didn't. He begged off having dinner at Coach's with the rest of the team and went to the school physician for some antacid. After taking the tablets he was given, he got horizontal and tried to sleep, but it was a long time before he could clear his mind.

"WHAT a complete and total dick," Peyton said.

Rollins Morehouse nodded. "I wish I had the guts to say something at the time, but I just sat there like everyone else and kept painting."

"Don't be too hard on yourself, Rolly. The implied threat of physical pain is a powerful deterrent. And thanks for telling me."

"Well, you and Blue don't seem so close these days, but I thought you'd like to know."

"You did well, dear boy. Blue's pissed and will only talk to me about official play business, but I'm not going to let him be destroyed by a bunch of junior frat boys."

"What are you going to do?"

"Hell if I know, but I'm going to do something. Those preppie assholes get away with everything and I'm tired of it."

"We can't go against the natural order."

"Why not? And what's so natural about it?"

Rolly shrugged pudgy shoulders. "It's just the way it's always been."

"I'm tired of that too."

"I think the power of being student director has gone to your head."

"Don't be absurd; that's my style. Why do you keep fidgeting?"

"I got a piercing and it still feels weird."

"How did I not know about this?"

"You've been kind of unavailable this year with the paper and the play and stalking people."

"Have you missed me?"

"Actually, yes."

"Then I'll make more of an effort to spend time with you."

"Do I have to play Nancy Drew with you?"

"Do you want to?"

Rolly grinned. "Yeah, I do kind of."

"Then we'll definitely be spending more time together."

CHAPTER 6

"HEY, do you have a light?"

Blue turned from the view of the nighttime campus spread out below to see who'd joined him on the roof of the theater. Astor Aldrich stopped beside him and held a cigarette to his mouth. Blue flicked his lighter, the sudden brightness throwing Astor's aquiline nose and full lower lip into stark relief.

"Thanks," Astor said. "I quit this summer, but this play is driving me to smoke again."

"You're really...regal as the duke," Blue said. "When you're in character, it's hard to believe it's you under the fake mustache."

"Thanks again. You're really good as Rosalind."

"Yeah, right."

"I mean it. When Peyn first brought you in, I wanted to smack him, but you're really good."

"So I make a good girl, huh?"

"Not exactly. I don't think you could pass for a woman, if that's what you mean. But you do say the lines with the feelings I imagine Rosalind would have, especially when you're speaking as Ganymede."

"Um, thanks," Blue mumbled.

"I mean it. Some people at this school might give you a hard time because of the way you look, but I think it's cool that you do your own thing."

"Give me a break. You're like the most conservative guy here. Isn't your dad on the board of trustees?"

"He's the head, but so what? Does that make my opinion less credible?"

"No, I was just surprised."

"Cool. Sometimes I get pissed off about the whole Prince of the Preppies thing. I didn't get a choice about the family I was born into, you know."

Blue hesitated a moment before he replied. It was so strange to be having a normal conversation with Astor Aldrich. "I was coerced into acting, but the more I do it, the more I like it."

"Wait until you hear your first applause and know those people are clapping for you."

"Um, I don't know if I'll like that part or not. Don't tell anyone, but I'm terrified of performing in front of an audience. Peyn seems to think I'll go on autopilot once the play starts, but I don't know."

"We're doing enough rehearsal that you should be able to play this role in your sleep."

Blue smiled. "It's kind of fun in a weird way, playing a girl playing a boy."

Astor smiled back. "I like the way you put that. Hey, do you drink coffee?"

"I used to live on black coffee and cigarettes."

"My sister sent me some Kona beans from Hawaii. Why don't you stop by my room sometime and I'll make a pot?"

"If I have time," Blue said vaguely, and headed for the door to the stairwell. "We should probably get back before Peyn comes looking for us."

"Yeah, I guess we should. I just wanted you to know that it's fun working with you," Astor said, as he followed Blue down the short flight of stairs.

"Yeah, you too."

Blue looked over his shoulder and smiled as he reached the bottom of the steps. Peyton looked up from a sketch of a new background for the rustic cottage and his heart felt like the fish must feel when the hook sinks in deep. Then Astor emerged from the stairwell and Peyton's fist clenched, crumpling the piece of paper. There was no mistaking the interest in the look the other two young men exchanged, even if they didn't realize the significance of it. Peyton thought his head might literally explode. It was too rich that Heydn would throw Blue away just so Astor Aldrich could pick him up. That was like going from the trailer park to the palace in one swoop. And once again, Peyton was on the outside looking in.

"Hey, Blue," Peyton said, as practice broke up. "Can you hang around for a minute?"

"Sure." Blue put his backpack down and waited until the rest of the cast was gone. "What's up? Do you have some new pages for me?"

"No, I want to apologize. I acted like an ass when you were with Heydn. I understand why you had to pull back from me, but if you ever wanted to be friends again, I'd be honored."

"You know, it's pretty cool that you never said 'I told you so.'"

"Why would I do that?"

"Because you were right. You tried to warn me and I shut you down."

"I would rather have been wrong than see you hurt."

Blue's head drooped, but he didn't speak.

"I'm sorry," Peyton said.

"Thanks. I thought I was going to die for a couple of days, but when that didn't happen, I got on with what I had to do. As long as I'm in class or at rehearsal or painting scenery, I'm okay."

"I wanted to be there for you, but I didn't think my sympathy would be welcome."

"I appreciate you leaving me alone. And I appreciate that you tried to save me, but honestly, I was so in love with him that I wouldn't have listened to anyone."

"I can't blame you for wanting to be loved."

Blue's chin dropped to his chest and his hair fell forward, throwing his face into shadow. "I loved him so much. I gave him everything and he…"

"You don't have to tell me," Peyton said.

Blue took a deep breath. "He said he outgrew me, not in so many words."

"That son of a bitch. So you were just an experiment to him?"

"That's what he said."

"That dumb son of a bitch. I almost feel sorry for him. He threw away the best thing that will ever happen to him and he's going to spend the rest of his life in denial."

"You're actually cheering me up."

Tentatively, Peyton reached out and squeezed Blue's shoulder. "Just don't cry," he said. "Not only will you look like a raccoon, but I'll start crying too and that's not a pretty sight."

Peyton's kind touch undid Blue. His tears started to fall and he couldn't seem to turn them off. When Peyton put gentle arms around him, Blue put his head on Peyton's shoulder and let the weeping run its course. Tenderly, Peyton rested his head against Blue's and held him until his sobs abated.

"Thanks," Blue said, as he pulled back. He wiped at his face with his sleeves and looked at Peyton. "How bad is it?"

Peyton tried not to laugh, but couldn't hold it in. "I'm sorry," he said, with his hand over his mouth. "But you look hilarious. Here." He held out his compact mirror.

Blue looked at his red-and-white-blotched face and swollen eyes ringed with smudgy black and a smile broke out. "What a mess."

"If we were doing Macbeth, you'd make a great witch."

"I've missed your smart-ass remarks."

"You don't have to. It's not like me to beg, but I'd really, really like us to be friends again."

"Me, too."

A short silence was broken by Peyton. "I really missed you at Halloween. The party at Giddie's was off the rails. Twelve people came dressed as a dragon."

"I was planning on being there, but I had the big fight with Heydn and I just didn't feel like going out after that."

"Can I ask what the fight was about?"

"My Halloween costume, supposedly. He thought it was too slutty."

"Asshole."

"I don't know. I think he's just…confused about a lot of stuff."

"Are you actually making excuses for the jerk that broke your heart? Don't you hate him?"

"I want to, but I just can't. I'm mad as hell sometimes and sometimes I hurt so much that I just want to disappear, but I don't want revenge or anything like that."

"I would. I'd want to hurt him as bad as he hurt me."

"I don't want to hurt Heydn."

"You're too good," Peyton said. "Hey, it's not too late. Why don't we catch the bus and go get a smoothie or something?"

Blue shook his head. "Not tonight, okay? I'm tired and I still don't have scene three by heart."

"Another time then."

"Let's plan on it after rehearsal tomorrow."

"Fine," Peyton said casually, as if it didn't mean the world to him.

Blue shouldered his backpack and headed for the exit. "See you tomorrow."

"Hey," Peyton called as Blue pushed open the door. "What were you going to be for Halloween?"

"I made a Kat Kaoru costume. Combat mode."

Peyton swallowed, picturing the skintight black clothing on Blue's lithe frame. "Ears and all?"

"Of course. I said combat mode, didn't I?"

"I'd love to see it sometime."

"You might have to wait for a year, unless an anime convention comes up within traveling distance."

"Maybe we could have our own con at Acton."

"You're a lunatic," Blue said, as he went out the door. "I like that."

Peyton basked for a few moments in the warmth of the renewed friendship and then went to collect his laptop and master script. Mr. McIntyre had been very good about leaving the student production to the students, only dropping in a couple of times a week to check on their progress. Peyton was enjoying the chance to stretch his creative impulses and the unlimited access to the theater department's resources. He'd been joking with Blue about holding an anime convention, but the idea lodged in his brain like a piece of grit in an oyster. By the time he reached his dorm, the notion had grown layer by layer into a concept for a play. Flipping open his laptop, he began to type.

CHAPTER 7

"ARE you ready?" Peyton reached out and adjusted one of Blue's cascading ringlets.

"This wig is heavy and hot."

"It's definitely hot," Astor Aldrich said as he arrived backstage.

"Eat me," Blue said automatically, as he'd responded to everyone's comments on his first appearance in full costume and makeup.

"Have you got a spoon?" Astor replied.

"Where's your hat?" Peyton asked before Blue could speak again. He loathed it when Blue and Astor got into one of their little banter sessions. The sexual tension made him want to scream at them to just go get a room and get it over with. In the interests of cast morale, he was not above using his power as director to nip the repartee in the bud. If anyone were going to be witty, it would be him.

"Buckles is putting another feather on it," Astor said, smoothing his false mustache.

"Stop touching that," Peyton barked. "And you," he turned to Blue. "Leave the wig alone."

"It seriously itches under there."

Peyton took a mechanical pencil from an inside pocket. "Here. Use this to scratch with. Carefully."

"It's just the dress rehearsal, Crane," Astor said. "It doesn't have to be perfect."

"Yes it fucking well does, Aldrich."

"Easy, Peyn," Blue said. "It's too early to blow a fuse. Wait until the third act at least."

"It would just be nice if everyone in this production shared my commitment to excellence."

Astor snorted. "You should be on stage."

"Why would I want to act when I can use actors as my puppets?"

"Are you trying to piss me off?"

"We're all nervous," Blue said. "I'm going to go get some water and look at my first lines again."

"I guess I'll go see if my hat's ready," Astor said.

"Good," Peyton said. "Sorry I got sharp with you. I just want this play to be a success."

Astor nodded. "No harm done. I'll be right back."

Peyton asked Blue to bring him a bottle of water and went to peek around the curtain at the token audience of stage crew, musicians, and Mr. McIntyre. He took a few calming breaths and reminded himself not to make the mistake he'd made with Heydn. Bad-mouthing Astor would only drive Blue away again. Maybe Blue would never love Peyton the way Peyton loved him, but Peyton would go on loving him anyway and he still wanted to be part of his life. If that meant he had to smile occasionally through a cute story about something Astor said or did, then he would swallow that bitter pill wrapped in the sweetness of Blue's company.

The dress rehearsal went well with only a few minor hitches that could easily be fixed before tomorrow night. While most of the cast was getting out of costume, Blue hurried out the rear exit and lit a cigarette. Looking up at the stars, he blew a long plume of smoke in a relieved sigh.

"I thought you quit that nasty habit."

Blue's blood froze in his veins and it took a monumental effort to turn his head and look at Heydn. "What are you doing here?" he asked, his lips cold and stiff.

"Takin' a shortcut to the lakeshore path." Heydn paused. "God, look at you."

"I'm in costume for the dress rehearsal."

"I figured. How can you humiliate yourself like this?"

"What do you care?"

"Of course I care. Do you think I can just stop carin' about you? What kind of person would that make me? I just can't be with you."

"Then what I do is none of your business."

"There are people at this school that might make it their business."

"I can't believe you're threatening me." Blue blinked, willing his tears not to fall. "All I've wanted since you walked away from me is a chance to talk to you, to try and find a way to get you back, and now that we're talking, I remember why you walked out and I know that nothing I say will make a difference."

"That's because you're smart." Heydn paused and finally looked Blue in the eyes. "We had a lot of fun together though, didn't we?"

Blue drew breath to answer, but was interrupted by a shout from the south corner of the building.

"Hey, Case!" Logan yelled again. "Allie's here. Move your ass."

"Guess you'd better get that ass moving," Blue said, throwing down his cigarette. He suddenly couldn't stand the taste and ground it out viciously with the toe of his dainty slipper.

"We're goin' on a run."

"So run."

"Case, what the hell are you doing?" Allerton shouted. "No time for a hand job, bro. Come on!"

Blue opened the back door, gathering his skirt with one hand. He stepped on the hem anyway and stumbled, going down on one knee and banging his head against the doorframe.

"Sorry, Case," Allerton called. "I didn't know you were getting a blowjob. Take your time."

Heydn hurried to where Allerton and Logan stood as Blue got slowly to his feet. "Come on; let's go," he said.

Allerton led the way past the barn to the beginning of the bridle path. "Just what were you doing back there?" he asked as they started jogging.

"I forgot a couple of things when I switched rooms."

"Things like your sperm bank?" Logan snickered.

"Shut up, Logan," Allerton said. "Did you remember to invite Heydn to the party?"

"It slipped my mind."

Allerton smacked the back of Logan's head. "Here's what's happening," he said. "Logan's girlfriend is back at her daddy's place and he's off skiing with some bunny that's about a year older than her. She's understandably pissed and needs help destroying his liquor cabinet. She'll pick us up, but she can only take four and I've included you."

"Thanks. Sounds like a blast."

"Bennie's going to try and get some of her friends to show up, too," Logan said.

"Finally, some pussy." Allerton patted his crotch. "Wake up, boy; the bitches are coming."

"Just remember; they're not all nymphos like Bennie."

"Are you really going to marry her?"

"Hell, yes. First of all because of the aforementioned nymphoism. Secondly, because Bennington Shoshanna Kaplan is richer than I am, and third, because it will royally piss off my mom."

"Nymphomania," Heydn said.

"What?"

"The condition is called nymphomania, not nymphoism."

"I don't give a shit," Logan said. "I've got a lifetime pass on the debutante ride."

"Do you love her?"

"Yeah, I guess. She's hot in a Jewish princess kind of way. Nice tits. She throws a hissy once in a while, but I figure I'll buy her a diamond bracelet or whatnot and the meat curtains will open again."

"I can tell you have a lot of respect for her and women in general."

Allerton slapped Heydn on the back. "Hey, bro. No teasing of the Logan. He's not equipped to fight back, you know?"

Neither are your victims, was on the tip of Heydn's tongue, but he didn't say it. "Maybe he needs to go back to the shallow end of the pool then."

Allerton laughed. "You're a pistol, Case, as my daddy would say. You should meet him sometime. He'd like you."

"I'd like to meet him."

"Yeah? Then you'll have to come home with me for Thanksgiving. Unless you already have plans."

"No plans. I'd love to have Thanksgiving with your family."

"Then it's settled. I'll call Mumsy and tell her to tell the staff to put out another plate."

"What about me?" Logan asked.

"You can come if you want to, but I thought you were going to Cancun with Bennie."

"Guess she'd be pissed if I blew her off."

"Probably," Allerton said. "And you're starting to lag already. Come on; let's pick up the pace."

The three young men increased their speed and conversation ceased until they finished the run. Heydn said goodnight to the other two and headed for his dorm. He felt pretty low for not standing up for Blue, and even lower for not giving him a hand when he tripped, but to offset his guilt was the promise of a Thanksgiving holiday with the King family. He would finally walk into one of the mansions of the people his mom worked for and as a guest, a friend, an equal.

"HEY, whoa," Astor said, as Blue brushed past him. "Peyton's been looking for you."

Blue kept walking toward the dressing room and Astor followed. The rest of the cast had finished changing and Blue and Astor were the only two in the room.

"Are you going to the dress rehearsal party?" Astor asked as Blue shucked his gown and put it on a hanger. "I hear there's free pizza."

"I'm not hungry. I'd just like to change in peace, okay?"

"You want me to go?"

Blue leaned on the dresser, covering his face with his hands. "I don't know what I want," he mumbled.

"You were very good in rehearsal tonight." Astor paused. "Can I help you get your makeup off or something?"

Blue looked up when Astor stopped next to him. "Could you just get the wig off?"

"Sure." Astor concentrated on removing pins, giving himself time to absorb the shock of seeing tears in the other young man's eyes. He had the nearly overwhelming urge to put his arms around Blue and hold him close. "Man, Thomas put this thing on to stay," he said, just to be saying something.

"Tell me about it," Blue said as he began slathering cold cream over his stage makeup.

"You don't look like you're up for a celebration."

"Not really. I'm kind of tired, in fact."

"Not surprising. Dress rehearsal is a very stressful experience. You need to unwind, but maybe being around a bunch of people isn't the best idea."

"No, I'd rather just go home and lay down."

"Can I get you anything to make you more comfortable?" Astor asked as he put the wig on a stand. "Aspirin? Caffeine?"

The thought of a hot cup of something sounded very appealing. "I wouldn't mind some coffee."

"Then come with me and I'll brew you a cup of heaven."

"You got a new bag of beans," Blue guessed as he finished cleaning off the last of the pancake.

"From Sumatra. Very dark and smoky flavor."

"Sometimes you sound like you're forty years old...and doing a commercial."

"You take that back." Blue smiled and Astor felt like a cloud shadow had passed letting the sunshine return. "Come on," he said. "Get dressed and let's get out of here."

The two young men left the building by a side door and no one saw them except Rolly, returning to look for Blue again at Peyton's behest. Blue and Astor kept walking past the sidewalk that would take them to Mr. McIntyre's on-campus cottage where the pizza party was being held. They went up the path to the dorms and Rolly went back to the party.

"You got a mini-fridge," Blue said as soon as they entered Astor's room.

"Yeah. My mother thinks I'm going to starve here and keeps sending me food."

"That's nice."

"It'd be even nicer if she sent things I like now, instead of things I liked when I was ten." Astor went to the table that held his coffeemaker and ground some beans. In a few minutes, the aroma of fresh coffee permeated the room. Astor poured two cups and brought one to Blue. "Have a seat," he said, sinking down to the floor.

Blue sat cross-legged and sipped his coffee. "Good," he approved.

"You want some cookies or something? Mom sent a box of assorted shortbread."

"Sure."

Astor opened a large tin and Blue picked out a couple of cookies. The rich, buttery shortbread melted in Blue's mouth and was the perfect complement to the dark-chocolate taste of the coffee.

"Really good," he said as he finished a third cookie.

Astor smiled. "You've got some crumbs on your upper lip," he said, leaning close.

Blue froze as the other young man put a hand on his shoulder and brushed their lips together. The soft warmth felt good, but he couldn't quite believe that Astor Aldrich was kissing him. Never during the time they had rehearsed or the few times they'd hung out had Blue ever suspected that Astor was gay.

"Sorry," Astor said, as he pulled back. "But at least I got those crumbs."

"Astor…"

"It's okay. I just don't turn you on, that's all."

"Are you going to give up that easily?"

Astor cocked his head, gray eyes gleaming in the scant light. "Are you daring me?"

"Would it help?"

"I'm no good at this. Just tell me if you want me to kiss you or not."

"I'd like it if you kissed me again. I'll be ready this time."

"I'm glad you're not freaking out. I thought maybe you'd be into it, but I wasn't sure."

"I thought the whole campus knew I was gay."

"I don't listen to gossip." Astor grinned. "Well, I do listen to gossip, but I don't give it any weight."

Blue leaned forward and closed the gap between them. As gently as he preferred a first kiss to be, he covered Astor's mouth and moved his lips subtly, as if tasting an elusive flavor. Astor opened his eyes as the kiss ended and smiled at Blue.

"That was really nice," he said, as he cupped a hand at the back of Blue's head. "My turn."

Blue put his arms around Astor as the other young man took his lips, feeling the tip of Astor's tongue and opening to him. Their tongues slid together and heat filled Blue's skin like helium in a balloon. Abruptly, he couldn't wait to sample all of Astor.

"Whoa," Astor said as Blue grabbed for his crotch. "You in a hurry?"

"I'm very horny. Is that a problem?"

"Hell no!" Astor wrapped his arms around Blue and kissed him again as they groped each other. Lips and tongues and fingers were everywhere, moving feverishly, seeking pleasure in every nook and cranny. Mostly they found it and things came to the predictable conclusion very quickly. "Damn!" Astor breathed, as Blue let Astor's sated cock slide from between his lips. He stopped stroking Blue's shaft, slippery with the seed Blue had squirted a few seconds ago. Pulling the other young man up into his arms, Astor fell back onto the futon. "Damn," he said again.

"So it was good?" Blue asked, arranging himself so he could pull his underwear up.

"Hell yes. Hey, what are you doing?"

"Just covering up a little."

"Well, don't, okay? I want to look at you."

Feeling a little self-conscious, Blue left his briefs where they were, hobbling his ankles, and lay back. Astor propped himself on one elbow and gazed down at Blue. Lightly, he traced the curve of Blue's softening cock with one finger and stirred the dark curls of his pubic patch. Blue repressed the urge to laugh when Astor stuck a fingertip in his belly button, but when the fingers trailed over his ribs, he couldn't hold it in. "I'm a little ticklish," he confessed.

"You're beautiful," Astor said.

Astor's words were sweet, but Blue wanted to hear them spoken in someone else's voice, a voice with a hint of Texas twang. When Astor burrowed a hand between Blue's thighs and worked his fingers into the crack, Blue fidgeted. Astor took the hint and stopped.

"Sorry," he said. "Didn't mean to trespass."

"No big deal. I just don't feel like doing anything else right now."

"Hey, I'm not complaining."

"Should we just be hanging out like this? What about your roomie?"

"Rhodes will stay after the party and help Mr. McIntyre clean up. We've got plenty of time."

"Peyn thinks Rhodes has the hots for Mr. McIntyre."

"Rhodes is as straight as the straightest thing you can think of, but he is a bit of a brown-noser."

"I never would have guessed you were gay."

"I'm not sure I what I am, but I sure like doing what we just did."

"You may be the sanest person I know."

"You've got to stop insulting me, or I won't do this again." Astor gently stroked Blue's cock.

"I should go," Blue said, sitting up. "Peyn's feelings will be hurt if I don't check in with him before I go to bed."

"What's the deal with you two?" Astor said, moving over so Blue could climb off the futon.

"What do you mean? We're friends."

"You're not fuck buddies?"

Blue looked up from fastening his trousers. "What?"

"I can see by your stunned expression that the answer is no."

"Why would you think that?"

"It's not that far-fetched. You're two gay guys isolated in the wilds of New England and he's got the biggest crush on you."

"Get out. He does not."

"How could you not notice?"

"Peyn likes older men. He's having some kind of kinky thing with a junior law partner at his dad's firm. His dad has been having an affair with his mom's best friend for years and his mom is doing it with her yoga instructor. His family is pretty wiggy."

"Mine's boring. Would you like to meet them?"

"You make it sound like so much fun."

"Seriously though, I'm going home for Thanksgiving. Want to come with?"

"I don't know. I usually stay here during holidays. I like Acton when there's no one around."

"Think about it, okay?"

"I will." Blue looked around to see if anything had fallen out of his backpack. "I should go. It's after eleven."

"Can we do this again sometime?"

"No guarantees, but probability is high."

"I won't be pushy, but I really want to be with you again."

Blue stopped fussing with a buckle and looked at the other young man. "In light of what just happened, this is going to sound stupid, but we don't really know each other that well. I kind of got carried away tonight and I had a good time; don't get me wrong. I just don't want to rush into anything."

"I'd like to know you better. Come home with me for Thanksgiving. I'll tell you all about myself."

"I'd like to know you better, too." Blue grimaced. "God, this is such a soap opera line, but it's the truth. I just broke up with someone and I'm not ready to be with anyone else yet."

"Yeah, I thought it might be something like that. I thought you and Peyton had a falling out or something from the way you both were acting."

"He didn't like my choice in men."

"I'm sure he didn't. He wouldn't like any man you chose unless it was him."

"I'm telling you, you're wrong about that. I'll see you tomorrow."

"Big day," Astor said, as Blue went to the door. "We have our premiere tomorrow night."

"Really? I forgot."

Astor laughed. "See you tomorrow."

Blue slipped out the door and went upstairs to his room. Quickly, he changed into fresh clothes and hurried back out. In less than ten minutes, he was walking across the quad toward the row of cottages. There were still several members of the cast and crew at Mr. McIntyre's, listening to music and wired on diet soda. It wasn't hard to find Peyton, who was holding forth in the kitchen. Among his audience was the Drama Club sponsor, listening intently. When Peyton took a breath, Mr. McIntyre spoke up.

"I agree with you in principle, Peyton, but the methods you advocate would make you no better than those you call Philistines."

"True, but I'd just like to see how they like it when the boot is on the other foot."

"I'm sure that would be satisfying, however briefly, but it's still not the civilized way to handle a problem. We're not cavemen, after all."

Someone in the crowd hooted like an ape and a spate of snickers broke out.

"That's exactly the response I was expecting," Peyton said, as he caught sight of Blue. "You may not think this affects you because you're not homosexual, but it's the kind of thing that spreads. I'm talking to you, Sebastian Wong. What if the preps decide they don't like Asians?"

"I'll go kamikaze on their asses," Sebastian Wong laughed.

"Bastian," Mr. McIntyre reproved. "That's a completely inappropriate thing to say."

Peyton sidled around the kitchen table until he met up with Blue. "I think we can count on Mr. McIntyre to continue fighting the good fight. Where have you been?"

"I felt a little sick after rehearsal and I went to lie down." Blue lied without thinking twice about it. For some reason, he didn't want to tell Peyton about Astor.

"Nerves," Peyton said. "You got through rehearsal fine though. You'll do great tomorrow night."

"I hope so. Everyone has worked so hard; I don't want to be the one to ruin it all."

"You won't. You're good, Blue. You really are."

"Thanks, but if everything goes right, it'll be because you pulled it all together."

"Flattery will get you everywhere. What shall we do to celebrate the premiere?"

"Well, there's the cast party."

Peyton made a noise with his lips and tongue. "Lame. I was thinking we should go somewhere after."

"Somewhere like Giddie's?"

"Somewhere exactly like that."

"Let's see how it goes. We might be too tired to go into Eastburn."

"Fine. By the way, where did you go to lie down? You weren't in your room."

"No, I…. I went to…"

"You're the worst liar. Come here." Peyton pulled Blue into the hall. "I couldn't fail to notice that Astor looks at you the way a dog looks at an unattended steak. Since you're not with Heydn anymore, you're a free agent and you can see whoever you want."

"I'm not seeing him."

"Let me rephrase then; you can get busy with whoever you want."

"You don't have anything negative to say about him?"

"At least he's not a jock."

Blue smiled. "Come on. Walk me home."

"Sure." Peyton led the way out to the tiny porch and they walked away side by side.

"So you knew Astor wanted to get with me? Because I was surprised as hell."

"You take people at face value, Blue. It's part of your charm, but it's really naïve."

"I'm not naïve."

"Okay, you're not naïve. Listen, I've been writing this play and…"

"What? How did you keep this a secret?"

"I wanted to be sure I could write it before I told anyone about the idea. It's too good to just throw out there. It deserves just the right words."

"Do I get to read it?"

"Before anyone else. I want you to play the main character."

"Can you tell me his…or her name?"

Peyton smiled. "Foxboy."

"Foxboy?"

"That's his name."

"Now I'll be consumed with curiosity," Blue said as they walked into the dorm. "When can I read it?"

"Soon, I think."

"Well, I can't wait." Blue stopped at the staircase. "Goodnight, Peyn."

"Sweet dreams, fairest Rosalind."

Blue laughed and waved at Peyton over his shoulder as he climbed the stairs. It was funny how life just went on and on like an infinite set of steps. He kept doing things. He got up in the morning. He put on clothes. He ate. He went to classes. He acted in the play. He cried. He painted scenery. He smoked. He watched videos. He laughed. He sucked Astor's dick. He slept. None of it meant anything because he didn't share it with Heydn. He wondered if it would be like this for the rest of his life, or if it would eventually fade like the deaths of his parents. It had taken years and years, but the sharp pain of loss and even the dull empty aching had diminished over time. He hoped it wouldn't take as long to get over Heydn, but he hurt as badly as if someone close to him had died. As always, just before he fell asleep, he admitted to himself what he really hoped. He hoped that this was all a long and terrible nightmare and he would wake in Heydn's arms.

CHAPTER 8

ON the night that the Drama Club's very well-received production of *As You Like It* premiered, Heydn Case was a hundred miles away at a multi-millionaire's so-called cabin. The split-level stone and timber chalet had eight bedrooms and every convenience known to man. Music poured from the sound system controlled by a panel that also regulated the lighting, the temperature, the window shades, and who knew what else. Heydn had already drunk two beers he'd never heard of before and been in the pool and the hot tub. He'd just finished drying off and was pulling on his jeans when someone opened the guest-room door and walked in.

"Woopsie!" Robin Douglas said as her gaze headed south. "Nice six-pack."

"Thanks. I'll be dressed in a second and you can have the room."

"Is that Case?" Allerton called from the hallway. "Robin, quit blocking the door."

Robin moved and Allerton came in with his arm around a petite blonde girl. "Heydn, did you meet Clarissa? This is Clarissa Albright. She's twenty."

"Hi," Heydn said. "Is the party moving in here?"

Allerton held up a bottle of liquor. "Here's your second clue," he said, as he deposited the wobbly blonde co-ed on the bed. "Clarissa wants some action and who am I to deny her?"

Heydn picked up his shirt and his wet towel. "I'll clear out," he said.

"Why?" Allerton asked, looking up from his task of removing Clarissa's pastel angora sweater. "She doesn't care. In fact, why don't you and Robin get down? This bed's plenty big enough."

Robin raised an eyebrow at Heydn. "Sounds like fun to me," she said.

"Yeah, it does," Heydn said. "But I'm starving."

"What a dweeb," Allerton said. "Hey, Robin. You want to play with me and Clarissa?"

Robin grabbed the hem of her dress and pulled it over her head to reveal a tanned, trim body in matching red bra and panties. "Good timing. The ecstasy kicked in about five minutes ago," she said.

"Heydn," Allerton called from the bed. "How can you walk away from this?"

"I seriously need to get some food in me, bro. I'll be back." Heydn went downstairs and filled a plate from the table piled with snacks. He strolled around while he ate, keeping on the move until he saw Allerton return to the party. When they met up later, Heydn excused himself by saying he'd gotten into a game of pool. Allerton told him he was a sucker and smacked him on the head.

"Listen," Allerton said. "Clarissa needs a favor. She drove her dad's car up here and she's too wasted to drive it back and it has to be there when he gets up in the morning. You never drink much so I thought you could drop it off. Bennie's going to take the rest of us to the bus station. Here's a hundred. Call a cab to bring you back to school."

"Okay," Heydn said slowly. "Is it very far out of the way?"

"No. You could walk from her house to a bus stop, but they only run once every hour at this time of night. I figured since you're doing a favor, you could take a cab instead of waiting around."

"Thanks. Who's got the keys?"

Allerton reached into his trousers pocket and handed Heydn a set of keys. "It's the green Jag," he said. "You can drive a stick, right?"

"No problem. See you at school."

"Take your time. Wind the Jag out a little. Just make sure it's there by six." Allerton gave Heydn directions, and Heydn said goodnight.

Heydn had been driving for about twenty minutes and thoroughly enjoying the experience when he saw the lights of a police car in the rearview mirror. Dutifully, he pulled onto the shoulder and waited for the officer to come to the window. He took out his wallet and felt a twinge of nerves when he saw that his license wasn't there. He was looking in the glove box for the registration when the patrolman harshly ordered him out of the car. Alarmed by the man's tone, Heydn got out, leaving the door open.

"Was I speeding?" he asked.

"Were you speeding?" the officer said. "No, I don't believe so. But if I'd just stolen a car, I wouldn't call attention to myself either."

"I didn't steal this car."

"Well, somebody did. The owner reported it stolen just about an hour ago."

"That's impossible. It was sitting in my friend's driveway an hour ago."

"What's your friend's address?"

"I don't know exactly," Heydn said. "I know how that sounds, but I was at a party at a house I've never been to before."

"And that's where you stole the car."

"No! A friend asked me to drive it home because she was too drunk."

"That's a good one. Thieves usually say they borrowed the car from a cousin."

"I'm not a car thief."

"You've got no ID and you're driving a car reported stolen. That makes you a suspect in my book."

"Just call Bennie's house and ask for…. Shit, they're probably already on the bus. That doesn't matter; I have Allerton's cell number. Just call him and he'll tell you…"

"Son, you can call anybody you want as soon as we get to the jail."

"Jail! You're taking me to jail?"

"Where did you think we were going? The prom?"

"But I didn't steal this car."

"Then you'll get a chance to prove it. Do I have to cuff you?"

"No, sir."

"All right then. Just climb in the backseat there and I'll be right with you."

The officer called for a tow truck and drove Heydn to the county lockup. Heydn was booked, which was a much longer process than shown on television, and put in a cell by himself. After a little while, someone came and took him to a phone. He called Allerton's cell and told him the whole story. Allerton told him not to worry and hung up.

"Was that Case?" Logan asked, as he opened the door of the dorm for Allerton.

"Yeah," Allerton smirked. "He's sitting in a county jail cell right now."

"Good one, Allie. Reporting Bennie's dad's car stolen was brilliant. Case'll miss the meet in the morning, and Coach will have to drop his ranking."

"Case is getting too cocky, but this should knock him down a peg or two."

"You think he's in the cell with some big, hairy ex-con?"

"I hope so. Case is a punk."

"Fuckin' A. Why do you even pretend to be his friend?"

"Why not? If people think you like them, they'll be less likely to expect an attack."

"That makes sense. I still think he's a fag."

"You think everyone's a fag."

"You know, they say that one in eleven guys is a homo."

"They? Well, it must be true then. Let's see; how many guys are there at Acton? Around three hundred, right? How many homos is that?"

"I'm not good at math."

"That's what accountants are for. So did you decide whether you're coming with me for Thanksgiving or spending it porking Bennie? I'm leaving right after the meet."

"Bennie wants me to go to her grandmother's in Miami. She'll pitch a bitch if I don't."

"Then you'd better go," Allerton said as they reached the end of the hall. "Hey, Morehouse! What are you doing here?"

Rolly closed the bathroom door behind him and edged past the other two young men. "I was walking by and I really had to take a piss."

"Are you sure you weren't hiding in our john so you could get a look at our cocks?" Logan asked.

"I have a weak bladder," Rolly said.

"Then get out of here before I make you piss down your leg." Logan took a step and Rolly hurried away.

"One in eleven, huh?" Allerton said as he watched the rapidly departing figure.

*   *   *

"Heydn Michael Case, you're free to go," said the officer who unlocked the cell door.

"What happened?"

"Your bail's been paid."

"Thank you, Allie!" Heydn whispered fervently as he followed the officer and collected his belongings. Since he'd already missed the track meet, he used the hundred dollars to buy a bus ticket instead of wasting it on a cab. He arrived at campus just after lunchtime and went directly to the shower. Feeling almost normal again, he got dressed and went to find Allerton to give him his change.

Allerton was in his room packing. "Where's your bag?" he asked.

"You still want me to meet your parents?"

"Sure. We just won't mention your criminal record."

"Thanks, man."

"Don't mention it. Now go get your shit. The car service will be here in fifteen."

Heydn ran back to his room and grabbed the bag he'd packed two days ago. "I didn't even ask where we're going," he said when he returned.

"Oh yeah, I forgot to tell you. My sister got engaged, so we're going to this hotel her fiancé owns on Nassau."

"I didn't pack a bathing suit."

"Don't sweat it. We'll get you a pair of trunks when we get down there. There's a Versace store right in the lobby."

"But the plane ticket…"

"Hey, I invited you to spend Thanksgiving with me. It's not your fault plans changed. If you don't want to go, I understand, but your ticket is bought and there's a room booked for you at the resort."

"The Bahamas," Heydn mused.

"Yeah, bro. Come on. Seize the day!"

"You're sure?"

"Absolutely." Allerton grinned as a car horn blared. "There's our ride."

Heydn told himself to go with the flow and followed Allerton to the limo.

"WHERE are we going and why do we have our bags with us?" Blue asked as he followed Astor out to the deserted paddock.

"This is where our ride is picking us up and taking us to New Hampshire."

Blue looked around. "Are we going by helicopter?"

"As a matter of fact, yes, we are."

"That's pretty cool."

"My mother doesn't trust public transportation so we have a jet and a helicopter."

"She sounds interesting."

"You know, for a Goth you're very diplomatic."

"Why does everyone think I'm a Goth?"

"It's probably the hair and the eyeliner."

"I'm so used to wearing it. Do you think I should wash it off before I meet your parents?"

"I couldn't care less. Just be yourself."

They heard the sound of the helicopter's blades and the wind of its descent blew their hair into witchy tangles. The copilot hopped out and took their bags. They climbed aboard, fastened their seat belts, and the chopper rose into the sky again. Drinks were offered from a large cooler and then the two young men sat back in the comfortable seats and watched the landscape below. Blue was disappointed when the ride was over, but stunned by the beauty of the countryside they landed in.

"It's gorgeous, isn't it?" Astor said, after they got far enough from the helicopter. "The painter Maxfield Parrish lived not too far from here and he used these woods in a lot of his paintings."

"I can see why. This is a beautiful place."

"Come on. You can meet Mom and Dad and we can go for a swim in the lake before dinner."

"I don't swim."

"Don't be ridiculous. Everyone knows how to swim. It's all we do for the first nine months of our lives."

"Yeah, well I forgot how."

Astor laughed and threw an arm around Blue's neck as they climbed the steps to the big house. "I love your sense of humor," he said.

"Darling!" a woman called in a faded British accent as she came out the front door and across the verandah. "It's so good to hear you laughing."

"Brace yourself," Astor whispered. "It's Hurricane Lil."

Lily Bancroft Aldrich threw her arms around her tall son's neck and kissed him on both cheeks. After a flurry of affection, she let go of Astor only to stand at his side with an arm around his waist. "And this must be your friend Blue. He looks a perfectly ordinary color to me."

Blue smiled hesitantly. "Pleased to meet you, Mrs. Aldrich," he said.

"And I'm very pleased to meet you," she replied, taking one of Blue's hands between hers. "Astor has very nice things to say about you. I've had a wonderful chum since I was a girl and we still correspond and meet in London twice a year. As you go through life, you'll find there's nothing so comforting as an old friend."

"I'm sure you're right, ma'am."

"Oh, I do like you," Lily said. "And you have such a sweet face."

"Mom." Astor's voice held a warning note.

"Oh, dear, am I embarrassing you again?"

"Of course not, but most teenage boys don't want to hear that they look sweet."

"What do they want to hear, darling?"

"I've always wanted to be sinister," Blue blurted out.

Lily laughed, a charming sound that made Blue glad he'd decided to come home with Astor. "I wanted to be a pirate when I was in the nursery. Do you know who you remind me of, dear? No, of course you don't, but you look the way I imagined Peter Pan's lost boys."

"I guess that's a little better," Astor said. "Is Dad here yet?"

"He was delayed at the last minute. The project designer in New York needed to consult with him."

"Dad's construction company is turning some old warehouses into low-cost housing," Astor told Blue. "I'm feeling kind of hungry; how about you?"

"I'm a little thirsty."

"Why don't the two of you go on into the kitchen?" Lily said. "I'm going to have a lie-down before dinner, but I didn't want to miss your arrival." She kissed Astor on the cheek, told Blue to feel at home, and left them alone.

"You didn't tell her my real name?" Blue asked as they walked toward the back of the mansion.

"Sure I did, but I also told her you preferred to be called Blue."

"Most adults just go ahead and call me Brooke."

"Mom's a little different."

"I thought you said your parents were boring."

"You'll see," Astor said as he opened the doors of a huge stainless-steel refrigerator. He handed Blue a bottle of water and got one for himself. "Deviled egg?" he asked. "Or how about some crackers and cheese, or some fruit? Cook has this fridge stacked with hors d'oeuvres."

"Water's fine for now."

"Let's go down to the boathouse then. It's my favorite place here." Astor took an apple and led the way across the tiered expanse of rolling lawn, under majestic oaks and past natural-looking landscaping down to the shore of the lake. The boathouse was a large structure with covered slips for several boats and a large deck outfitted for entertaining. Astor pulled Blue into the small cabana and found a pair of swim trunks for him among the motley assortment of forgotten apparel. Quickly, Astor changed into a pair of baby blue board shorts and hung his clothes on a hook. "What are you waiting for?" he asked a still-clothed Blue.

"I told you; I don't swim."

"Look, if you're embarrassed about showing your body, you don't have to be. You look just fine without any clothes on."

"What kind of fish are in this lake?"

"Well, there aren't any sharks, I can guarantee that."

"What about eels?"

"No eels."

Blue sighed and changed into the red and white trunks. "Are you happy now?"

Astor put a hand on the small of Blue's back, pulling him close. Looking into Blue's dark eyes, Astor kissed him tenderly. "Now I'm happy," he said. "Come on. Last one in the water owes a blow job."

Astor spun around and dashed out to the deck. After a slight hesitation, Blue followed. Astor leaped to the railing and dove cleanly into the water. Blue climbed over the wooden rail and stood at the edge, staring into the lake until Astor surfaced.

"Come on. Get in." Astor's auburn hair was sticking to his face and his skin sparkled with droplets.

"How cold is it?"

"It's not warm. Hang on a second and I'll see if I can pee."

"Ass." Blue chewed his lower lip for a few moments. "Honestly, I've always been kind of scared of any body of water bigger than a bathtub."

"You're not just playing with me?" Astor swam to the ladder and started climbing up.

"It's stupid, I know."

"It's not stupid to be scared." Astor put an arm around Blue's shoulders. "But it's kind of silly to keep being afraid when it's easy to get over it."

Blue gave Astor an inquiring look.

"Just get in the water with me. I promise I won't let anything happen to you. In fact, you can have a life jacket if you want."

"Can I go down the ladder instead of jumping?"

Astor chuckled. "I guess it would be okay just this one time. I'll go first." He went down the ladder and swam away a bit, treading water and looking up at Blue. "Come on." He held out his arms.

Blue turned his back to the lake and put his foot on the first rung, moving slowly downward until he touched the water. Astor came closer and put a hand on the ladder.

"Take your time," he said. "I'm right here to catch you."

"I feel like such a wuss, but would you take my hand?"

"Anytime." Astor took Blue's right hand and tugged gently. "Just keep climbing down until you feel yourself start to float."

"I had swimming lessons when I was little, but I never liked it. Something about having my head under water freaks me out. I had my fortune told once and supposedly I drowned in a past life."

"You're too cute. Come here." Astor put his arms around Blue and very gently pulled him away from the ladder. "You okay?"

Blue nodded, holding on to Astor, trying not to clutch at him.

"Kick your feet a little and we'll stay up. If you go back toward shore, you'll be able to touch bottom real fast. So you see there's nothing to be worried about."

Astor's arms felt incredibly warm contrasted with the chill of the lake and Blue was content to just tread water and be next to him for several long moments. He could tell Astor was angling for a kiss and tilted his head for better access. A baritone voice broke the relative silence in a warning to look out below. Immediately afterward, something big hit the water a few feet away, liberally splashing both young men. As they moved a little apart, a man's head broke the surface a few feet away and Astor rolled his eyes.

"Very funny, Dad."

"I couldn't resist." Mr. Aldrich shook water from his short salt-and-pepper hair. "You never heard me coming."

"You got us good," Astor said. "I'm sure you made an impression on Blue."

"So this is Blue." Mr. Aldrich held out his hand. "Pleased to meet you."

Blue let go of Astor's arm and shook Mr. Aldrich's hand. He found he could stay afloat on his own and tried not to think about what might be swimming around below him wondering if his toes tasted good.

"Call me Avery," Mr. Aldrich said. "And my wife prefers to be called Lily."

Blue nodded and then grabbed for the ladder when Astor dunked his dad. An aquatic wrestling match ensued, which Blue watched from the dock. Avery Aldrich's love and pride for Astor showed clearly in his face and actions as they played. Blue put his feet in the water and was content to sit there in the pale but warm autumn sunshine and watch father and son. When a bell rang up at the house, Avery and Astor raced for the ladder and Blue climbed quickly up, but didn't escape a soaking as the other two teamed up on him.

"Dinner's ready," Astor said, throwing a towel over Blue's head. "Mom gives Cook the day before Thanksgiving off and makes dinner herself. It's always an adventure."

"You didn't warn him before you brought him here?" Mr. Aldrich feigned shock.

"He eats in Acton's cafeteria, Dad. I'm sure his stomach can handle one of Mom's creations."

"Don't worry," Astor's father said, putting a big hand on Blue's shoulder. "There's a pizza place not too far away that delivers."

Blue smiled up at the tanned, fit man with the laugh lines around his eyes and mouth. "I'm not as picky as Astor," he said.

Avery Aldrich laughed heartily. "So you've noticed our boy's taste for the finer things. Did you know that he refused to drink from a plastic bottle when he was a baby? They had to be glass."

"That's not true," Astor told Blue.

Mr. Aldrich leaned toward Blue as they crossed the lawn and spoke in a confidential tone. "Can you believe the disrespect? You'd never call me a liar, would you, Blue?"

"No, sir."

Astor shot Blue a comic look of betrayal as they bounded up the back steps. Blue grinned at his friend as he listened to Mr. Aldrich's goofy description of what his wife might be serving for dinner. They parted in the hall and Astor gestured for Blue to follow him up to the third floor.

"Your room's right there," he said, pointing to a door. "Right across from mine. Your bag's been brought up, so get changed and we'll go have dinner."

Blue loved his room with its sloping white ceiling dancing with reflections from the lake. He changed into soft black pants and a logo-less ash gray pullover, laying his wet bathing suit on a towel. Astor knocked at the door and Blue called out for him to come in as he slipped his feet into shoes.

"Is the room okay?" Astor asked as he went to one of the tall windows.

"I really like it. This quilt is wild."

"It's Shaker or something. All this furniture has been in the family for hundreds of years. Isn't that kind of weird? The idea of our things outliving us."

"I never thought about it, but I knew this girl whose grandmother had a parrot that outlived her. The old lady had to leave the bird to someone in her will."

"Weird. You ready to go down?"

"I think so. What do you think?" Blue held his arms out from his sides.

"I think it's a crime that I can't jump you right now, but this is one of Mom's big moments." Taking Blue's hand, Astor led him to the door and they walked down the stairs hand in hand until they reached the dining room. Blue pulled his hand from Astor's and moved a little away from him.

"Hello, darlings," Lily Aldrich said. "I've put you across the table from each other. Blue, if you'll sit here? Lovely. Both of you look very handsome. And you as well, Avery."

Astor's father smiled fondly at the elegant auburn-haired woman. "Thank you, Lil. Are you ready for me to pour the wine?"

"If you would." She tilted her cheek for a kiss as her husband passed by.

Dinner was a soufflé of myriad elusive flavors, a pasta dish with meat that might have been chicken or pork, and a wilted spinach salad with homemade dressing that was neither sweet nor sour, but some uneasy blend that baffled the tongue. Mr. Aldrich kept pouring the wine, opening a new bottle for each dish, remarking each time that no one had to drive home. By the time dessert was brought out, Blue knew he'd had too much to drink and hoped he didn't say anything embarrassing.

"You outdid yourself this year, Lily," Mr. Aldrich said, when his wife returned to the table with coffee. "That was the most interesting pre-Thanksgiving dinner yet."

"Thank you, dear. I'm a bit proud of the pasta. I substituted rattlesnake for the chicken in that one."

Blue exchanged a glance with Astor.

"She's not kidding," Astor said. "Mom likes trying new things."

"Life is short," Mrs. Aldrich said. "And there are so many things to be experienced. Now, what would you two lads like to do after you've had your pudding?"

"No plans," Astor said. "It's nice just to be here at the lake."

"You're a good son," Mr. Aldrich said. "Remind me to thank whoever raised you."

"We haven't played charades in ages," Astor's mother suggested.

"No one plays charades anymore, Mom."

"Actually, that sounds like fun," Blue spoke up. "I'd play if everyone else wanted to."

"Well, we are all a little tipsy," Mr. Aldrich said. "The perfect state in which to play charades."

"Oh, all right," Astor said. "Blue's a really good actor; I warn you."

For the first time since Blue had met Mr. Aldrich, the man's bluff demeanor faltered. It was just a small frown, a twitch of facial muscles, and then the smile was back in place, but Blue could feel the chill of disapproval and it centered on the word actor. Then Mrs. Aldrich rose and the moment passed. They went into the game room and had a silly, good time until Astor's father looked at his watch and checked it against the clock.

"I'm afraid I'll have to call it a day," he said as he stood. "I have to go back into New York for a couple of hours in the morning."

"I'm coming to bed, too, dear," Lily said, as she bent to kiss Astor. Blue was surprised to feel the brush of her lips against his cheek as well as she said goodnight and then she was gone, leaving behind the ghost of her perfume. She took Avery's arm and they walked away together.

"Your parents are great," Blue said. "A little square, maybe, but really nice."

"It would kill them to not be polite."

"It's more than that. They really made me feel at home."

"Good. I'm glad you feel at home here. I'm hoping this won't be the last time you visit."

"Me, too."

"What do you want to do now?"

"I don't know. It's only ten-thirty."

"When I'm here, I like to go out at night and sit on the dock for a while. Want to come with me?"

"Sure," Blue said and they walked down to the shore again under the light of the moon.

Blue was expecting Astor to make a move and didn't flinch when the other young man's arms went around him as soon as they were on the dock. Astor held Blue against his chest and looked over Blue's shoulder at the tiny lights of the homes on the other side of the large lake. Blue could feel Astor's warm breath on his neck and it felt good to be held like this with the chill wind fresh on his face, listening to the water lap at the pilings. He wished it didn't remind him of the afternoon he and Heydn had spent on the banks of the lake at school, and just for a minute, with Astor behind him, Blue pretended Astor was Heydn. He imagined Heydn's hands were sliding down to his crotch and squeezing his cock, that Heydn's mouth was sucking softly at the side of his neck, that it was Heydn's hard-on pressed against his butt. Then Astor spoke and Blue felt a pang of guilt for using him like that.

"You are without a doubt one of the coolest people I've ever known."

"You must not know many people."

Astor's arms tightened fiercely around Blue's lower belly. "You're beautiful, smart, and talented, and I'm glad you like me."

"I'm glad you like me, too."

"You want to go into the boathouse?"

Blue turned to face Astor and brought their mouths together. "If you want to," he murmured against Astor's lips.

Astor pushed his tongue into Blue's mouth, inviting Blue's tongue to play, as he grabbed a double handful of Blue's ass and walked him over to the boathouse door. Blue hooked his fingers in Astor's belt loops and yanked him closer. Astor pressed Blue against the weathered wood as the kisses grew more urgent, shoving a knee between Blue's thighs, grinding their crotches together. Blue reached behind him and turned the knob and the door swung inward. Astor lurched, recovered, and plunged after Blue into the glimmering gloom of the boathouse.

"Here," Astor said, jumping down into a powerboat and holding out a hand to Blue.

Blue climbed aboard and sat next to Astor on the comfortable cushions in the stern. They made out for a long time, exchanging slow sloppy kisses with their hands in each other's pants, prolonging the sweet torment until they couldn't stand any more.

"Strip down and sit on my lap?" Astor requested in a breathless voice.

Blue shoved his unfastened trousers and his briefs down to the floor and stepped out of them as Astor shed his khakis.

"Facing me," Astor said. "So our dicks can touch."

Astor leaned back as Blue straddled him and lined their cocks up. Resting a knee on the padded bench seat, Blue rocked his hips, rubbing his hard-on over Astor's balls and up the length of his shaft. Astor groaned and slid his hands under Blue's soft shirt to toy with his nipples. Blue leaned in for a kiss as Astor ran a hand down his flank and over his hip to his ass. Astor's fingers crept into Blue's cleft, stroking and squeezing as the kiss went on. Blue whimpered into Astor's mouth when Astor fiddled a fingertip around Blue's hole. Astor took hold of the root of his cock and bent it down, rubbing the head against Blue's entrance.

"I want you so much," he said, as he broke the kiss.

"I don't want to fuck."

"Neither do I, but I'd like to make love with you."

"Call it whatever; I'm not into it right now."

Astor prodded Blue's hole gently with the tip of his leaking cock. "Are you sure I can't change your mind?"

"Knock it off."

"I'm sorry," Astor said, letting go of Blue's hips. "We can go up to the house now if you want."

"Like this?" Blue pointed to his hard cock.

"You aren't mad at me?"

"I would be if you hadn't stopped."

"I'm not a rapist."

"I know. I'm just not ready for that yet."

"It's cool. Taking someone's dick is a big trust issue. I won't push it."

"Sometimes you sound like a lawyer."

"I thought you were going to stop insulting me." Astor put a hand on Blue's arousal and began stroking it lazily.

"Guh, that feels good," Blue said as his knees went weak. "I need to sit down."

Astor was surprised, but greatly pleased when Blue sat on his lap again, even if he was facing away. Blue drew Astor's shaft up between his legs and clamped it tightly with his thigh muscles. He bounced gingerly a couple of times and Astor got the idea. Reaching around to take a firm hold on Blue's rod, Astor planted his feet against the deck and lifted his pelvis. Blue spat in his palm and rubbed it over the head of Astor's cock, as it emerged from the vise of his thighs.

"Ho…lee…shit," Astor breathed, as he pumped his hips. "That feels amazing."

"Don't forget about me," Blue prompted.

"Right, sorry." Astor began stroking Blue's cock again. "But that really does feel good."

Blue sensed the power he held over Astor in that moment; he could give or deny pleasure with a flex of his muscles. The thought had never occurred to him while he and Heydn were together. He had simply concentrated on giving Heydn as much pleasure as possible without considering the implications. Heydn had gobbled it up and held out his hands for more. Astor was touchingly grateful without being a kiss-ass. Astor accepted him the way he was. Astor was handsome and good company. Why couldn't Astor make him feel like his blood was going to boil away in his veins, like his insides had turned to hot honey, like he'd die if he didn't touch him?

"Oh God," Astor groaned, thrusting in short rolls of his hips, buttocks squeaking against vinyl. He held on to Blue's dick as if it was a joystick, letting his thrusts push the hard length of flesh into his fist. Blue leaned forward and rested his hands on Astor's knees, levering himself up and down. "Oh yeah!" Astor cried out. "Yeah! Jesus, Blue! Don't stop. I'm going to cum a gusher."

Blue cupped the end of Astor's hard-on, flicking his thumb across the sensitive slit. Astor shuddered, his hand jittering on Blue's cock as his climax broke over him like a tsunami. He continued to thrust, sliding his cum-slippery shaft between Blue's trembling thighs as Blue came in three powerful spurts. Astor let go of Blue's dick and spread his hand across Blue's taut lower belly, feeling the spasms that tightened the other young man's muscles in waves.

"I love the way you cum," Astor said, drawing Blue to lie against his chest. "You don't hold back."

"Mmm," Blue purred. "I love how you can't stop touching me after we cum."

"In that case…" Astor trailed his fingers down Blue's side from his collarbone to the top of his thigh. Curling his fingers around Blue's hipbone, he craned his neck and took Blue's lips in a deep kiss. He walked his hand down Blue's sparse treasure trail and fondled the silky skin where his legs joined his torso. As the caresses continued, Blue's cock stirred. "Looks like you're ready for more," Astor smirked.

"We've been out here for a while. Are you sure no one's going to come looking for us?"

"Is that your way of rejecting me gently?"

"I think I'd expire if one of your parents walked in on us. It was bad enough that your dad saw us practically making out in the lake."

"Don't worry about it."

"I saw the way he looked at me when you said I was an actor."

"Oh, that. Dad thinks acting is a waste of my time since it'll be of no use to me in my career."

"And what would that be?"

"Building things."

"Building *things*?"

"*Big* things."

"Like the pyramids?"

Astor smiled. "Like hospitals, and museums, things like that."

"I've never heard you mention wanting to build things."

"Because I don't, particularly. I love acting and I'd love to be a director someday, but I have to be realistic. My choices affect a lot more people than just myself."

"You're a Chinese monk in a teenage-boy suit, aren't you?"

"You make me feel good, Blue Barclay. I hope we're friends for a long time."

"I'd like that."

"Honestly, I'd like to be more than friends."

Blue sat up quickly. "I want more, too," he said, as he scooted to sit on the edge of the cushion. "I just need to take it slow."

"Understood." Astor sat up as Blue stood and rescued his trousers. "Was it Heydn Case?"

Blue froze for a split second and then finished pulling his pants up. "What do you mean?"

"Is he the one that hurt you?"

"Is it imperative that we talk about this now?"

"Of course not. You don't have to tell me anything you don't want to." Astor drew his khakis up and buttoned them. "I don't own you."

Blue didn't answer. He went to the door of the boathouse and stepped onto the deck. The wind off the water cooled his face and made a constant, soothing noise in the trees. He stood there with his eyes closed, just listening to the hum of the Earth as it rotated until he heard the door close behind him. He could feel the heat radiating from Astor at his back and slowly leaned until he was supported by the solid warmth. Astor crossed his arms around Blue's chest and Blue reached up to wrap his fingers around Astor's wrists.

"I'm sorry if I went too far," Astor said in Blue's ear. "I don't ever want to fight with you."

"We're not fighting. I'm not mad."

"Good." Astor took a deep breath of the fresh air. "Are you as hungry as I am?"

"For leftover snake?"

Astor made a face. "I can't believe Mom didn't tell us. Just once I'd like to see her make spaghetti, or meatloaf, or something normal."

"I think your mom's great."

"Then maybe you should marry her," Astor teased.

Blue looked interested. "Are she and your dad having problems?"

"I just can't top you." Astor paused as he realized what he'd said. "That's a hell of a double entendre."

"I just got it," Blue snickered. "That's terrible."

"Come on. Let's go find some real food."

Astor and Blue raided the refrigerator, brushed their teeth, and went to bed. Blue had been asleep a couple of hours when Astor sneaked into his room and they went at it again on the enormous four-poster bed. They fell asleep tangled together, but Astor woke up early enough to rouse Blue with a hand job and still get back to his room before anyone was moving around the upstairs hall. They showed up for breakfast with matching auras of supreme satisfaction and hearty appetites.

Mr. Aldrich was already gone and Mrs. Aldrich was on her way out to shop for a few last-minute items to make Thanksgiving dinner perfect. Astor and Blue spent the day canoeing, hiking, and looking through the house's library of books and films. They found an ancient Pong game on the top shelf of a closet and hooked it up, playing until Astor's father came home and dinner was served. The table was beautiful and the food was delicious, but more than anything else about that Thanksgiving, Blue remembered how it felt to be welcome. After they ate, they sat for a long time and talked, and Lily's gracious manners drew Blue into the conversation. *Maybe Astor and Heydn were right,* Blue thought, as he looked around the table. Maybe he needed to be a little more realistic. Maybe he needed to stop wishing for his soul mate and be thankful for the blessings being showered on him. Why couldn't he just forget Heydn?

Blue tried again that night to block out the memory of Heydn with the reality of Astor in his bed, and both of them went to sleep satisfied, but it was only skin deep in Blue's case. After Astor woke and went to his room, Blue lay awake until morning. He got up, got dressed, and found himself alone with Mrs. Aldrich at the breakfast table.

"Avery's off again," she said lightly as she poured coffee for Blue. "He works too hard."

"I'm sorry he's not here. I wanted to thank him, too. I've had a wonderful time here."

"Thank you, dear. It was lovely to have you. I can see that Astor is very fond of you and I can't tell you what it means to me that he's let someone in at last."

"Ma'am?"

"Oh dear. If he hasn't told you, I really shouldn't. Perhaps just the facts. Astor had a cousin one year younger who was his best friend. Archer was nine when he died in an accident at summer camp. We were all devastated of course, but I was beginning to think that Astor was never going to get over it. He stayed out of school for a year and would hardly leave his room."

"He's never mentioned it."

"Then perhaps you shouldn't bring it up."

"No, ma'am, I won't. I'm really sorry."

"Thank you, Blue. You say that as though you truly mean it."

"Truly mean what?" Astor asked as he walked into the dining room.

"That I think I can help you," Blue answered.

"And exactly what needs to be fixed?"

"We can't tell you, darling. It's privileged information."

Astor pretended to be miffed, but he was thrilled that his mom seemed to have a rapport with Blue. He let them tease him through breakfast, secretly glorying in the attention of the two people he loved most in the world. After eating, they heard the helicopter arriving and Astor volunteered to go upstairs for their bags. Mrs. Aldrich waited in the foyer with Blue.

"You really care about my lad, don't you?" Lily asked.

Blue looked at the floor.

"It's all right, Blue. I've known for some time that Astor isn't attracted to girls and I've made peace with the fact. I only hope you'll be careful with his heart."

Blue was glad when he heard Astor coming down the stairs. He took the hand that Mrs. Aldrich held out, but he couldn't look her in the eyes. Astor kissed her cheek and they picked up their bags and went to meet the helicopter.

"YOU having a good time?" Allerton asked as the waiter put two more drinks on the glass-topped table.

Heydn looked over at the outdoor floor show of half-naked women dancing to a song from last year's American top 40. "Sure. Free room, free wardrobe, free booze. Why wouldn't I be having a good time?"

"You looked a little bored."

"Well, it is the same show we saw last night."

"True; same old titties. Want to go prowling for fresh pussy?"

"Where?"

"We could just take our drinks and walk down the beach."

"I thought Christophe said we shouldn't go too far away from the resort."

"Christophe is stupid enough to marry my bitch whore sister. Let's go find some action."

"I don't think it's a good idea."

"Who cares what you think?" Allerton picked up his drink and staggered away from the beach bar behind the hotel.

"Shit," Heydn said as he stood and went after Allerton. "Wait up."

"Look, there's a fire farther down the beach."

"I see it."

"Maybe there'll be some hotties there, 'cause there's fuck-all at the resort."

"Okay. We'll check it out, but it's pretty far away."

Allerton didn't even get halfway before he sat down in the sand and threw his empty plastic coconut at the ocean. "What the hell are we doin' so far from the bar?"

"It's a mystery." Heydn sat down next to Allerton.

"We're out of booze."

"That's indisputable."

"Shit."

"We might as well."

Allerton laughed. "Got any smokes?"

"Neither one of us smokes."

"What the hell are we doin' way out here?"

"We're drunk."

"Tell Logan to get some more beers."

"Logan's not here." Heydn sighed. He didn't think he'd ever seen a human being as drunk as Allerton. "Let's just sit for a few minutes."

"I need a drink."

"We'll get you one soon."

"I hate the fuckin' beach."

Heydn sighed again. "Listen, you never let me thank you properly for bailing me out."

"What?"

"I just wanted to say thanks."

"If you want to show your appreciation, you can suck my dick."

"Very funny."

"You said you wanted to thank me. Can't blame a guy for tryin' to get a little head."

Knowing it was a mistake, but unable to stop himself, Heydn put a hand on Allerton's inner thigh. When the other young man didn't punch him, Heydn let his hand drift until he found Allerton's cock. Neither of them said a word; they both stared at the moonlight on the waves as Heydn worked his hand up the leg of Allerton's shorts and under his briefs until he touched bare dick. Without a sound other than the surf mingled with Allerton's heavy breathing, Heydn stroked his friend's hard shaft. It took a few minutes, due to the amount of alcohol consumed, but Allerton shot his wad with a harsh grunt and Heydn withdrew his hand. Before long, they stood and headed back to the lights. The incident was not mentioned by either as they went to their rooms. In the morning, they boarded a plane back to the mainland. Allerton was massively hung over and refused to take his sunglasses off, causing a minor scene at customs. It was over quickly, and they were on their way home with tans and, in Allerton's case, a small amount of potent marijuana. A cab dropped them off at campus, they separated on the quad in front of the dorms, and Heydn went to his room to catch a nap before classes started.

CHAPTER 7

PEYTON opened his door, saw Blue, and yanked him inside.

"I've been looking everywhere for you," Blue said.

"I haven't been everywhere. I've been right here. I'm under house arrest."

"What?"

"Dean Whittaker told me to stay in my room until I'm sent for."

"What did you do?"

"What did *I* do? They're the ones that are violating my freedom of speech."

"What's this about, Peyn?"

"Censorship."

"They wouldn't publish his exposé," Rolly said from his seat by the window.

"I thought we agreed you wouldn't go on a crusade," Blue said.

"I didn't agree to anything." Peyton sat down on his bed and looked up at Blue with something close to worry in his green eyes. "Some people are pretty pissed at me."

"Tell me what you did."

"He has pictures of some homophobes in compromising situations," Rolly said.

"You spied on people and took pictures?" Blue sat on a chair opposite Peyton. "You dumbass! What were you thinking?"

"I was thinking that I'd show them up for the hypocrites they are. I had one picture of a teacher and a student."

"They'll expel you."

"I have copies," Peyton said coyly.

"Who did you have pictures of?"

"I could show you on my laptop."

"You have the file on your computer? You really are a dumbass."

"No, I have several disc copies and a flash drive."

"Well, don't show it to me. I don't want to be involved in something like this."

"Yet you want to know who was in the pictures."

"So I'll know who's coming after you, idiot. Seriously, what were you thinking?"

"He tried to run the press by all by himself," Rolly said. "It would've been so cool if he could have printed a few hundred copies and spread them around."

Blue shook his head. "Why didn't you just make some fliers with your printer?"

"It wouldn't have the same impact," Peyton said.

"Do you want to get beat up?"

"Of course not. That would hurt and I'm not a masochist."

"Then stop doing crazy things."

"I thought you loved me because I was crazy."

"Stop it, Peyton. Just stop it, please."

Rolly got up and went to the door. "I forgot something in my room," he said as he fled the scene of an incipient confrontation between his friends.

"Stop what exactly?" Peyton asked. "Stop standing up for my rights? Stop fighting bullies? Stop caring about injustice?"

"No, just stop…making people angry."

"It's not intentional; it's just a side effect."

"You call too much attention to yourself and to everyone like you."

"Is that what this is about? Are you afraid I'll mess things up for you and the Prince?"

"That's part of it, sure, but mostly I don't want to visit you in the hospital."

"Blue…" Peyton paused and turned away, looking out the window. "I wish things were different, too," he said at last. "But this is how they are."

Blue stared at the back of Peyton's head for a long time before he spoke. "Is there anything I can do to help?"

"Just be my friend."

Blue crossed the room and put his hands on Peyton's shoulders. As if expecting a rebuff, he put his arms around his friend in stages, letting his hands slide down a bit at a time until he circled Peyton's chest. Peyton was stiff at first, but he relaxed gradually and let the hug be what it was and nothing more, just one friend offering comfort to another. He stilled the storm of butterfly wings in his middle and rested his cheek against Blue's forearm. It occurred to him that wanting someone that didn't want you back might be the hardest thing in the world to comprehend and accept.

"Blue?"

"I'm right here."

"I need my laptop."

Blue let go of Peyton and moved back. His friend went directly to his computer and began typing.

"What trouble are you stirring up now?"

"What?" Peyton looked at Blue as though he'd forgotten the other young man was in the room. "Oh, I just had an idea for my play. Do you mind? I'd like to write it down before it goes away."

"I don't mind. I think you should stick to writing plays instead of inflammatory journalism."

"Okay, just close the door on your way out." Peyton's eyes never left the screen.

Blue smiled as he left his friend's room and headed up the stairs.

"HEYDN."

"Yes, Coach?"

"I've been giving a lot of thought to your brush with the law. By the rules, I should suspend you from the team, maybe even bar you from competing in sanctioned meets. The fact is that you're the fastest man on the team, even if you lack training. You run like all hell was chasing you and Acton needs you if we expect to place in the top three."

"What did you decide, sir?"

"I have to keep you on the sidelines for a couple of weeks, but then we'll ease you back into the lineup."

"Thanks, Coach."

"Just try and stay out of trouble. You shouldn't be drinking while you're in training."

"No, sir."

Coach was quiet for a minute and Heydn was about to ask if he could go when the man spoke. "I hesitate to bring this up, but since we're talking ethics and morals, we might as well clear the air. I've heard a couple of rumors about you and I'd like to give you the chance to refute them."

"Sure."

"I'm certain you can understand why we can't have homosexuals on the team. Sometimes when you travel, you have to bunk together. Enough said, right?"

"Yes, sir."

"Then I can assume the gossip is just trash talk?"

"Yes, sir."

"Good. I've already sent your stats to some people I know at good colleges. We both know you don't have the same kind of funding as the rest of team and it would be a shame if you lost your ride before you even got it."

Heydn nodded.

"All right. Just because you're not competing doesn't mean you can skip practice. I'll be expecting you to work twice as hard as everybody else."

"You can count on it."

"You're excused."

Heydn walked down the hall from the coach's office and out of the gym building into the late afternoon sunlight. He moved like a blind man, avoiding obstacles as though he had radar. When he picked his head up, he saw that he was on the path that led to The Monks. Feeling as though he could use some solitude, he kept going, picking up his pace on the leaf-strewn track. Just before he came out of the trees, a flash of color warned him and he stopped. Peering through the foliage, he saw two young men in Acton uniforms welded together at the mouth. He recognized Blue immediately and in another moment, he came up with Astor Aldrich's name. Astor squeezed Blue's butt cheeks and Blue moaned his approval. The sound went right through Heydn's ribcage like a well-aimed arrow. He was blindsided by pain of a magnitude he'd never felt before. Dropping to his knees, he fell forward onto his hands and tried to get rid of his lunch. It was a little while before he got to his feet, shaky and weak, and wobbled back to the campus. He tripped on the threshold of his dorm and someone put a hand under his elbow to steady him.

"Damn, Case, you look like hammered shit," Peyton said.

"I thought you were confined to your room."

"Dean Whittaker moved me to an empty room in this house to be fair to my roommate."

"Poor guy. I can't imagine what it would be like to have you around twenty-four/seven."

"It's good to know the feeling is mutual."

"You were against me from the beginning."

"That's your paranoia talking."

"No, you bad-mouthed me from day one. It took me a while to figure it out though."

"You figured something out? Won't that get you disqualified from sports?"

"God, I hate phony snobs like you."

"Really? Then how do you explain Allerton King? He's your best bud now, right? And the biggest snob I can think of."

"At least he didn't leave me hangin' in jail."

"What?"

"Maybe you haven't heard," Heydn said bitterly. "I was arrested."

"No, I knew about that. In fact, I'd bet I was one of the first to hear."

"You're always digging up dirt on somebody, aren't you, you twisted shit?"

"Give me a moment while I contemplate the mental image your words have instilled in my brain."

"Fags," Heydn sneered. "You can't do anything straight, can you?"

"At least I'm not stupid enough to believe Allerton King would bail me out of jail."

"I called him and he took care of me."

"Wow, you really are as dumb as I think you are."

"Get out of my face, asshole."

"Sure. You look like you could use some rest. When you're refreshed, you can intimidate me some more with your manly muscles."

"Spare me your concern for my welfare, dickweed."

"My pleasure, jackhole. There's a lot more I could tell you about recent skullduggery, but I'm happy to leave you alone."

"Thank you." Heydn slammed the door of his room in Peyton's face.

"What the hell?" Heydn's roommate woke up with a start and knocked his books over.

"You fell asleep studying again, Judson."

Judson Lenoir yawned and glanced at his watch. "Only fifteen hours until the history test."

"Why don't you just read the book at the beginning of the year?"

"Maybe that works for you, but facts don't stick to my brain. Hey, are you all right?"

"Yeah. I'm just tired."

"You look like you had a heart attack."

Heydn stretched out on his bed and closed his eyes. Judson's choice of words pierced him to the core. It was a kind of heart attack that he'd had. The sight of golden boy Astor Aldrich kissing and putting his hands all over Blue had hit Heydn like a massive coronary. A powerful need to feel Blue's warmth in his arms made Heydn's body ache like a bad tooth. Blue's absence made expulsion from the track team seem trivial. "That's just your dick talkin', buckaroo," he whispered fiercely.

"What?" Judson turned in his chair to look at Heydn.

"Nothin'. Just tryin' to motivate myself."

"Oh. Well…good luck with that." Judson put his head down over his book again.

Heydn closed his eyes again and tried to put Blue out of his mind by concentrating on his goal of getting into a good school without bankrupting his mom. It didn't work. Turning onto his side, he put his back to Judson and faced the wall. Stealthily, he slid a hand under the waistband of his track pants and cradled his cock and balls. He remembered the way Blue's fingers had always been cool at first, but warmed up very nicely. He remembered how right Blue's touch felt on his skin seducing him to the belief that there was nothing wrong in what they were doing. He remembered Blue's eyes the first time he'd entered him.

"You sure you're all right?" Judson asked.

"Yeah, I'm sure. I'm tryin' to go to sleep."

"You were groaning."

"I was havin' a nightmare."

"Okay."

Heydn let out a big breath and took his hand off his dick. He must have been crazy to pull something like that. At least Judson had the couth to wait until he thought Heydn was asleep. However, Heydn could see that sleep would not come quickly tonight. "Hey, Jud, you ever see *Demon Armageddon*?"

"Sounds like a horror movie."

"So you haven't seen it?"

"I don't think so. Why?"

"Never mind."

Judson went back to his history text as Heydn rose and went down the hall to the bathroom. He took a quick shower, just long enough to jerk off and rinse. When he turned the water off, he heard the outside door slam shut. Taking his towel off the hook, he dried off and began getting dressed. The voices of the two young men using the toilet echoed off the tile, coming clearly to Heydn's ears. He tried to ignore them until he heard his name. Draping his damp towel over his shoulders, he walked barefoot into the next room and stopped a few feet from the pair of junior track team members.

Copeland Graham elbowed Sloan Spalding. Sloan turned from the urinal and saw Heydn. Copeland shook off and zipped up, walking quickly to the long row of sinks. Sloan brazened it out, smirking at Heydn as he finished up.

"Have a nice shower?"

"I could swear I heard you call me Allie King's butt boy."

"Well, you know, with the water running, you probably misunderstood me."

"Then what did you say?"

"He said you were King's best bud," Copeland blurted out.

"I wasn't talking to you." Heydn continued to stare at Sloan. "Is that what you said, Skip? That me and Allie are best buds?"

"Sure. Everyone knows that."

"It also sounded like Logan told you I suck a mean dick."

"Well, Allie told Logan..." Copeland stopped speaking when Sloan glanced at him.

"Forget it, bro," Sloan said. "You just misunderstood, that's all. Come on, Cope; let's go."

Heydn stood there, trembling with rage, and let them walk away. Their laughter drifted back to him as their footsteps faded down the hall and he nearly choked on his bile, but they were just stooges. He knew who the spiteful mastermind of this smear campaign was and that's where he'd direct the blast of his anger.

CHAPTER 19

"Do you believe that shit?" Heydn said as he finished lacing up.

Allerton exchanged a droll glance with Logan. "Peyton Crane is nothing but trouble," he said. "Always has been, always will be."

"Unless somebody got rid of him," Logan said, slamming his gym locker shut. "Then he wouldn't be any trouble to anybody."

"You watch too much TV," Heydn said. "I'll take care of Peyn Crane my own way."

"See, Newcombe." Allerton punched Logan. "That's class. Case cleans up after himself."

"Whatever." Logan shrugged. "Let's run."

The trio left the locker room and joined the other team members on the track for a few minutes before they broke away. As they turned onto the sidewalk that led to the bridle path, they saw two pedestrians ahead. At six foot-three, Astor Aldrich was hard to miss, and he had his arm around the shoulders of a familiar dark-haired figure.

"What a you want a do, Allie?" Logan asked eagerly.

Allerton eyed Astor's long frame for a moment before he answered. "Go around," he said grudgingly.

The three runners parted, taking to the grass as they passed the couple on the path. Blue and Astor stared after them, a little startled by the suddenness of their advent and their departure. In their wake, Blue imagined he could smell Heydn's unique scent.

"Are you cold?" Astor asked when Blue shivered. "We could go inside and have a hot chocolate or something."

"No, I want to walk. I like looking at the trees when the leaves are falling, seeing the skeletons poking through."

"I knew you were a Goth."

"Shut. Up."

"Oh, come on. You're really into all that bare branches against a bleak sky with a dead bird in the gutter kind of thing. Admit it. You have a journal in a drawer full of poems about despair and alienation."

"Nope."

"Really? I do."

Blue poked Astor in the ribs. "Did you even notice that my eyeliner has become quite discreet?"

"Well, you don't look like a raccoon, if that's what you mean."

"Ha-ha." Blue poked Astor again. "For real though, I just don't feel the need to provoke a response from anyone anymore."

"You provoke a response from me. I like to call it the Blue Elevator."

Blue pretended to contemptuous. "What kind of foolish name is that?"

"Well, Blue is you, of course, and elevate is what you do to me."

"I make you go up?"

"Exactly." Astor stopped as soon as they were out of sight of the campus. He took Blue's mittened hands and brought them to his chest. "Hey, I know you've been worried about Peyton, and I wanted to do something for you to cheer you up."

"Peyton is the one who needs cheering up. They threatened his grade point average."

"According to him."

"Well, whatever the administration said to him worked. He's keeping a low profile right now."

"It's hard for me to believe that the deans would deliberately trash a student's record. If he really did have evidence that an instructor was being inappropriate with a student, he'd have them over a barrel."

"I'm not sure what's going on between Peyton and the staff. After bitching me out about never spending time with him, he doesn't have time for me."

"That gives you more time for me."

"No hardship there. I hope we start on a new play soon so we can work together again."

"I'd love to play Romeo opposite you."

"They both die though. I'm not into tragedies as much as I used to be. It'd be really cool if Peyton finished his play soon."

"That's right. We were talking about taking your mind off poor pitiful Peyton."

"No, *you* were."

"Yes, I was. What are you doing for Christmas?"

"Same as usual. I'll go to New York, buy myself some presents, see a show, stay in a really nice hotel and come back here."

"Why don't you ever go home?"

"I don't really have one. I have houses, but no home."

"Your mom and dad?"

"Gone. A long time ago."

"Do you have any family?"

"Not living."

"Wow. I never thought to ask. I just assumed that since you didn't mention them that you didn't get along with them or something."

"I barely remember them. They got into my dad's private plane the day after my second birthday to fly down to Rio de Janeiro. I've been told my dad was a good pilot, but something malfunctioned and they went down in the ocean."

"I'm sorry, Blue."

"Seriously, it was a long time ago. I don't like broadcasting it, because people always treat you different when they find out you're an orphan. You can practically see their eyes welling up with tears and you know they're thinking, 'oh, you poor thing.'"

Astor let go of Blue's hands and put his arms around the other young man. "Yeah, I know how it can be. You know they're just trying to be nice, but you want to scream at them to leave you alone."

"Yeah." Blue rested his cheek against the soft fabric of Astor's jacket.

"So, if you can bear to break with tradition, would you like to spend Christmas with me?"

"No, I wouldn't like that…. I'd love it." Blue laughed. "You should have seen your face."

"I don't have any defenses where you're concerned," Astor said. "So take it easy on me, okay?"

"I'm sorry. I didn't mean to hurt your feelings."

"I'm kidding." Astor kissed Blue's forehead. "Well, half-kidding anyway."

Blue looked up and rubbed his nose against Astor's. "I would never do anything on purpose to hurt you."

Astor slid his hands inside Blue's long coat. "You can turn me on so easily," he said. "The first time I saw you, I wanted you."

"When was the first time you saw me?"

"Orientation two years ago. You got out of a limo and stood there looking like a character out of a ghost story. I could never get your image out of my mind after that. I never thought we'd end up involved, but I always thought you were intriguing."

"Intriguing," Blue repeated. "I like that."

"Are you sure you don't want to go to your room where it's warm?"

"You're only saying that because you know I don't have a roommate and you want to be inappropriate with me."

"Yes, I certainly do. Let's go sit on your bed and make out for a couple of days."

"Well…" Blue pretended to consider. "I do still owe you a blow job from Thanksgiving."

"I love you," Astor laughed, as he leaned in to give Blue a brief kiss.

"Aren't you afraid someone will see us?" Blue asked, avoiding the issue of saying the words back to Astor.

Astor looked around. "We're out in the woods, and if someone did see us and had the bad taste to mention it, I'd just say I lost a bet or something like that."

Blue shook his head in admiration. "You're so cool," he said.

Astor had been hoping Blue would say something else, but he accepted the accolade graciously. He had no illusions that Blue felt the same way that he did, but he did hope that would change. Brooke Barclay was someone that Astor could imagine spending the rest of his life with without ever being bored. He told Blue that he'd never marry a woman, because it would be a sham, and he refused to treat the bond of marriage so shabbily. If the laws ever changed, he would marry Blue, if Blue would have him, for he also knew that he was not meant for a solitary life. He needed a companion to share his joys and sorrows and, for whatever reason, his nature dictated that the companion be male. "How did you get so far under my skin so fast?" he murmured against Blue's hair.

"I can't lie to you any longer," Blue said dramatically, as he moved away, tugging on the end of Astor's muffler. "You have already guessed the truth. I am a vampire, a child of the night, with powers beyond those of mere mortals. It is a little-known fact that vampires inject an anesthetic anticoagulant when we bite. That's why you didn't feel the fangs going in." He continued walking backward down the path.

"I knew it was something like that. Am I going to rise from the dead too?"

"I don't plan on killing you. I'm going to keep you around so I can suck you whenever I want."

"That works for me."

Blue and Astor went to Blue's room and spent the next hour in languid play. Astor never tired of watching Blue's face as he caressed him; they had developed a game of stretching out the foreplay until one of them surrendered helplessly to his climax. Blue usually lost because Astor was very good at maneuvering them into a position where he could fondle Blue, but Blue was hampered. There were times when Blue protested the unfairness of it, but being loved so completely was a heady thing and mostly he was content to let Astor get his fill of touching and looking until the tension in his groin became unbearable. He didn't even have to say anything; a single look and Astor slid down to take Blue in his mouth and finish him off, swallowing like a man taking communion. Afterward, Astor was happy to lie on whatever surface was available, holding Blue until their time was up. The only difference this time was the banging on the door right after Blue came.

"I know you're in there, Barclay. I can smell brimstone and sulfur," Peyton hollered.

"Give me a minute. And keep your voice down."

"I can't. I'm too excited. Open the damned door."

"I'm not alone, Peyn."

"Duh, you big slut."

Astor zipped up, yanked his shirt down over his head, and opened the door.

"Oh, it's you," Peyton said.

"Who's a big slut?"

"Please." Peyton brushed past the taller boy. "As if you weren't just enjoying the benefits of my friend Blue's generous sexual nature."

"That's none of your business."

"If you say so. Hey, Blue, when you finish getting dressed, have a look at this." Peyton held up a disc.

"What is it?" Blue left off buttoning his shirt.

"Pop it in and see."

"Tell me you finished your play."

"I finished my play."

Blue threw his arms around Peyton's neck and hugged him exuberantly. "Congratulations!"

"Save the compliments until after you read it."

"I guess you'd like some time alone now," Astor said.

"What?" Blue looked up from loading the disc in his laptop. "No, you don't have to go. I doubt if Peyton minds, since you'll probably have a part in this."

Peyton shrugged. "I hate throwing a man out in the snow right after he's gotten some."

Blue rolled his eyes at Astor. "Peyn thinks he sounds sophisticated."

"Only compared to everyone else at this school," Peyn said.

"So it's called *Menagerie*?" Blue asked, turning his gaze to the screen.

"Yeah. It's a strictly candy-ass name. My original title was *Flesh in Common*, because that's the theme."

Blue gave Peyton an inquiring look over his shoulder.

"Well, you know, even if I like guys and Rhodes likes girls, we both bleed red. That's what all humans have in common, no matter what we choose to believe, or who we choose to love. We all feel pain and that alone should give us more compassion for one another."

"Wow," Astor said, sitting down on Blue's bed. "That's what your play's about?"

"That's my theme, yeah."

"I'm impressed."

"Me too," Blue said. "And I'm only on page two."

Peyton glowed quietly for about two seconds. "Thanks, but I really hate the title. Even *Flesh Menagerie* would be better."

"Why'd you change it?" Blue asked.

"I told Mr. McIntyre about it while I was on the way over here in an exalted state. I'll need his permission to put this play on. He was excited about doing a play written by a student, but he insisted that the name had to go."

"I agree with him," Astor said. "You want to be provocative, but you don't want to put people off. If the play was on Broadway, *Flesh in Common* would be a great name, but at Acton…"

"Say no more," Peyton waved a hand in Astor's direction.

"This is really good," Blue said. "It reads like a fable."

"Good, because it *is* a fable. Still want to be my Foxboy?"

"I'd pay you."

"No need for that." Peyton turned to Astor. "I need someone tall," he said. "Care to participate?"

"As long as I'm not Mooseboy or Giraffeboy or something like that."

Peyton smiled. "I wish I'd thought of that, but no, you're one of the Bear Boys. Not one of the Bully Bear Boys though; you're a Sugar Bear."

"Now you've really got my interest," Astor said, standing and reading over Blue's shoulder.

"It's about a village populated by nothing but young men between the ages of thirteen and nineteen and a few wise elders," Peyton said. "Or would you rather just read?"

"I wouldn't mind a quick synopsis," Astor said. "I have a student council meeting at seven."

"Uneasy lies the head that wears a crown," Peyton quoted. "So we have this isolated village of boys and they spend their time learning to be men. They absorb the wisdom imparted by the elders and compete in tests of mental and physical skill. They're encouraged to win at all costs to ensure that they'll be strong enough to go out into the cold, cruel world beyond the walls of the village. Into their midst comes someone different; he's not a Bull or a Bear. He's Foxboy: smaller, faster, and a little cleverer than the rest. Naturally, the others resent him when he refuses to compete in their games. They shun him at first, but later, they begin to persecute him."

"Persecute?" Astor interrupted.

"I know that's a strong word, but it fits. Eventually, they drive Foxboy out into the cold to starve. One day the youngest Sugar Bear falls into the river. It's freezing cold and he's going down for the last time when Foxboy appears. Foxboy jumps in and saves him, but Foxboy is exhausted from not eating and he drowns."

"Wow," Astor said. "That's really sad."

Peyton shrugged. "It's supposed to be."

"Does it end with the Bulls and Bears being sorry they picked on Foxboy?"

"I just told you the ending. Foxboy drowns."

"I don't mean to be critical, but shouldn't the bullies learn a lesson?"

"Not in my experience."

"This is your play. Make it happen the way you want it to."

"Why don't you write your own play?"

Blue looked up from the monitor. "Hey, guys, let's not get into some big literary discussion, okay? Let's talk about the rest of the cast. I can't wait to get started learning my lines."

"Are you in, Aldrich?" Peyton asked.

"All the way."

Peyton grinned. "This is going to be the most epic event in the history of this miserable place."

"It'll raise a few eyebrows, that's for sure," Astor said. "I gotta get going." He leaned over and kissed the top of Blue's head. "Call me before you go to bed."

"Don't I always?" Blue said as Astor went to the door.

"Goodnight, Peyton," Astor said.

Peyton waved and went back to looking over Blue's shoulder as the door closed. After a few minutes, he found a bottle of water and picked up one of Blue's comic books. He flipped through the flimsy magazine and stood up again. "This is torture," he said.

"Go for a walk or something."

"I'd better not. Since I've been given my freedom, I keep running into trouble whenever I go out."

Blue looked up in alarm. "What kind of trouble?"

"I phrased that badly. I just seem to run into people I don't particularly care for."

"You're not going to let me read, are you?"

"I ran into Heydn Case a couple of nights ago, just before I got off confinement."

"Is this random, or are you coming to a point?"

"I just thought you'd like to know that he looked terrible. I heard he got suspended from the track team over that car thing."

"As if Heydn would steal anything. I really appreciate you letting me know as soon as you heard about it. He doesn't belong in a cell."

"Neither do we, but look where we are."

"Stop being melodramatic."

"I can't. It's in my blood. Don't forget that Mommy was an actress."

Blue turned 180 degrees and rested his arms across the back of his chair. "Before I get too into this… are you sure the school will let you do this play?"

"Mr. McIntyre read the synopsis and he's excited, to put it mildly. I was careful to keep the story in allegory form so nothing is explicit, but people with a brain will get the message."

"I really want to do this, but not if it's going to get you into more trouble."

"Life would be boring without challenges."

"You're not going to listen to me, are you?"

"Why do you keep asking me questions you already know the answers to?"

"It serves me right. I didn't listen when you warned me about Heydn."

"This is different." Peyton paused. "You and Astor look like you're getting along well."

"He's nice…and a lot of other things. I don't want to talk about Astor."

"Why not? He doesn't seem shy about the way he feels about you."

"Why can't you understand that some things are personal?"

"I understand plenty and I can tell when you're lying. You don't want to talk about Astor because it makes you feel guilty."

"And why would that be?"

"Because you're using him to get over Heydn."

Blue was silent for a long moment. "That hurt," he said at last.

"But it's true, isn't it?"

"No. I'm not using Astor to get over Heydn, because that's never going to happen. I'm with Astor because being with him keeps me from going crazy."

"Exactly."

"Why are you being such a dick? Do you think this is how I want it?"

"I'm just being honest. Truth hurts."

"Yeah." Blue sighed. "Do you ever wish you could be like ten or twelve again?"

"God, no! How horrible!"

"I just think life was easier then."

"No, it wasn't. You've just forgotten what it was like."

"You're really depressing me now. Let's talk about the play."

"No. I have to go. I told McIntyre I'd meet him with a copy of the entire play, but I promised you that you could read it first."

"I'm honored. Truly."

"As well you should be." Peyton jammed his hat onto his head as he crossed the room. He stopped with a hand on the doorknob. "Hey, what show are you seeing this Christmas?"

"I'm not going to New York. Astor invited me to his house."

"I thought he might. He bores the hell out of me, but he treats you well."

"Thanks for tolerating him."

As soon as Peyton was gone, Blue finished reading the play. It made him cry like a baby. Like Astor, he would have preferred an ending where Foxboy's sacrifice resonated a little more. He didn't like the bleakness of the character giving his life without causing a change. Maybe he was a little too conventional, but the ending as written was cathartic but unsatisfying.

Blue looked at the time in the corner of the screen and reached for his phone. In a few minutes, he was listening to Astor talk him to sleep in his sonorous Boston accent. He dreamed of pristine fields of snow, of the scent of evergreen, and the jingling of silver bells. Sometime before dawn, his dreams morphed into the wet kind and he saw Heydn's face hanging over him, as beautiful and as remote as the moon while Heydn's cock plunged in and out, ceaseless as the tide. He woke to sticky sheets and the realization that he'd told Peyton the truth. He wasn't going to get over Heydn Case.

CHAPTER 11

"BLUE," Lily Aldrich greeted the young man. "How lovely to see you again."

Blue let the Aldrich's chauffeur take his bags and put them in the trunk with Astor's luggage. "Thanks. I'm really looking forward to this visit."

"Avery isn't here, of course," she went on. "So you'll only have me to put up with for a while."

"I don't mind," Blue said.

"Hey, are you two getting in, or are we spending Christmas Eve in front of the airport?"

Lily and Blue both turned to look at Astor, who was already in the car sipping a soft drink. They exchanged a smile and climbed in. Mrs. Aldrich spoke to the driver and they pulled away from the curb.

"Thanks for coming to meet us," Astor said.

"I wanted to, darling," Lily said. "And it gave me a chance to pick up a few last-minute presents."

"That explains all the shopping bags in the trunk."

"It just didn't look as if there were enough gifts under the tree with Blue's name on them."

"You didn't buy me presents!" Blue exclaimed.

"You wouldn't deny me the pleasure, would you, dear?"

Astor smiled at Blue. "It's okay. Mom and Dad know we haven't had a chance to do much shopping. Just look happy when you open your gifts and everything will be fine."

"I'll do my best."

Lily chuckled. "I've never heard a boy sound so glum at the thought of prezzies. Blue, dear, you've already given me the most wonderful gift by befriending my lad here." She squeezed Astor's hand.

"He's not all that bad," Blue said.

"Don't embarrass me with effusive praise," Astor replied.

"Like you need help embarrassing yourself."

Lily laughed again. "I miss having young men around. Perhaps we should invite some more of your school chums to visit when we're at the lake this summer."

"We'll talk about it, Mom." Astor looked out the window at the Berkshires. "Any good powder in the mountains yet?"

"I'm afraid I don't know, darling." Lily pointed to the cabinet that hid the electronics. "You can look at the weather channel if you like."

"Or I could get my laptop out," Blue said.

"It's not critical. I don't really care if we get to ski or not. I'm looking forward to two days of lying around and pigging out."

"Surely you're going to show Blue the sights." Lily paused when the two young men snickered. "Have I said something amusing?"

"No, Mom." Astor smirked at Blue. "I'll show him the sights. All the natural wonders."

The lodge was a chalet-style building of wood, stone, and glass on a grand scale. Perched on the side of a mountain near the tree line, it had a large back deck cantilevered over a sheer drop of 300 feet. It made Blue feel queasy when Astor jumped up onto the wide top railing and walked to the corner.

"Could you come down from there?"

"It's the best view."

"It's making me a little nervous."

"I'm not going to do a tap dance. I'm just looking. Why don't you come up here with me?"

"Screw that!"

Astor turned to face Blue. "This is a lot wider than, say, a balance beam, for instance."

"You nearly gave me a heart attack just now. Please come down."

"Are you really that worried about me?"

"Yes." Blue held out his hand. "Please?"

Astor jumped lightly down to the deck and took Blue's hand. "Sorry."

"I'd feel terrible if anything happened to you."

"Then I guess I'd better cancel those skydiving lessons."

"Parachutes are fine. Just don't go dancing on the rims of any volcanoes."

"I'll scratch that off my list of things to do before I die." Astor leaned toward Blue.

"Are you going to kiss me?"

"Planning on it. Objections?"

"You don't care if your mom or someone sees us?"

"Not really. Mom knows and doesn't care. Dad.... I'm pretty sure Dad knows, but thinks it's something I'll outgrow."

Blue lifted his head and offered his mouth, glad his back was to the wall of glass. Astor framed Blue's face in gloved hands and bent his neck to brush their lips together. Blue opened his eyes as Astor drew back a little.

"You know what I'd really like for Christmas?" Astor smiled impishly.

"I think I can guess. No promises on that one."

"I'll just have to wait and see if Santa thinks I was a good boy."

"I think you're a good boy." Blue pulled Astor's head down for another kiss. "But Santa's a tough sell. Thanks again for inviting me to spend Christmas with you."

"If you hadn't come home with me, I would've followed you to New York."

Blue gasped at the idea of being alone in New York City with Astor. "What a great idea!"

"What?"

"You and me in a big New York hotel bed with room service?"

"That sounds nice."

"We could see a show, go to the zoo, eat falafel, and stay up for twenty-four straight."

"Well, maybe not straight," Astor said.

Blue grinned. "We have to do this. What about spring break?"

"We'll have to talk about it later. Are you hungry? I have a craving for ice cream."

"Any time is a good time for ice cream."

Astor and Blue went to the kitchen and were given big bowls of homemade peppermint ice cream. They joined Mrs. Aldrich in front of the great room's fireplace and did their best to eat the ice cream before it melted. The two young men began talking about the new play and Astor's mother insisted on hearing all about it. They were enacting a brief scene when her change of expression warned Astor.

"Hi, Dad," he said brightly as he turned around.

"Hello, son," Avery Aldrich said. "Good to see you again, Blue. Lily, can I talk to you for a few minutes? Sorry, guys; I won't keep her long."

In less than ten minutes, a bell rang announcing dinner and Astor led the way to the dining room. His parents joined them and they enjoyed a delicious meal, but despite Lily's skill at keeping the conversation light, Blue could feel the tension between the three Aldriches. They played charades after dinner, but no one's heart was in it, and Astor was the first to bow out. Yawning hugely, he claimed to be tuckered out and headed for the stairs.

"Hey, Blue," he called as he started up. "Would you mind getting the flash drive with the pictures I took at the museum?"

Blue scrambled to his feet. "No problem. Goodnight, Avery and Lily," he said as he joined Astor. "I thought you were throwing me under the bus for a minute there," he said as they reached the top of the stairs.

"Never." Astor opened the door to his room. "Care to come in?"

Blue walked into Astor's room with a glance over his shoulder. "Just once I'd like to have sex someplace where I didn't feel nervous about getting caught."

"Did you think we were going to have sex?"

Blue punched Astor's shoulder. "Very funny. I can just imagine what my face looks like. Was it good for you?"

"Well, I did get you."

"Yes, you did. Now stop gloating. It doesn't look good on you."

"Put this on." Astor pulled a down parka from his closet.

"Why? Do you have some fetish for the Michelin Man?"

"No. It's so you don't have to go to your room and get your coat."

"Are we going somewhere?"

"Yes." Astor went to a window and opened it.

"Does it have anything to do with why you disappeared when we first got here?"

"Yes."

"Do I have to climb?"

"Yes." Astor went out the window and waited for Blue.

Blue leaned out. "Are you going to say anything besides yes?"

"Yes." Astor caught Blue and kissed him before setting him on his feet. "Come on."

Blue held onto Astor's hand as they walked a squeaky-crunchy path in the snow to the edge of the front yard and into the trees. There were lampposts at regular intervals, throwing pools of saffron light on the ground between the evergreens and up into their skirts. After a short climb, they reached a thicket of beeches and Blue stopped, staring in wonder. The bare branches of the trees, illuminated from below, shone like polished glass, each twig sheathed in ice, dripping with fragile jewels.

"Did you do this?" Blue breathed.

"A hose, a pump, and several gallons of water, plus the time and the temperature, and boom!"

"It's like magic."

"Me and my cousin used to do this when we were kids. We'd add food coloring to make different colors and break off the icicles and eat them. We were always disappointed when they didn't have any flavor."

Blue put his arms around Astor. "This is the most beautiful thing anyone's ever done for me."

"Then it was worth freezing my balls off."

"You froze your balls off? Then what are these?" Blue grabbed at Astor's crotch.

"I grew a new set spontaneously when you smiled at me."

"Ugh, that was bad. Cute, but bad."

Astor hugged Blue tighter. "Can I tell you something?"

"Of course. I'm supposed to be getting to know you better, remember?"

"Did you know I'm nineteen?" Astor began. "I'm a year older than everyone else in our class because I was out of school for a year when I was ten. My cousin Archer died that year. He was just five months younger than me and we were best friends from the cradle. After his funeral, I decided I wasn't going to participate in a world that made no sense."

"I know that feeling."

"I can see that. That's what really attracted me to you. I always liked the way you looked, but I never would have come on to you if we hadn't been in the play together. Most of the time you keep your head down and your hair is in your face, so no one can tell what you're thinking. But when you're acting, your soul is right there in your eyes. I could see that you've been hurt like I have. I thought we might have even common ground to build a bridge between us."

"I'd say you have some of your dad's talent for construction."

"You know what I'm asking you."

Blue sighed. "I don't have an answer for you right now."

"It's all right," Astor said unconvincingly. "I can wait. It gives me a reason to stick around."

"When you said you didn't want to participate in the world, you meant that you withdrew, right? You didn't mean…suicide, did you?"

"That's something that we never figured out, my therapist and me. I took a rowboat out on a day when there was this huge storm. There were whitecaps on the lake and then the rain came bucketing down. It was impossible to row against the wind. I lost my sense of direction and just stopped paddling. A couple of big waves capsized the boat. I was hanging on to it when it occurred to me how easy it would be to let go. It would be out of my hands whether I lived or died, and, if my parents' faith hadn't lied to me, I'd see Archer again when I died. Dying seemed like the better option at that point."

"But you lived," Blue pointed out the obvious.

"My dad found me. He and some other men in powerboats went out in the storm to look for me. The next day, I was mortified when I realized that my little stunt had endangered the lives of several people. If any of the search party had been lost, that soul would be on my conscience."

Blue hugged Astor a little tighter, but he didn't say anything.

"After that, I tried very hard to never be any trouble to anyone. I soon found that it was easier if I had limited contact with people. It makes things so much less complicated, you know?"

"I do."

Astor shivered. "I'd really love it if you never left."

Blue looked up, inviting a kiss, taking the lead and easily persuading Astor that the time for talking was over for a while. As their lips parted, their breath emerged in pale plumes that mingled and dissipated as their mouths came together again. Blue clutched at Astor's shoulders, tipping his head back, hair catching on bark, as the other young man pushed up his jacket and shirt and licked at his nipples. The sensation was exquisite as the wet buds furled tightly in the sharp cold sending a bolt of intense pleasure shooting to the end of Blue's cock.

"Damn, you're beautiful," Astor said. "I wish I had a picture of this. Your black hair and white skin and your nipples so rosy with the snow and the beeches in the lamplight. I'll never forget this."

"Let's go back to your room and fool around," Blue answered.

HEYDN took a bottle of water from the refrigerator and held it to his forehead as he left the kitchen and went out onto the back deck. With his mom stuck in Japan, he'd stayed on campus and accepted an invitation to a party at Bennington Kaplan's house. He hadn't seen Bennie since he'd arrived at the house and he knew her boyfriend Logan had gone home for the Christmas holiday. It occurred to him that Bennie might not even know about the party and that he should probably go in and get his jacket. But the cold felt good, like it was waking him up from the dullness of two hours spent in rooms filled with dense smoke and denser music. Only when his teeth began to chatter did he go back inside.

"Hey, I know you." A blonde girl waved at Heydn and lost her balance. She pitched forward and he caught her, getting a nose full of liquor fumes.

"It's Clarissa, right?"

"I knew I knew you. I spilled my drink."

"Want some of my water?"

"What's in it?"

"Minerals, I think."

"No, I mean, like is there like some X in it or something?"

"We're definitely failing to communicate."

"Who're you?" Clarissa looked blearily up at Heydn.

"I'm the guy that got arrested for doing you a favor."

"What?"

"The last time I was here you asked me to drive your dad's car home so you wouldn't get in trouble. You were drunk then, too."

"It's a freaking party, man. Lighten up."

"Yeah, I guess it's not your fault that your dad reported the car stolen."

"What are you talking about? My dad lives in Connecticut."

"Do you remember giving me a set of keys at another party here?"

"I remember some frat boy I boffed giving you the keys to Bennie's car."

"Bennie's car!"

"Yeah, she just got a new one. I guess what's-his-name thought it would be a good joke on her to make her think it was stolen."

"It was a joke?"

"More like a prank. He called the cops from the bedroom right after we did it."

"Clarissa."

"Yeah?" She peered up at him again.

"Why would the cops need to be involved to pull a prank on Bennie?"

Clarissa's kittenish features scrunched up as she thought hard. "Guess there wasn't any reason to call them," she said at last. "Wow, that was a pretty mean trick to play on you."

Heydn shook his head. "I can't believe it. Why would Allie do that?"

"I don't have a clue, but I feel kind of sorry for you. Want to get a room?"

"No, thanks. I need to find a ride to the bus stop."

"Aw, poor…" Clarissa paused. "Who are you, anyway?"

"Nobody," Heydn said. "Don't bother learning my name."

He propped Clarissa against the wall and walked out of the party. Shrugging into his jacket, he jogged the half-mile to the highway. It was another mile to the bus stop, but he barely noticed. His mind was occupied by the implications of the chance conversation with Clarissa. Why would Allerton set him up to spend a night in jail? That little prank had caused him to miss the track meet and nearly cost Acton a victory. Surely, Allerton wouldn't harm the team deliberately; that made no sense. None of it made sense. In fact, nothing had made sense since he'd walked away from Blue. Everything he'd done since then had been phony. He'd pretended to be something he wasn't to fit in with the kind of guys that bullied anyone weaker, the kind of guys who took their good fortune for granted, the kind of guys that would smile to his face and stab him in the back.

Heydn reached the bus stop and glanced at his watch as he jogged in place. He didn't have long to wait and he could kill time with a set of cool-down exercises. As his body went through the familiar routine, Heydn's mind strayed again to the days when he'd come in from running and Blue would caress him while he got his breath back only to steal it from him again. Blue had always been honest about what he wanted, honest about everything. Heydn felt the burn of tears behind his closed eyelids. Had he really given up love for a free ride to college? Yes, he had. He hadn't believed, hadn't recognized it for what it was, hadn't been strong enough or honest enough with himself to admit that Blue was what he wanted.

"You screwed that up, sure enough," he whispered, as the bus came around the bend. He climbed on for the long ride back to school, kept company by unwelcome thoughts.

Heydn had seen Blue with Astor Aldrich around campus and it was obvious to him that they had become very cozy. He didn't see any reason he should even try to get Blue back. It was a no-hope situation. He'd just have to live with the knowledge of how badly he'd screwed up. It was small consolation, but he understood now some of the things his father had tried to explain when he told Heydn why he couldn't be with him. Heydn actually found himself feeling some sympathy for a man he'd hated most of his life. It was hard to swallow, but Heydn could accept now that his father had made a mistake in the heat of the moment, that he had never wanted children, that it was probably better that he wasn't around to breed strife from his dissatisfaction. Heydn could see these things quite clearly now, but they were no comfort to the child who had cried for a father that would never come. He was a young man now, beyond childhood's unreasoning fears, and here he was, making the same mistakes his old man had.

Heydn looked out the window at the lights of Acton as the bus hissed to a stop. He'd really hoped it would be different here and, for a while, it had been. Now, it was a big, tangled, stinking mess that he wanted to turn his back on and run away from as fast and as far as he could go. Maybe if he called Mom, she'd send a ticket to Tokyo. Of course, the money would have to come out of their savings and Mom hated touching the savings account.

Heydn clenched his hands into fists as the bus grunted away from the curb. He wasn't going to run the way his father had. Maybe he'd never fit in with the yacht-club crowd, but so what? The ones he'd met weren't all that nice anyway. Maybe he'd never get Blue back, but that didn't mean he couldn't try. If others laughed at him for his efforts, he'd ignore it. Public humiliation was the thing that made him cringe, but if he had to, he'd parade naked around the track holding a sign that proclaimed how he felt. He loved Blue Barclay and if he didn't fight for him, he'd regret it for all time.

CHAPTER 12

"MERRY Christmas!" Lily Aldrich said merrily as Blue opened a box tied with a plaid bow. "That one is from me."

"Mom, you bought all of them," Astor reminded her.

"Yes, but they're not all *from* me," she said. "Would you pass me another croissant, darling?"

Astor carried the platter of pastries, croissants, and biscotti over to where Lily sat. He settled on the rug in front of the chaise not far from Blue's chair. "Well, what did Mom get you?" he prompted.

"It's…" Blue looked up, his eyes wide. "It's a Count Bloodscar action figure. The original one from the Korean TV series. It's even got the dagger."

"Do you like it, dear?" Lily asked.

"Like it? I can't tell you…. Do you have any idea…? This is…"

"I think he likes it," Avery Aldrich drawled. "No one's that good an actor."

Astor shot his father a look, but didn't add to the comment. Blue pulled the boxed figure out of the wrapping, anxious to break the tension that had been growing between father and son all morning.

"I don't see anything under the tree from you," Lily nudged Astor with her foot.

"Blue and I exchanged gifts last night," he said. "It's a tradition we're starting."

"That's lovely, darling." She held up her Bloody Mary. "To many more Christmases together."

Mr. Aldrich took a drink of his nog, but he didn't echo his wife's wish this time. Instead, he became engrossed in a book about ancient architecture that Lily had given him and the rest returned to the unwrapping of the presents. The fire crackled cheerfully. The snow fell outside the picture windows. The cook came in with gingerbread warm from the oven and mulled cider with cinnamon sticks standing in the stoneware mugs. Just after midday, a stag and three does picked their way carefully across the drive and melted into the evergreens on the other side. It was Christmas the way Blue had dreamed it when he was little, right down to the silver glass star at the top of the tree. The only thing that marred it was the undercurrent of bad feeling that never quite rose to the surface, but lurked near enough that Blue could see the shadow now and then. He felt guilty for being relieved when Mr. Aldrich excused himself to make some phone calls that wouldn't wait on the season.

"It's not Christmas everywhere, you know," he said, as he kissed Lily's cheek on his way out.

"Well, it bloody well should be," she said, as he passed out of earshot. "Don't you think so, lads?"

When Astor didn't speak, Blue cleared his throat. "I think it's nice to set aside at least one day a year as special and do nothing but be with the people you love."

"That's lovely, Blue. Very well-said." Lily took a small box from the pocket of her quilted satin robe. "Here's one last gift from me. It's small, but I'm hoping you'll like it best of all."

"You've already given me too many presents," Blue protested.

"Then give them back and take this one."

"You can have it all, except for Count Bloodscar."

Lily and Astor laughed and she reached down to tousle his auburn hair. "Just open it," she commanded.

Blue opened the small box and took out a pin made of silver and tiny jet and crystal beads forming a spiderweb hung with dewdrops. "This is cool."

"It's from the early nineteen hundreds and it's meant to be a tie bar," Lily said. "But of course you can wear it anywhere you like. Have I said something amusing again?"

"No, Mom," Astor said, imagining the pin resting in Blue's belly button. "I'm just having a good time."

Lily looked down at her son and smiled fondly. "I'm so glad, darling."

Astor put his cheek against her knee for a brief moment and everything was all right again, or at least as all right as it could ever be again. He took Blue for an exhilarating snowmobile ride and showed him the frozen waterfall. They made out for a little while on the warm seat of the machine as a territorial bird scolded them from an unseen vantage. The sun went west and they went back to the lodge for dinner. They said their goodbyes to Mr. Aldrich, who would be leaving very early, and everyone retired to their rooms, too full to do anything else but lie down. Still, Blue wasn't surprised when Astor slipped into his room half an hour later.

"I missed you," Astor said, as he got beneath the covers.

"It's been thirty minutes."

"I know. I can't believe I stood it for so long."

"Easy," Blue said, grabbing Astor's wrist. "How about a little warm-up before we jump right into the game?"

"Sorry, it's just that what we did last night was so good, and when I say good, I mean cosmic. I got so excited thinking about it that I'm a little ahead of you."

Blue put a hand on Astor's cock. "So I feel. You could crack coconuts with this thing."

"I wasn't thinking about using it for anything quite that violent."

Blue drew his fingers lightly up and down the underside of Astor's shaft. "What were you thinking of doing with it?"

"Don't tease me, please."

"Honestly, I'm a little sore from last night, but if you use a lot of lube and take it real slow, don't go too deep or anything, it should be all right."

"No problem. I brought lube with me."

"I had a feeling. Let me have it." Blue squeezed gel onto his fingers and reached between his legs. Carefully, thoroughly, he lubricated his sheath, stopping suddenly when the bedside lamp came on.

"Please keep going," Astor said, easing the sheet back.

"I feel pretty self-conscious with my fingers in my own butthole."

"It's the sexiest thing I've ever seen." Astor trailed a finger down Blue's cock and over his balls to his crack. "I can't wait to be inside you."

"Just give me a minute."

Astor wrapped a hand around Blue's shaft and pumped it. "It's okay with you that we're skipping the foreplay?"

"Could you wait?"

Astor shook his head. "My dick feels like it's going to explode."

"Then let's take care of that, and we can have after-play."

"Sounds good." Astor moved between Blue's thighs and lifted one of Blue's legs to rest on his shoulder. "God, I thought about this all day."

A swift little shiver tightened Blue's lower belly as the head of Aston's cock touched his hole. Gently, Astor pressed with his thumb, dimpling Blue's flesh and pushing the tip of his arousal through the elastic ring. Blue expected some discomfort, but he was surprised by the burning sensation as raw tissues were forced to stretch. Instead of relaxing, his muscles resisted, clamping down on the intruder. Astor groaned with pleasure and thrust instinctively. Blue yelped, pushing at Astor's thighs as the hard cock sank deeper.

"Stop," he gasped.

Astor halted and started to pull back.

"No. Don't move. Just…"

"I'm almost there," Astor said in a strained voice. "Just one more and I swear I'll come. Just one."

Blue shook his head as Astor's cock slid back another few centimeters before it was sheathed to the hilt. Astor's eyelids fluttered as he came, his seed spooling out deep inside Blue. He took several panting breaths before emptying his lungs in a long exhale. Lowering Blue's foot to the mattress, Astor carefully disengaged and lay down beside him.

"I'm not exactly a great lover, am I?" he murmured, circling one of Blue's nipples with a forefinger. "Two thrusts and I'm out."

Blue batted his hand away. "Are you deaf?"

"What?" Astor looked down into Blue's face. "What's wrong?"

"I told you to stop."

"Right. As in, stop for a second and let me catch my breath."

"No. As in, stop, this is very painful."

"I hurt you?"

"Yeah, you hurt me."

"I'm sorry. If you'd said something…"

"What did you think I meant when I asked you not to move?"

"I didn't think I was hurting you. I'm so sorry, Blue. Is there anything I can do to make it better?" Astor took hold of Blue's shaft.

"Please don't," Blue said. "Just let me lay here for a little while."

"Can I hold you?"

Blue shook his head. "I just want to lay here."

"I'm really sorry. I don't know why I didn't stop. Maybe I heard what I wanted to hear."

"Astor, please stop apologizing. I just need time to adjust."

"Sounds like you've had a little therapy yourself. Sorry. I won't say another word."

Several minutes crawled by like ants awaiting a signal to attack. Finally, Blue uncurled and turned to face Astor, his thick lashes clumped together with tears. "I do believe you misunderstood me. I don't think you meant to force me to do anything, but…"

"Oh no," Astor said. "This can't be good."

"The truth is that you did force me and that's going to be hard to forget, even though it's already forgiven." Blue gazed into Astor's eyes. "This isn't easy to say. I've never told anyone else."

"You can tell me. It can't be worse than being suicidal."

"When I was twelve, someone tried to rape me. He hit me really hard and got my pants off while I was dazed. A proctor saw us before anything else happened and pulled the kid off. He was the same age as me, so the grown-ups sent us both to counseling and the authorities were never involved. Technically, I wasn't raped, but I'll never forget how it felt to be helpless and I don't ever want to feel that way again."

Astor put his hand over his heart. "I swear. I'll never make you feel helpless."

"I'm giving you the benefit of the doubt. You can hold me now if you still want to."

Astor swept Blue into his arms and hugged him fiercely. Blue returned the embrace, but the security he'd felt in Astor's arms was diminished, no longer certain. He and Astor knew a lot more about each other now and there were many things they had in common, things that would make a good basis for a long-term relationship, but Blue was still undecided. When he was with Heydn, everything had a feel of rightness about it, as if he'd found his place in life and needed to do nothing but exist and love Heydn. No matter how right for him Astor might be, Blue didn't get that same feeling with him. Once again, he wondered if he was foolish for yearning after something that would turn out to be a mirage, but in his heart, he knew that what he felt for Heydn was true love, unselfish and pure. He was trying to be mature and make the smart choice, but something held him back each time he thought he could commit to Astor. He just couldn't make himself say the words that Astor wanted to hear.

"Hey," he whispered. "Are you awake?"

"Yeah."

"Maybe you should go back to your room now."

"Sure, okay." Astor got up and pulled on his briefs. "Blue, I'm…"

"I know," Blue said quickly. "Go to sleep, Astor. We have the whole trip home to talk."

Astor nodded and left quietly. Blue pulled the covers up to his chin and closed his eyes. Life wasn't getting easier, as he'd imagined it would when he was an adult. It just got more complicated, but at least he could be sure of a handful of hours when he was free of difficult choices. Blue fell asleep and if he dreamed, he didn't remember in the morning.

CHAPTER 13

"EVERYONE please settle for just a minute," Mr. McIntyre gently called the Drama Club to order. "Now you know that my policy is to let the students themselves do all of the work of preparing a play and then I step in on opening night and take all the credit, but..." He was interrupted by laughter and a few calls of protest. "Thank you. As you know, our new play was written by our very own male version of Dorothy Parker, Peyton Crane. If you don't know who Dorothy was, Peyton will be happy to explain later. I only have a couple of things to say and then I'll be out of your hair again for a while. First, the board of directors of the school has raised objections to the script I sent for approval." He waited for the noises of dismay to die down. "However, I've set up a meeting wherein I believe I can stroke their egos sufficiently to make those itchy objections go away." He waited once more for laughter to dissipate. "The second matter is our lack of an actor to fill the role of Bully Boy Primus. You'll be happy to know I've found someone and he'll be at practice today. That is all, except to say that you're doing an excellent job. If anyone has questions or suggestions, I'll be in my office for the next hour."

Blue looked at Peyton, but he could tell by the other young man's expression that Peyton didn't know about either of the announcements. He watched Peyton follow Mr. McIntyre and return almost immediately. Peyton came to where Blue was directing a couple of juniors in the assembly of a bizarre jungle gym structure. Before Peyton could speak, the side door opened, admitting a strong shaft of sunlight and Heydn Case. Blue looked quickly away, as Heydn walked toward the stage.

"What's he doing here?" Blue whispered harshly to Peyton.

"Auditioning."

"What?"

"He asked McIntyre about joining the Drama Club and here he is."

"No way."

"Yes way." Peyton looked over Blue's shoulder. "Case, what a surprise, or it would be if McIntyre hadn't announced you. Tell me; I'm curious. What was it that made you realize that you'd always wanted to be on the stage?"

"My guidance counselor says it'll be good for my self-confidence *and* spiff up my permanent record," Heydn answered. "Hi, Blue."

"Hello," Blue said and gave his attention back to the project.

"That would go together easier if you laid it flat on the ground and then raised it into place with some ropes and pulleys, or somethin'."

"Are you here to audition for the cast or crew?" Peyton asked.

"Wherever you can use me."

"Over here," Peyton gestured and walked to the far side of the stage.

Blue waited until Heydn was gone and then directed the builders to lay the painted PVC tubes out on the floor. The sections of the combination playground toy and combat training apparatus were much easier to fit together and didn't require any ladders. Seeing how quickly the work was going, Blue left his crew for a few minutes to talk to Peyton. He tried not to look at Heydn, but his eyes were drawn to the other young man and he saw how Heydn's hair was the color of aged honey in the sun and that his eyes were the blue-gray of a storm cloud, the way his upper lip curled at the corners as though he kept a couple of extra smiles tucked away there, the little scar on his right cheekbone like a tiny divot in the soft skin...

"Blue," Peyton said again. "Did you want something, or are you having some kind of out-of-body experience?"

Blue blinked. "The slayground piece will be ready soon. Do you want it in place or should we just move it aside for now?"

"Oooh, I'm tempted to say set that sucker up, but if it gets damaged…"

"We'll fix it," Heydn put in. "It's just plastic painted to look like jagged metal, right? We can saw off anything that gets broken and weld it back together with PVC cement. Nobody's actually going to be crawling around on it, are they?"

"Of course not," Peyton said. "There isn't enough liability insurance in the world."

"It looks amazing. Great job on the painting. It reminds me a little bit of the decaying techno city in Extro Metro Mortuary."

"Thanks," Blue responded curtly to the compliment. "Peyton, what's the word?"

"Put it in place," Peyton decided. "If it breaks, we'll let Heydn the Handyman fix it."

"Fine." Blue turned and walked away.

Peyton made a show of hugging himself and shivering dramatically. "Did you just feel a chill?"

"Look," Heydn said. "If you want to poke at me because I was stupid enough to let Blue go, all I can do is wonder why you picked such an easy target."

"You look." Peyton took a step closer to Heydn and lowered his voice. "If you came here thinking you'd find a way to get Blue back, you're wasting your time, and if you screw up my play…" His voice trailed off.

"What?"

"I haven't thought it through that far yet. Don't make me have to come up with some fiendish revenge."

"Fair enough. I did come here to be near Blue. I'm pretty sure you're right and I don't have a hope in hell of even getting him to talk nicely to me, but I don't know what else to do."

Peyton narrowed his eyes, glaring at Heydn for a long moment. "The maddening thing is that you'd make a perfect Primus. I need you in my play."

"So I can stay?"

"Until you screw up."

"That shouldn't take long."

"Here's your script. Don't lose it. We're here every day starting at five. I hope that won't interfere with any of your other activities."

"I quit the track team."

"Do tell."

Heydn shrugged. "I had questions about their ethics."

"Are you serious?"

"What do you care?"

"Good point. Okay, I'm done with you."

"One question?"

"Go ahead."

"Am I the villain?"

Peyton smiled and Heydn had his answer. Heydn nodded and went to find a corner to start memorizing his lines. Astor arrived from a student council meeting and nearly collided with Heydn on his way out.

"What the hell's he doing here?" Astor asked Peyton.

"Case has graciously consented to take the part of Primus."

"You're kidding."

"Do I look like I'm kidding?"

Astor glanced over at Blue. "I wonder what sparked Case's interest in the theater."

Peyton snorted. "I almost feel sorry for him."

"I don't. It's going to cause quite a bit of tension having him around."

"I took that into consideration. I trust my actors to channel their emotions into their performances."

"You're very slick, Peyton."

"May I take that as a compliment?"

"Sure, why not?"

"While we're talking, I'd like to see a little more arrogance in your portrayal of Big Teddy. It's true that he's the nicest guy in the play next to Foxboy, but he's still an entitled heir of the elite class."

"I'll see what I can do. Any more surprises?"

Peyton shook his head and Astor went to where Blue was putting tools away at the side of the stage. Astor knelt and began helping.

"You look awfully elegant in that vest."

Blue smiled without looking at Astor. "It was a Christmas present," he said.

"From someone with good taste obviously."

"Obviously." Blue closed the toolbox and stood. "That muffler looks great with your jacket."

"A close personal friend gave it to me."

"Close *and* personal?"

"Very."

Blue smiled again, glad to see Astor in a playful mood. Since Christmas, Astor had been vacillating between buoyant hours filled with exuberant sex and plans for the future, and hours when he seemed to disappear into his thoughts, remote and uncommunicative. Blue had tried to talk to Astor, guessing that the trouble involved Mr. Aldrich, but Astor denied it. He blamed his moodiness on the recurrence of his asthma and Blue backed off, trusting Astor to talk when he was ready.

"Did you see Heydn?" Astor asked as he walked with Blue to the storage room.

"Yeah. It was unexpected, to say the least."

"Are you okay with it?"

"It's not my decision." Blue set the toolbox on a shelf and turned the light off.

"Want to hang out in here for a while?" Astor put a hand on Blue's nape and massaged gently.

"No time. We have practice and then we have to get the dining hall ready for the Founders' party."

Astor stopped before they reached the area where the rest of the cast was gathering. "Are you sure it won't bother you to have Heydn here?"

"It'll bother me, but we need him. Don't worry about it. I'm a trouper." Blue paused. "Is it going to bother you?"

"It already does, but I won't let it affect the play."

"Me either."

"Sorry. I didn't mean to imply that you couldn't handle it."

"We'll just have to see. Come on. Peyn's giving us the evil eye."

Practice started with Heydn's introduction to the rest of the cast and then he was plunged into the thick of it. Peyton showed no mercy, but although Heydn had to read his lines, everyone was impressed with the presence he gave the character of Primus. Heydn took Peyton's direction to act like the top predator in the food chain and translated it into a menacing stance and a flat hard-edged tone. Grudgingly, Peyton included him in the praise at the end.

"You're actually good as Primus."

"Don't hurt yourself," Heydn said. "You don't have to be nice to me."

"No, I don't, but you're part of the cast now and your morale is my business. So in my own best interests, I'm going to tell you when you're doing a good job. There's not really anything you can do about it as long as I'm in charge."

"Yeah. I figured you'd enjoy having some power over me."

"Don't you dare analyze me. I'll take you to school, cow kicker."

"You're so sure you're smarter than everybody else, aren't you?"

"It's useless to argue with the self-evident."

"Yeah, well, being clever doesn't mean you've got any sense."

"This is too tiresome," Peyton said.

"Quitting already?"

"Please. That's fourth-grade rhetoric. Why don't you just come out and call me chicken?"

"What's going on over here?" Blue asked, stopping by Peyton's side.

"Just going over some things with the new boy."

"Normally, he'd give the new boy's things a going-over," Heydn said.

"The new boy is sassy," Peyton continued.

"Add it to his list of bad habits," Blue said. "We need to get over to the dining hall and finish decorating."

"Whoa," Heydn said. "I'd like to know more about this list of bad habits."

"Are you sure you have time? It's kind of long."

"Cute," Heydn said. "What's number one?"

"You're a hypocrite," Blue fired his worst insult.

"Then let's introduce Mr. Kettle to Mr. Pot. You call me a hypocrite for joining the track team, yet you hang out with Astor Aldrich, a guy that you used to refer to as the Prince of the Preppies. What's the difference between us?"

"You don't know anything about Astor."

"Look," Heydn said point-blank. "I know I'm not as good as Astor and I never will be, but I love you. I wish I was someone better, but I'm not. You'd be a fool to take me back when you could have him. All I can tell you is that I love you. That's all I've got to say."

Whatever Blue had been expecting Heydn to say, *I love you* was not among the possibilities. He stood in silence, staring at Heydn like a sleepwalker hearing his name.

"Blue," Peyton said, a warning note in his voice. "Don't you dare; don't you even think about it. Bailing him out was bad enough. I won't let you make this mistake again."

"You won't *let* me?" Blue glanced at Peyton.

"Maybe I phrased it badly."

"Maybe you should butt out of a private conversation."

"Blue, don't be an idiot."

"Peyn, don't judge me."

Peyton mimed zipping his lips and walked away, but not so far that he couldn't keep an eye on Blue and Heydn.

"Before you say anything," Heydn said, "did you bail me out of jail?"

"Yeah."

"Why?"

"Peyton told me you'd been arrested and I really didn't even think about it. I just called a lawyer and arranged it."

"Thanks."

"I didn't do it because I wanted your gratitude."

"So I can eliminate gratitude from the list of possible reasons?"

"Don't be funny."

"To paraphrase our director, I *am* funny and there's not much you can do about it."

"I can leave."

"It's what I deserve." Heydn paused. "But I wish you'd stay."

"Where do you get the balls to say something like that?"

"I don't know. I swear I don't, but I'm a desperate man."

"Cut it out. Seriously."

"I'll try, but I can't help how you affect me."

"I'm leaving." Blue turned and saw Astor waiting by the door.

"Need any help with the decorations?" Heydn called after Blue.

"Ask Peyton; he's in charge." Blue hurried off, keenly aware of Astor's gaze.

"What did Case have to say, if it's any of my business?"

"He wanted to know if we needed help in the dining hall."

Astor stopped on the path outside the theater. "Blue, you don't have to spare my feelings. I'd almost bet that Heydn was making some sort of apology for being stupid enough to dump you."

"How'd you know?"

"It's what I would do if I were ever that stupid." Astor smiled. "Of course, I'd show up with a loaded pizza, the first edition of *Scarlet Defender* comics and the latest Nightsteed CD."

"You can't buy me," Blue said haughtily, as he started walking again, nose in the air. His sudden grin marred the affronted demeanor somewhat. "But keep trying."

"Have I told you I love your sense of humor?"

"It was one of the first things you said to me, as a matter of fact." Blue bounced up the dining hall stairs.

"Well, I meant it." Astor swung the left-hand door open and waited for Blue. "God, how could I possibly forget what this place smells like?"

"Your subconscious blocks it out like any other memory that's too horrible to bear."

"Hey!" Peyton called from the middle of the large hall. "If you two could take a break from making out, you can hang these nets of balloons."

"I hate the Old Fart Party," Astor said, as he held a ladder for Blue.

"You'll get to see your mom and dad."

"Yeah, but we have to stand around talking with a bunch of blowhards. Don't get me wrong. Some of them are related to me and I love them, but the more they drink, the louder they get, and it's always the same old crap."

"I usually leave right after the buffet line starts."

"Stick around tonight?"

"Sure, I'll save you from the terminal boredom."

"You're a good man, Barclay."

In two hours, the hall was festooned for a celebration and the young men of Acton-Pierce Academy's senior class assembled in their best evening wear to mingle with the members of the board of trustees, descendants of the academy's founders, and prominent alumni and their guests. A group of students from the school orchestra played chamber music and against one wall was a long row of tables covered with dishes and manned by the kitchen staff. A few of the bolder students asked daughters and sisters to dance, and opened the floodgates for their shyer fellows. Before long, the dance floor was crowded and the boys and girls were pairing off in private conversations. The Aldriches were late and Blue stuck by Astor until he had to relieve himself of a half-dozen ginger ales. As he returned from the men's room, he saw Lily standing alone at the edge of the dance floor.

"Hello, Blue darling," she said, embracing him with a kiss on each cheek. "You look very handsome."

"Thank you. You look beautiful."

"I had my hair highlighted. I'm not certain I like it, but Avery says it looks very natural."

"I thought you'd been to the beach or something. Have you seen Astor?"

"He's right there, dear." Lily pointed discreetly to the dance floor. "Isn't Cecelia lovely?"

Cecelia was lovely. She was tall, blonde, and willowy with narrow hips and small breasts, a body made to display designer clothing. Her long legs easily kept up with Astor's stride as he spun her in a waltz step. She laughed fetchingly, large white teeth and bright blue eyes catching all the light in the room. The air practically shimmered around her in her silvery slip dress. "She's beautiful," Blue said.

"Just picture my grandchildren," Lily said softly.

Blue froze, unable to take his eyes from the dancing couple to look at Mrs. Aldrich and see if she was joking or serious.

"Oh, dear. I didn't mean to let it slip like that. Astor…Astor cares very much for you and he made us promise not to say anything until he'd spoken with you."

"I need to be excused," Blue said.

"Blue, wait. You don't understand." Lily caught his hand. "Astor is my only child. He's the only son in Avery's family. I don't mind, I truly don't, that you and he have a special bond. I would never object to it, but you musn't deny me my grandchildren."

"I don't feel well, Mrs. Aldrich." Blue tugged his hand free. "Excuse me please."

"Blue!" she called after him, but he didn't turn around.

Blue brushed past Rolly at the door and hurried down the stairs, taking the path that led to the lake. Rolly found Peyton in the kitchen and told him Blue had left the party looking shaken.

"We're not following people around anymore," Peyton said.

"Yeah, but I thought you'd want to know about this."

Peyton sighed. "Why do I put myself through this? Here." He threw his clipboard at Rolly. "Make sure the custard goes out by nine." Peyton brushed off his jacket and went into the hall in time to see Astor having an animated conversation with his mother while a thoroughbred stunner looked on. Astor pushed the girl's hand off his arm, gave his mother a look of reproach, and headed for the doors. Peyton sighed again and went back into the kitchen.

Astor dashed down the stairs and stopped where the walkway split into three. Given what he knew of Blue, he took the left-hand path away from civilization. Risking a broken ankle on the icy trail, he ran into the woods, calling Blue's name. He found him at The Monks.

"Can I talk to you?" he asked.

"If you'll tell me everything you've been hiding from me since Christmas…or whenever."

"Will you hear me out?"

"No guarantees. Just be honest. Who's Cecelia?"

"Okay, nothing but the truth. Cece is…. I've known her for a long time. Her mother and Archer's mother were sorority sisters and best friends. They joked all the time about their kids getting married someday."

"So now you're going to marry her?"

"Probably."

"Keep talking. I need to hear how you justify this."

"Blue, please—this isn't easy for me."

"It isn't? Because I'm having the time of my life."

"Point taken. I know you thought I was having problems with my dad, but those issues are old ones. My mom's the one who's been on my case lately."

"I thought she understood about you."

"She does, but she still wants grandchildren."

"We don't all get what we want."

"No, that's sure as hell true." Astor moved closer to Blue. "We could make this work," he said. "Cecelia knows I'm gay. She won't mind if I have a lover, if I don't mind hers. We could still be together."

"How?"

"I've given it a lot of thought since I met you. I'd have to maintain a residence with Cece, but that doesn't mean we couldn't have our own place, or places all over the world."

"You're fooling yourself. You don't think your folks and hers aren't going to be coming over for dinners and whatnot? And what about grandchildren? Is she going to be artificially inseminated, or are you going to do the deed?"

"I'm not going to sleep with her."

"As far as I know, anyway."

"Blue, that's ridiculous."

"This whole situation is ridiculous. You really think I'm going to be your dirty little secret?"

"Don't say that. That's not true."

Blue overcame his fear of losing his security and spoke with painful candor. "I won't accept half a life, Astor. I'd rather be alone again, pretending I like it that way."

Astor bowed his head. "Here's the rest of it. Archer's mom and mine were sisters," he said. "After Archer died, my Aunt Rose killed herself. My mom still feels like she should have seen it coming and been able to stop it. If a baby of mine will make her feel…"

"I don't want to hear any more," Blue interrupted. "I can see that you think you have good reasons for doing this. I just can't be part of it."

"So you're too good to do something so disgusting?"

"Yeah, and so are you."

"I have to do this."

"I understand."

"Please, don't make up your mind right now. We're really good together and a lot of people are happier with a lot less than we'd have."

"I couldn't live like that. Not now. Not after New Year's in New York."

Astor closed his eyes and savored the memory of standing in Times Square with Blue, their arms around each other, counting down the seconds with the crowd, and kissing in full view of anyone who cared to look. "I'll never forget it."

"That's the way it should be. We shouldn't have to hide and it wouldn't be fair to either one of us if I agreed to this scheme. You should think about it again."

"This is going nowhere and I need to get back. Can we talk again?"

"Yes, Astor. We can talk again."

"Walk back with me."

"I'd rather stay here for a while."

"I don't like the idea of you being alone out here at night."

"I'm a child of the night, remember?"

Astor didn't smile. "Come on back with me."

Blue sighed. "Okay. You can walk me to the dorm."

Astor left Blue outside his building and went back to the party. Peyton saw him return and waited what he considered a reasonable time before calling Blue's cell. He got voicemail and hung up without leaving a message. As soon as he could, he left the celebration and knocked on Blue's door.

"Come on!" he called through the wood. "Let me in. There are ogres out here."

"It's not locked, Peyn."

Peyton turned the knob and came into the room. As he'd expected, Blue was on his bed, back to the wall, his face lit by the glow of his laptop. Peyton brought the bottle out from behind his back. "I have here a very fancy red wine that somehow didn't get opened with the rest of the case." Peyton switched on a lamp and prowled around until he found two plastic cups. Taking a corkscrew from his pocket, he opened the wine and poured. "Here," he said, offering a cup to Blue. "Take two of these with bed rest and you'll feel better."

"I'm fine."

"Bullshit. I know you a little. I know that look on your face."

"I'd kind of like to be alone."

"I don't think so. I think that's the last thing you want. Drink up and tell your wicked Uncle Peyn all about it. I might not be able to help, but I'll help you heap abuse on who or whatever."

Blue took a sip of the wine. "Got anything to eat?"

Peyton pulled a plastic bag of cheese cubes from his right pocket and tossed it to Blue. "Do I know you or what?"

"A little."

"So…what are you perving on?"

Blue closed the laptop. "Nothing."

"Good. Then I'm not interrupting."

Blue nibbled a piece of cheese and took a big drink of the wine. "What's wrong with me?"

"Not a whole lot. You want unconditional love, but that's not very realistic and so you get disappointed. Only our mothers ever love us like that, and we spend the rest of our lives chasing it."

"Psychobabble."

"Yeah, but I really don't think you're any more screwed up than anyone else."

"Thanks." Blue scooted back and leaned against the wall. "How did I get here?" he asked as he held out his cup for more wine.

"This is where your parents wanted you to go?"

"No. I mean…at the end of the summer, I knew who I was. Now, I have no idea. I've done and said things that I never thought I would. I've got two guys who claim they'll do anything to be with me. Me. A scrawny, snarky space case being chased by two guys."

"You forgot to mention that the guys are totally hot."

"Sadly, that is a factor. Now I feel shallow."

"Well, you're not." Peyton pushed his luck and moved from the chair to the bed. He settled next to Blue and propped the bottle between his legs. "You're the best person I know."

"Someone else said something like that to me not long ago. I told him he probably didn't know many people."

Astor rolled his eyes. "Tell me what happened tonight."

"More wine." Blue held out his cup as he popped another cube of cheese into his mouth. "You don't have any chocolate, do you?"

"Oh, crap." Peyton reached into his left pocket. "It's a little melty."

"I'll lick it off the wrapper. Hand it over."

"Leave me a couple of fingers," Peyton said as Blue grabbed the candy. "So does your mood have anything to do with Case declaring his undying love in the theater?"

"That shook me, but it was just a warm-up compared to Astor's surprise. He's getting married."

Peyton almost spilled his wine as his head swung toward Blue. "What?"

"Not tomorrow, but someday. His mom already has the bride picked out. She'll make pretty babies."

"I'm flabbergasted."

"It's the timing that's killing me. Over Christmas, he told me he loved me and that he wanted to spend the rest of his life with me, that he'd never be one of those pathetic gay men that get married and sneak around. And less than a month later, I find out he's practically engaged."

"I'm sorry. I really am."

"I'm just staggered, you know. I believed him and the hell of it is that I still do. He doesn't really want to get married. He's doing this for his family and he's going to be miserable for the rest of his life."

"So you can't even hate him."

Blue shook his head and a teardrop fell to darken a spot on his trousers. Peyton set his cup on the floor and put his arm around his friend. He took Blue's empty cup and put it down, pulling Blue's head to his shoulder. Blue let the tears fall, but he stayed composed. "Thanks for coming to check on me."

"I care. It's my curse," Peyton said airily.

Blue lay down and put his head in Peyton's lap, staring at the toes of his high-tops. "All I want is a barbarian warrior prince who'll appear on his flying stallion and take me captive to serve his pleasure. Is that too much to ask?"

"My dream man's an international jewel thief who wears skintight black outfits when he's working and gambles in a tux at Monte Carlo when he's not. Does yours have a big sword?"

Blue smiled. "I can always count on you to bring it back home."

"As if you're not as big a horn dog as I am."

"Once I started having sex, I went a little overboard, huh?"

"I wouldn't say that. I'd say you're pretty normal for an eighteen-year-old boy, especially considering you're a late bloomer."

"Did you just call me normal?"

"I take it back."

"Good. I'm really not in the mood to kick your ass."

"So what were they like?"

"What was who like?"

"Case and Aldrich. How do they measure up in the sack?"

"I'm not going to give you a blow-by-blow, but I have no complaints about either."

"Bor...ring. I'd tell you."

"I wouldn't listen."

"Boring times infinity."

"Yes, I'm boring and I'm tired." Blue sat up. "Thanks, Peyton. I appreciate the shoulder."

"That sounds like goodbye." Peyton stood up and tousled Blue's hair.

"See you tomorrow," Blue said, as Peyton went to the door.

"One thing's for sure; play practice won't be boring." Peyton shut the door on Blue's groan.

CHAPTER 14

PLAY practice was anything but boring, but not due to any drama between any of the players. All the drama came from Peyton's script. The actors were excited to be performing something written by a peer. The language was current and the invented slang was fresh. Buckley Caldwell and his part-time assistants had started on the costumes and everyone loved the uneasy combination of distressed prep school uniforms and fur. Buckley's partner Carrington Foster was able to use makeup to suggest a blend of human and beast without using any rubber noses, and Blue gave him the Web address of a company that made inexpensive sets of fangs that didn't look cheap.

There was only one set, divided into sections that filled the stage with a bizarre tangle of elements both futuristic and primitive. The eye would light on a structure that seemed familiar, but it had been twisted, or truncated, or had disparate items attached that rendered it alien, creating in the viewer a sense of vague anxiety.

Peyton in director mode was demanding, but extremely pleased with how everything was coming together and his mood permeated the cast and crew. Mr. McIntyre sat back and basked in the glow of knowing he'd taught his pupils well. His main contribution was a brief conversation with Avery Aldrich, head of the board of trustees, in which he illustrated the unfairness of the board's intention to prohibit the staging of *Menagerie*.

Each day after the Founder's Party, Astor managed to corner Blue, speaking sincerely and at length in a determined effort to change Blue's mind. Blue told Astor at the outset that nothing he could say would alter the fact that what he proposed was deceitful. The lies they would have to tell were too much to pay. Astor knew this as well as Blue and yet was willing to lock himself in that closet. It was a brick wall between them that neither could see through and it grew thicker each day.

Blue resumed his habit of hanging out in anime chat rooms, staying online for hours with role-players from the UK, Japan, and Australia. When his eyes began to burn, he closed the laptop and often went outside to let the cold and the mindless rhythm of walking clear his head. Memories kept him from the lakeside path that led past The Monks, but one morning around five, he got tired of being herded by the past and took the downward trail. He could smell water and hear the lapping of wavelets on the shingle when he became aware of another sound. Running footsteps kept a muffled beat, growing louder as the jogger approached. Blue almost stepped into the trees, but at this time of year, they gave little cover.

Heydn stopped in his tracks when he saw Blue. "Hey," he said, exhaling a cloud of warm breath.

Blue nodded and started to walk around the other young man.

"Are you in a hurry?"

Blue shook his head.

"Could we talk for a minute?"

"I'm sick of talking."

Blue was standing close enough that it was easy for Heydn to take him by the shoulders and kiss him soundly. Taken completely by surprise, Blue stood quiescent as Heydn tenderly melded their mouths together, pouring all his longing into the caress. When Blue put a hand on Heydn's chest and pushed, Heydn let go of him instantly.

"Sorry," he said. "That was pretty stupid, huh? But when you said you were sick of talking, it just popped into my head and I did it."

Blue stared at Heydn, his lips parted, breathing in small puffs. Without warning, he took Heydn's head in his hands and pressed their lips together hard. Heydn tasted blood when Blue flung away from him.

"Ow," Heydn said.

"Now we're even."

"Does that mean if I grab your dick, you'll be compelled to grab mine, and so on?"

"Get out of my way."

"I'm not in your way."

"The hell you aren't." Blue licked his lips, still tingling from Heydn's kiss. "No matter where I go, or what I do, you're there in front of me."

"You mean that?"

Blue nodded.

"Oh, man! I thought you hated me, that you couldn't ever love me again."

"I love you, Heydn."

Heydn's eyes sparkled in the gloom. "You don't know what that means to me. I never thought we'd ever be able to…"

"Easy," Blue said softly. "Just because I love you doesn't mean I'm taking you back."

"Oh…. I thought maybe…. God, how stupid can one man be?"

"I don't think you're stupid. I think you bought into something and forgot who you were."

"Don't worry; I've been reminded."

There was silence until Blue broke it with a question. "I heard you quit the track team. Why are you out running at this forsaken hour?"

Heydn shrugged. "I like to run."

"It must have been hard for you to quit."

"It woulda been harder to stay."

Blue was curious in spite of himself. "What happened?"

"I started noticing things about my new friends that bothered me, but I ignored them. Maybe rationalized would be a better word.

Anyway, I heard some rumors that were circulating about me and I assumed that Peyton was the one spreading them. I told Allerton about it, which made me feel like the biggest fool in the world when I found out by chance that it was him who started the rumors. If I hadn't run into that chick Clarissa at Christmas, I'd probably still be walking around at the end of Allie's leash."

"You got fooled. Happens to everyone."

"Yeah, but it sure cost me."

"Pain is the price of wisdom, according to some guy in Humanities class."

"Does it have to hurt this much?"

"I'm…I'm sorry you lost your chance at a scholarship."

Heydn laughed. "Do you really think I give a shit about that anymore? College? It'd be just another place where you aren't. I'm not makin' sense."

"Don't make me the reason you give up on your dream."

"But you give the dream meanin', don't you get that? Without you to share it, it's nothin'."

Blue put his hands under the earflaps of his knitted hat. "I can't hear any more of this."

"Want a doughnut?"

"Do you *have* a doughnut?"

"Oh, so now you can hear me. No, I don't have one, but if we hightail it to the bus stop, we can be at the diner in about fifteen minutes."

"I hate Acton's 'no student vehicles' policy."

"I think everybody does. So, do you want to go?"

Blue thought for a minute. "It doesn't mean anything," he said. "It's just coffee and doughnuts."

"I know. Last one there buys."

Heydn sprinted away, leaving Blue staring after him. Blue shook his head at his own idiocy and ran after the other young man, intensely annoyed that he couldn't keep his gaze from Heydn's perfect ass.

"SO I have to hear from the grapevine that you're going with Heydn Case again?"

Blue looked at Astor in the mirror, his face made up to resemble a fox's impish features. He glanced to the side, but Carrington was at the far end of the room helping Buckles glue points on Rhodes' ears. "I'm not going with Heydn."

"Then why are you with him all the time?"

"I'm not. I spend just as much time with Peyton, but even if I was, it has nothing to do with you."

"It's not like you to be mean, Blue."

Blue turned in his chair and stared at Astor until the other young man dropped his eyes.

"I miss you," Astor said in a quieter voice.

"I miss you, too. There's a big hole in my life where you used to be."

"Take me back."

"Tell your mom you can't get married."

Astor's jawline hardened as he gritted his teeth. Taking a nebulizer from his pocket, he put it in his mouth and squeezed. He breathed deeply and after a moment, the pinched look of his features relaxed a little. However, his relief was short-lived.

"Blue," Heydn said, as he plopped down in the chair next to Blue. "Guess what's on the Sci-Fi channel tonight."

"Hi, Heydn," Blue said, looking at his reflection.

"Kamakura Kazui's *Sinbad*. It's not available on DVD, and I've been waiting for a chance to get some kind of copy."

"I'll capture it for you. No problem."

"I thought you'd be more excited. You love that movie. It has that badass CGI flying horse."

"I don't know. Maybe a guy on a flying horse just doesn't thrill me anymore."

"You're crazy. It'd be the coolest thing ever to have a horse with wings."

"Do you have any idea how large the wings would have to be to get an animal the size of a horse off the ground?" Astor asked.

"Really, really large?" Heydn guessed.

"No, they'd have to be really, really, *really* large," Astor replied.

"Oh, so roughly a wingspan about as wide as my dick is long?"

Blue snickered; he couldn't help it. Looking wounded, Astor opened his mouth to retort when Peyton came in. The director announced that he wanted all actors and crew out front in ten minutes and sent Buckley and Carrington into a tizzy. When everyone was gathered, Peyton had them sit in the audience while he took the stage.

"I got a note today," Peyton said, holding a crumpled piece of notebook paper up for all to see. "It's not signed, unless 'death to fags' is a name. The writer, using some rather creative spelling choices on the harder words, wants me to know what will happen if I don't stop spreading my queerness around. He includes everyone in the Drama Club, by the way. Apparently, if you're in the theater, it automatically makes you gay. Don't laugh. The person that wrote this is not funny. He's scary."

"Oh, come on," Rhodes said. "He wrote a note. All bark and no bite."

"The Saturday Killer wrote notes," Blue said.

"You're not comparing this jackass with a serial killer, are you?"

"Crazy is crazy, regardless of degree."

"You're the expert."

Blue smiled at Rhodes. "Now you're getting a clue."

"Eyes front," Peyton said loudly. "I'm telling all of you about the threats because you have a right to know. If anyone wants to drop out of the production, he can go to Mr. McIntyre's office and tell him."

"This is just a lot of melodrama," Rhodes said. "I'm not quitting."

"Thank you, Rhodes," Peyton said dryly. "All right, everyone. Take five and we'll get started."

Heydn leaned forward in his chair behind Blue's, interposing himself between Blue and Astor. "I've got a pretty good idea who's writing love letters to Peyn," he said.

"I'm sure Peyton does too," Blue answered.

"Think he'll tell anyone on the faculty?"

"Of course he will," Astor said. "Why wouldn't he?"

"Because it would give them a legitimate reason to close down the play?"

"Yes it would," Blue said. "For just a second, when Peyton started talking, I suspected that he wrote the note just to stir us up, but he wouldn't risk that. This play is everything to him right now."

"You're kidding," Heydn deadpanned.

Blue smiled and Astor frowned.

"We could be using this time productively," Astor said.

"How mature of you," Heydn said.

"Someone has to be."

"My whiskers itch," Blue said.

Heydn laughed and Astor frowned again.

"That's just the gum that's holding them on," Astor said, touching one of the plastic filaments with a forefinger.

"They're cute," Heydn said. "The ears remind me of your Halloween costume." The second the words were out of his mouth, Heydn knew they were the wrong ones. In his haste to one-up Astor, he'd reminded Blue of a bad memory.

"I think it's been about five minutes," Blue said as he stood. "I'm going to find Peyton."

Astor gave Heydn a long look behind Blue's back. He didn't know why, but the other young man's words had bothered Blue and even if Blue wasn't with Astor now, Astor still felt protective. Heydn met Astor's eyes and stared back as if he had all day and nothing else to do.

"You're a jerk," Astor said as he rose to his feet.

"Coming from the King of Jerks, that's a compliment."

"I don't want to get into it with you here."

"Okay. Where and when?"

"Why don't we leave it to chance?"

"That's what I thought. Believe it or not, I don't hate you, Astor. I actually think you're probably a pretty cool guy since Blue likes you, but you're just a little bit too polite."

"What's wrong with manners?"

"Nothing, but you couldn't keep Blue because you wouldn't fight for him. You're too nice to get your knuckles bloody."

"I sure hope so. Violence never solves anything."

"Maybe you're right, but sometimes you have to be willing to make a stand."

"Whenever the two of you are ready, we'll get started." Peyton's voice boomed out of the speakers.

Heydn and Astor gave each other a last look that made it clear that the conversation was just postponed. Practice went well, though Peyton had to make the decision to eliminate the whiskers from the costumes when the actors kept scratching their faces. Carrington was overheard to remark that the damned things couldn't be seen from the audience anyway and became the most recent recipient of Peyton's benevolent dictator speech. The group broke up in a good mood, splitting off with excited voices and bright laughter. The threatening message had begun the evening on a grim note, but the camaraderie of the production raised morale again .

"Blue," Peyton called as his friend exited the dressing room, followed shortly by Astor and Heydn. "Can you hang around for a few minutes?"

"Sure." Blue dropped his backpack and waved to the other two young men. "Catch you later."

"Yeah, bye," Peyton said.

"Thanks," Blue said, when Heydn and Astor were gone. "I was trying to think of an excuse to ditch both of them for a while."

"Now will you believe I have psychic powers? It occurred to me today that we haven't been to Giddie's together since school started. Why don't we live dangerously?"

"You mean be spontaneous?"

Peyton waggled his eyebrows. "Come on. I've got my credit card. Let's call a cab, get dressed up, and get our fine asses to Giddie's."

"Okay."

"Oh, come on, Blue, you never..." Peyton paused. "Did you say okay?"

"Call a cab; I'm going to change."

CHAPTER 15

"You changed?" Peyton said, eyeing Blue's white button-down shirt and dark trousers. "That looks the same as your uniform."

"No, it doesn't. This isn't an Oxford shirt and uniform trousers would never be this tight."

"True." Peyton ogled Blue's ass as he got into the cab. "It's just kind of conservative for Giddie's."

"Next time you can pick out my clothes."

"Don't think I won't." Peyton smoothed the front of his clinging long-sleeved T-shirt of black lace and Spandex.

The conversation continued in that vein until the taxi dropped them at the curb in front of Giddie's. The building looked exactly like the pre-fab warehouse it was on the outside, but the inside held five different theme bars and attracted business from the five closest counties. There was a disco, a honky-tonk, a sports bar, a show bar, and a lounge, all catering to a primarily gay clientele. Not only did it offer a veritable smorgasbord of eye candy and entertainment, the bouncers had selective trouble doing the math when examining the IDs of the more attractive underage males. Peyton insisted on buying the drinks on the grounds that he looked older than Blue and Blue soon had a line of cocktail glasses waiting as Peyton drained his as quickly as possible.

"You starting a collection?" a man asked as he stopped at their table in the disco.

"Just looking for the perfect Cosmo," Blue answered.

"You're cute."

"But not alone," Peyton said as he put two more pink drinks on the table and sat down.

"You're cute, too," the stranger said.

"How old are you?" Peyton asked baldly.

"Thirty-two. And my name's Garner, if you're interested."

"Do I look interested?" Peyton yawned.

"Would you like a drink, Garner?" Blue asked. "I have five."

"Sure," Garner said, picking up one of the Cosmopolitans. "Never had one of these before." The flashing lights from the dance floor gleamed in his sun-bleached surfer mane as he tipped his head back and sipped from the martini glass. "Tart, yet sweet," he said. "Kind of like the two of you."

"Handsome *and* witty," Peyton marveled. "How'd we get so lucky?"

"You must've been a real good boy."

"You'll never know just how good. If you've finished your drink, would you mind moving along?"

Garner leaned over the table, his shirt gaping open, showcasing his sculpted pecs. He smiled at Blue. "Would you like to dance to a song that was popular when I was your age?" he asked.

Blue smiled back. "As long as you don't expect much. I'm not a very good dancer."

"You are when you've had a couple of drinks," Peyton said.

Blue picked up two of the glasses. He put one to his lips and drained it in three gulps. The other drink followed and Blue thumped both glasses back down on the table. "There," he said. "Theoretically, I should be able to dance now."

Peyton finished the rest of the booze on the table as he watched Blue boogie with the bodybuilder. Blue moved differently from how he had the last time Peyton had seen him dance. He had more confidence, really occupying his space and even invading Garner's. When the stranger put his hands on Blue's hips from behind and bumped his crotch against Blue's butt, Blue laughed over his shoulder and bumped back. Peyton got up and went to the men's room. He relieved himself, washed his hands, and reached into his jacket's inner pocket. Taking out a small white tablet divided in the middle, he popped it into his mouth and dry-swallowed it. He knew that mixing diazepam and alcohol wasn't a good idea, but he'd done it before and lived. What he needed right now was to be numb enough not to care about anything.

When he found his way back to the right bar and the right table, Blue was nowhere in sight. "Have you seen my friend?" he slurred at the waiter.

"Am I supposed to know you?"

"He's my age, black hair, dancing with a blond guy that looks like he picks up extra cash making porno movies."

"Oh, you mean Garner. They went outside when the song ended. Lucky kid. I'd love Garner to look at me like that. You want another drink?"

Peyton was already halfway to the door. He burst outside and looked to his right and left. Blue was not on the sidewalk, or across the street. That left the alleys and the back parking lot. Figuring he'd circle the building, Peyton headed down the alleyway on the right. He saw a few couples, but no one he knew. The small back lot was full and there were no lights because the customers liked it that way. Peyton guessed that at least a third of the vehicles had fogged-up windows. He realized that he looked about as ridiculous as the father of a teenage girl roaming lovers' lane peering into cars, but he didn't care. He didn't even care that Blue would probably be angry. He had to find him.

"Damn, boy, you taste as sweet as you look," Garner said as he covered Blue's mouth with his again. Letting his hands slide down Blue's back, Garner grabbed his ass cheeks and lifted him to sit on the car hood behind him. Moving between Blue's thighs, Garner lifted one of Blue's legs on his forearm and leaned in. Blue was pressed back against the hood as Garner rubbed his hard-on against Blue's crack.

That's what Peyton saw as he reached the last row of cars parked in the shadow of the board fence. He kept moving forward on autopilot as Blue squirmed on the polished metal. It was impossible to tell if Blue was pushing Garner away or clutching his shoulders in passion, but Peyton had no trouble making up his mind what was going on. "Blue!" he called out.

Garner's head came up and he peered at Peyton in the moonlight. "What the fuck do you want?" he asked thickly.

"Let go of my friend."

"You want me to let you go?" Garner looked down at Blue.

"Kinda, yeah."

"Fine." Garner stepped back and let Blue up. "I thought you wanted to be dominated. My mistake."

"No mistake," Blue said. "Except on my part. I got in over my head."

"Is that so?" Garner reached out and put a hand on Blue's hair. "Tell you what, Peaches. When you feel like you're ready, come and find me. The owner of this place will have my number. He's a very happy and loyal customer. Not that I'd ever charge you a cent."

Blue nodded, his stomach fluttering at Garner's touch.

"I really hope you'll call," Garner said as he turned from Blue. He grinned at Peyton. "You're a good friend," he said. "But you need to get laid and keep your nose out of other people's love lives."

"Yeah, like I'm totally going to take advice from a pervert."

"Come back when you grow up...both of you," Garner said as he walked away.

"Peyn..." Blue sighed. "That was really embarrassing."

"I saved you from certain ravishment."

"Please."

"Your legs were up in the air. If I'd come out here five minutes later, he'd have been pounding your ass like he was drilling for oil."

"You're probably right. When he bent me over that car hood and I felt how strong he was…" Blue shivered. "I was a little nervous, but my insides melted and ran down into my dick."

"Gross. He had date-rape written all over him."

"Those were tattoos."

"Seriously, what were you thinking? He's a stranger."

"A hot stranger. Lighten up, Peyn; I'm just horny. Isn't this what all those funny gay guys in the movies do? Have casual sex anywhere, anytime?"

"You've had too much to drink. We're going home."

"*I've* had too much? You can barely stand up."

"I don't need to stand to wield my plastic wand." Peyton fumbled his phone out and called for a cab. "Did you leave anything inside?"

"Just my dignity."

"Maybe we should have one more while we're waiting."

"Cab drivers hate it when you puke in the car."

"I am a gentleman." Peyton held up one finger and it nearly over-balanced him. "I puke out of the window," he finished as he rocked on his feet.

Blue linked his arm with Peyton's. "Come on; we'll sit on the bench under the street-light."

"Like a couple of steaks in the butcher's window."

"I might be a steak, but you're a rump roast."

"That was truly lame, Barclay."

Blue got a good look at Peyton's heavy eyelids and slack features as they came out of the alley. "Are you on anything besides booze?"

"I may have taken a Valium."

"You're not sure?"

"Okay, I took a Valium."

"You're going to hurl for sure."

"I'm not a puker; you know that."

"Whatever. Have a seat."

"Yes, I am blithering drunk," Peyton said to a passerby that stared at him too long.

"Peyton, please sit down. If you make too much trouble you won't get a banana."

"Ha-ha." Peyton slumped on the bench. "Classic," he said. "I just got settled and here's our taxi."

After they climbed into the backseat and the cab pulled away, Blue turned to Peyton. "Hey, even though it wasn't necessary, thanks for rescuing me in the parking lot. Garner was right. You're a good friend."

Peyton nodded. "Yeah, that's me."

"I was kind of wondering what you were going to do if he got hostile."

"Call nine-one-one?"

Blue smiled in the dimness of the car's interior. "I should never have guzzled those two drinks. They hit me all at once and the next thing I knew I had a mouthful of tongue."

"So that kind of guy turns you on, huh?"

"I can picture him with a sword and a loincloth bending me to his will."

"Your fantasies are so fan-boy…but go on."

"You saw that body. He was muscular without being too pumped. Didn't you imagine him naked?"

"I might have."

"Give me a break. Haven't you ever daydreamed about a guy that desires you so passionately that he overwhelms you and takes what he wants?"

"Sure…when I was fourteen. Sorry. I was kidding. Go on."

"It's just a fantasy. Doesn't mean I actually want to be raped."

"I understand."

"How did we get on this subject?"

"It's all I talk about, remember?"

"Trapped in a cab with a sex addict," Blue moaned, pretending to cringe away from Peyton.

"Yes, you have fallen into my clutches, my pretty." Peyton loomed over Blue, forming his fingers into claws. "And I am insatiable."

Blue crossed his forefingers and held them up. "I repudiate you, evil one."

The taxi rounded a corner and Peyton fell onto Blue. Blue caught him and sat him up again. Peyton put his arms around Blue's neck and leaned until their foreheads touched.

"I may throw up," he confided, his breath redolent of alcohol.

Blue smiled. "We're out of town and on the freeway. No more bumps or corners."

"Good. Blue?"

"What is it?"

"You know I love you, right?"

"I love you, too."

Peyton squeezed the back of Blue's neck. "You're not hearing me."

Blue made a small startled noise when Peyton's lips covered his. The kiss was unexpected, skillful and wild with yearning. Peyton licked at Blue's lips in flickering little darts before his tongue slid inside. He tasted every surface of Blue's mouth, ranging wide and deep in a sensuous preview and Blue responded for a few seconds, tightening his arms around Peyton before letting go.

"Don't, okay?" he said, when their lips parted.

"Just once," Peyton said. "I'll never ask again; I promise."

"Are you bartering with me for sex?"

"Am I? I want you so much right now that my brain is scrambled."

"I can't."

"It felt like you were getting into that kiss."

"And then I remembered the cab driver."

"I'll tip him generously."

"Don't," Blue said again, as Peyton leaned toward him.

"Why not?"

"Because I don't want to have a sexual relationship with you."

"Just one time."

"You are *so* wasted and you're going to feel incredibly stupid in the morning."

"I don't care. You'll sleep with the jock. You'll sleep with the prep. You'll even get busy with some random stud, but you won't even kiss me?"

"You're my friend."

"I don't want to be your friend; I want…. That didn't come out right."

"No, it didn't."

"Blue…"

"Shut up, Peyton. You're very, very drunk and you've taken some of your mother's medicine. It'd probably be better if you just shut up now."

Peyton took a deep breath, opened his mouth and shut it again. Dense silence filled the vehicle and in less than five miles, Peyton passed out. He sagged toward Blue and Blue sat back, pulling Peyton's head to rest on his shoulder. When the car stopped, he got Peyton out with the driver's help and woke him up enough to walk him to his room. Blue put Peyton to bed and turned to go. Peyton reached up and tried to pull Blue onto the bed. After a few moments' struggle, Peyton collapsed and his eyelids fluttered closed. Blue said goodnight and went upstairs to his room.

"Hi," Heydn said, getting up from the floor beside Blue's door.

"It's two in the morning."

"Yeah, I've been waiting for a long time."

"Go to bed. That's what I'm going to do."

"I just want to tell you something."

"Speak," Blue said, turning the key in the lock.

"I saw you perform in the Shakespeare play. You didn't look ridiculous in the dress."

"That's it? That's what you waited up until two to tell me?"

"It seemed important to me."

"Well...goodnight," Blue said as he went into his room.

"Goodnight!" Heydn called. "You know, if I hadn't screwed up, I'd be home now."

"Am I supposed to respond to that?"

"This reminds me of the day we met. I'm nervous. You're sarcastic. The only real difference is the hickey on your neck."

Blue shut the door on Heydn and went to the mirror. He stared at the maroon patch of skin near the base of his neck and a slow smile curved his lips. Heydn was probably racking his brain right now, wondering who was responsible for the mark. Maybe it was petty, but Blue derived some small satisfaction from the thought.

CHAPTER 16

DESPITE tension among the cast, or maybe because of it, the opening night of *Menagerie* was electrifying. There were long moments when the spectators sat stunned, eruptions of laughter both delighted and horrified, and shouts of approbation when a line hit home. When the curtains closed on Foxboy's dead body, the audience was silent, unsure whether to clap or not. Peyton loudly called out "The end," and the applause began. The prevailing opinion among the students was that *Menagerie* kicked ass, pointing out everything that was bad about Acton and all boys' prep schools in general, though they didn't phrase it quite that way. The attending teachers were divided between admiration and outrage, internally and from one another. Peyton was exultant. Mr. McIntyre was not amused.

"Peyton Crane." The Drama teacher's voice cut through the excited babble around the director. Actors and crew fell back to make way. "I need to talk to you," Alan McIntyre said.

Peyton knew very well what the Drama Club sponsor wanted to talk about: the scene Peyton had inserted into the play at the last minute, the scene that suggested the character of Primus was coercing a Teddy Bear to give him head. It was nothing more than a hand gesture on Heydn's part, a motion as though he was pushing someone's head into his crotch. His back was to the audience and the actor playing Trey Bear had exited through a trap door, but the insinuation was clear to many who were watching, including Mr. McIntyre.

"I'm simply mystified," he said, when the others had moved away. "How could you betray my trust? You know the rules as well as I, Peyton. No unauthorized material is to be performed."

"I needed it to illustrate the rank hypocrisy of the ruling class."

"Don't be pretentious with me, Mr. Crane. You know that I agree with you about many of the problems at this school, but that is not the issue at the moment. I trusted you. No other student has had the autonomy that you've enjoyed as director. I thought you had enough character to blossom into a leader."

"The play is a success."

"Yes, but a leader tries to do what is best for all. In the end, you made the selfish decision."

"I don't regret it."

"You've given the board of trustees all the reason they need to censor student productions."

"Then we'll perform in the streets. Creativity will not be stifled."

"The streets? Don't make me laugh. You're a child of extraordinary privilege and I thought you might do something with the advantages you've been given, but…"

"But?"

"Never mind. I forget sometimes that you're only eighteen. That's a compliment, by the way."

Peyton pursed his lips. "I'm sorry if I got you in trouble," he said at last. "I'll tell the deans that you didn't know anything about it."

"That hardly matters. I'm your sponsor; that means I'm responsible."

"That sucks."

"Consequences, Peyton. Every action has them. Think about it."

"The play really was good though, wasn't it?"

"It was brilliant. Enjoy your opening night party." Mr. McIntyre turned away.

"Is it a closing night party, too?"

"That remains to be seen."

Peyton shook off the guilt until a more convenient time and went to celebrate with his colleagues and admirers. The performers were vibrant with the charge of enacting something daring and high on the applause of their peers. Peyton could hardly keep his eyes from Blue's glowing visage and wished for the infinite time that he hadn't made such an ass of himself in the cab the other night. Blue hadn't mentioned it, but it hung in the air between them like the diesel fumes of a runaway bus. He'd blown any chance he had of winning Blue's love; two and half years of ground work wasted in two minutes. Those dark eyes would never look at him with adoration or kindling desire. Those lips would never kiss him tenderly or open wide for his cock. He'd struck out as surely as his rivals had and with less excuse. After all, he knew Blue better than anyone did. Didn't he? A short while later, as he stood within a circle of admirers and watched Blue slip out with Heydn, he had to admit that perhaps his friend had changed and he didn't know him so well anymore.

"Are you sure this isn't a ploy to get me alone?" Blue's bubbly tone belied his words.

"If I'm lyin', I'm dyin'," Heydn said, as they hurried toward his dorm. "Allerton gave me a nugget of dank when we got back from that trip to the islands. I never touched it, so I imagine it's still at the bottom of my underwear drawer sealed in foil and tucked into an empty cigarette pack."

"It's been a while since I smoked."

"We're celebratin'. Let's shoot the moon."

Blue laughed just to let some of the high spirits out. "Okay. Let's do a couple of swats and go back to the party."

"It'll definitely make Peyn's wallowin' easier to take."

"Hey, come on; he earned it."

"Sorry if I'm just a tidge miffed over the dirty trick he played on me."

"If he'd told you the new scene hadn't been approved, would you have refused to do it?"

"Hell no," Heydn said honestly. "But he should've told me."

"Yes, he should've. I've noticed that people don't always do what they should."

"Fuck you."

"You wish."

"With every beat of my heart."

"Shut up. Hey, there's a light on in your room."

"Oh yeah, I kinda forgot that my roommate would be there. I'll just grab the stuff and be right out."

Blue took off his mittens and made werewolf paw prints in the snow until Heydn came back. Without discussing it, they took the path toward the lake, stopping as soon as they were out of sight of the campus. Heydn used three matches, but finally got the stubby joint to stay lit. He passed the roach to Blue, who inhaled a deep lungful and gave it back.

"Damn," Blue said in a tight voice. "That tastes like kryptonite. I doubt I'll need another hit."

"Sure?" Heydn glanced at Blue before he pinched the end off the joint and dropped it in Blue's jacket pocket. "For later."

"I think I might be over getting stoned."

"I never smoked much. It's a nice buzz once in a while."

"Mmm," Blue tilted his head back and looked up at the stars through the winter bare branches. "I like the floaty feeling. Kind of like when you've got a fever, you know?"

Heydn was gazing at the line of Blue's neck. "Yeah. Right," he said slowly.

"Whoa," Blue said as he looked back down. "I'm a little high."

"Yeah." Heydn grinned.

"Ready to go back to the party?"

"No, but if you leave, I'll follow you."

"Damn it, Heydn. Every time it seems like we're having a nice normal conversation, you have to say something like that."

"Yes I do."

"You won't wear me down with persistence."

"Doesn't matter. This is who I am."

"Are you somehow mocking me?"

"Not intentionally."

Blue gave the other young man an assessing look. "If I wanted to kiss you, could you let it be just that? A kiss and nothing more?"

"If you're asking me if I could sleep with you and not let it mean anything, the answer is no."

"Too bad."

"I wasn't finished. It would mean something to me because I love you, but it doesn't have to mean anything to you. If you're horny, I'm your man."

"I am horny," Blue confessed. "I had sort of an adventure a couple of nights ago and it…"

"Got your motor runnin'?"

"Yeah. Now I can't switch it off and jerking off doesn't make it go away."

"I can help with that. I'm a pretty good mechanic."

"If you say anything about looking under my hood or checking my oil…" Blue let it hang.

"Aw, you're takin' all the fun out of it."

"Then let's just forget it."

"No more puns," Heydn said quickly.

"It was a bad idea to begin with. I don't know what I was thinking."

"You were thinking that this feels pretty good." Heydn cupped Blue's cheek on his palm and drew his thumb along the silky line of Blue's eyebrow.

"It really does," Blue sighed.

Greatly daring, Heydn took a step closer and put his other hand on Blue's face. As though he expected to be caught and taken away in handcuffs, Heydn stole a kiss, brushing his lips so delicately against Blue's that the touch was almost subliminal. A soft moan escaped Blue's lips and he looked at Heydn with eyes that were dewy with need. Heydn didn't ask for any more permission. He covered Blue's mouth with his and acquainted the other young man with the depths of his desire.

"How do you do that?" Blue groaned as their lips parted. "I want you so much I can't make it back to the dorm."

"It's awful cold out here."

"Then warm me up."

Heydn took Blue's hand and pulled him to The Monks. Taking shelter from the wind in the lee of the boulders, Heydn and Blue embraced hungrily, devouring each other with mouths and hands. Kisses were urgent and covered all of the limited skin that was exposed to the elements. Blue slid a cold hand under Heydn's waistband and took hold of his burning shaft. Heydn groaned into Blue's mouth, pressing him against one of the huge rocks as he worked at Blue's zipper. Blue pulled Heydn's hard cock through his fly and slicked it with warm spit. Heydn shuddered as the saliva quickly cooled, but Blue chafed his rod back to quivering life. Clumsy with his gloved fingers, Heydn yanked Blue's trousers below the bottom curve of his ass. Putting his hands on Blue's waist, he lifted him to the slight incline of the boulder and held him there with his weight.

"Do it. Do it," Blue chanted under his breath when he felt the head of Heydn's cock at his hole.

Conscious of the lack of adequate lubrication, Heydn eased the tip of his shaft into the reluctantly yielding aperture. A thin whine emerged from Blue's throat, but he gripped Heydn by the biceps and let himself sink farther onto the hot length of flesh. Heydn widened his stance as Blue wrapped his legs around him, heels digging into the small of his back. Snow fell around them, but they stood in a blast furnace funnel of wind, swept up and away like cinders from a bonfire, dancing together in the currents of hot-blooded pleasure. Heydn wrapped an arm around Blue's back and pulled him closer, sheathed to the hilt, Blue's cock trapped between their bodies, sliding in a slick of its own making. Blue gasped and moaned, pulling at Heydn's hair, arching his back, pressing the soles of his feet against Heydn's buttocks for leverage as he single-mindedly sought greater stimulation. Spurred by Blue's abandoned enthusiasm, Heydn churned his hips and put his mouth to Blue's neck, placing his own mark on the smooth skin. Blue made a strangled little noise and dug his fingertips into Heydn's muscles. Heydn shortened his stroke and Blue cried out, his legs tightening around Heydn's waist. Burying his face in Blue's neck, Heydn thrust until he felt Blue shudder in the throes of orgasm and then slowed his cadence, sinking deep as the tight passage rippled along the length of his aching cock. Shivering at the exquisite caress, Heydn shifted his rod, savoring the small sounds that Blue made. Blue was wrung out by the powerful orgasm. Dreamily, he clenched and relaxed his interior muscles as Heydn slid in and out of him. In about five seconds of this treatment, Heydn shot his load. He stood on trembling legs, holding Blue up, as his seed spurted out in a seemingly endless stream.

"God damn," he breathed, as aftershocks tightened his abdomen in waves. "I think my legs are gonna give out on me."

Blue made a sound of protest as Heydn disengaged and set him on his feet. Quickly, Heydn pulled Blue's trousers up and fastened them before he did up his jeans. Then he swept Blue into his arms and kissed him until Blue pulled away.

"Bow howdy," Heydn grinned. "That was somethin' else."

"You definitely tuned me up," Blue said.

"Uh, if you don't mind me askin', did you cum without touchin' your dick?"

"Wild, huh?"

"So you came just from me, you know, puttin' my dick in you?"

"Well, you did have to repeat the action several times."

Heydn's grin widened. "No shit. That's cool as hell."

"It's not a miracle or anything. Don't call Ripley's or the Guinness people."

"You're wrong. A couple as sexually compatible as we are is a genuine miracle."

"How come sometimes you talk like a country boy and sometimes you sound like a talk show host?"

"I've missed your insults."

Blue took a deep breath. "This was just sex," he said. "Nothing more."

"Wrong again. That wasn't just sex; it was somethin' a whole lot better that there isn't a word for yet."

"I'm going back to the party."

Heydn fell in beside Blue, ebullient with the fact that he was walking next to Blue and with the afterglow of fantastic sex. He stopped at the entrance to the dining hall and pretended to inspect his friend from head to foot.

"What?" Blue asked.

"I'm afraid there's no way to hide it."

"What?"

"That well-laid look."

Blue punched Heydn's shoulder and walked past him into the party.

"I was looking for you," Astor said, as Blue took a soft drink from the tub of ice.

Blue opened the bottle and took a long drink. "I needed some air."

"I would've gone with you."

"Thanks." Blue took another long pull at the soda.

"Did either of your little playmates tell you why they thought it would be a good idea to spit in Mr. McIntyre's face?"

"No."

"Did you know about it?"

"No."

"That's the only word you have for me now, isn't it? It doesn't matter what you say; every word means no. How did we go from making love for hours to this?"

"You know how."

"This stalemate is driving me crazy."

Tired, sated, and with his inhibitions lowered by the marijuana, Blue's insecurities spoke for him. "Do you know how much it hurt me when I saw you dancing with that girl? It was like an icicle in my heart. Even if we could be together, you'd have to be with her sometimes, and every time you left me, it would be like that same icicle plunging into my chest. I can't live like that. Please take that as my final answer."

"You never cared about me, did you?" Astor whispered harshly. "You used me to get Heydn Case back and it worked perfectly. It probably took longer than you planned, but you got what you wanted."

Blue could only stare at Astor in disbelief. "If you really believe that..." he began and then gave it up as pointless. "I'm sorry," he said, as he moved away.

"Why do you keep humiliating yourself?" Peyton said from behind Astor.

Astor turned around. "I'd think you'd have more sympathy for me, considering."

"Considering what?"

"That Blue has never looked at you and wondered what it'd be like to fuck you."

"Touché. Feel better now?"

"Not really." Astor took a pull at his nebulizer. "Why can't Blue compromise?"

"I don't know, but I think it's why I fell for him."

"You know Case has snaked him again. I can't prove it, but I can smell it."

"Ew. I think you need a real drink. Come with me if you want to kill a few brain cells."

"We probably shouldn't be drinking alcohol on school premises."

"Granted; now do you want a drink or not?"

"Yeah." Astor followed Peyton to the kitchen.

Blue saw them leave together and nudged Heydn. "Check it out. Wouldn't it be ironic?"

"Thanks for putting that picture in my head. How are you doin'?"

"I'm fine." Blue gave Heydn an odd look. "How are you?"

"Me? Couldn't be better. Need another soda?"

"I think I'm over the dry mouth. Looks like the party is winding down."

"What do you expect from a sausage fest like this? The heteros get bored quick."

"You and Peyton must have been raised in the same gutter."

"Hey, me and him are the normal ones. You're a prude."

"You're saying this to the guy you just nailed up against a rock in a snowstorm?"

"You do have a point." Heydn grinned. "I love you," he added.

"Why don't you fags make out?" Rhodes said, as he passed by.

"Okay," Heydn replied. "But if you want to watch, you'll have to take a number."

Rhodes stopped and looked back and forth between the other two young men. "What do you get out of it?" he asked.

"The sarcasm?"

"No, the...being queer. I mean, it seems like you take an awful lot of shit for being gay and I was wondering what makes it worth it. Is the sex a lot better or something?"

Blue stared open-mouthed at Rhodes while Heydn tried to control his laughter long enough to answer.

"You don't get to pick." Blue recovered first. "I didn't choose to be homosexual; I just am. The way you're heterosexual."

"That just doesn't make sense to me," Rhodes shook his head.

"I guarantee you when I kiss Blue I feel all the same things you feel when you kiss your girl," Heydn said.

"No shit?"

"I'm crappin' you negative," Heydn said. "You can take my word as a bisexual."

"I still don't get it. The idea of touching another guy's dick does nothing for me."

"What about a guy touchin' your dick?" Heydn smiled slyly. "Head is head, right?"

Rhodes shook his head again. "Not to me."

"Hey, I'm just messin' with you," Heydn said. "I don't mean anything by it."

"For a minute there, you sounded like Allerton King or one of his goons."

"Just a bad joke, Rhodes."

"Glad to hear it. Carry on."

Heydn smiled at Blue as Rhodes walked away. "He thinks we're together."

"Yeah, he seems confused about a lot of things."

"Are you ready to get out of here?"

"I was thinking about it."

"Come on. I'll walk you home."

"Fine, but you're not getting any."

"That's what you say now," Heydn said, as they left the hall.

"You're pushing it."

"What have I got to lose?"

"I guess you could look at it that way," Blue said as they walked up the path to his building.

"Are you sayin' there's a chance you'd take me back?"

"If you don't think there is, why are you hanging around?"

"Because I made a vow to myself that this time I wouldn't run away. If you don't take me back by the time we graduate and go off to college, I'll admit defeat. Until then, I'm not givin' up."

Blue remembered how nice it felt to sleep beside someone, to know they'd be there when you woke up. "I can't stop you," he said.

"So," Heydn said, as Blue started up the stairs. "Do you think we'll get together again like we did tonight?"

"Are you asking if we'll have sex again?"

"I could get on my knees if that would make it clearer."

Blue smiled. "I'm not making any promises, but I think it's likely. If you think you can keep yourself under control."

"What do you mean? Like no jackhammer action or what?"

"You know what I mean."

"Come on, Blue," Heydn said softly, taking one of the other young man's hands. "We're so good together. You felt it out there in the snow, didn't you? We're meant for each other."

Blue gently pulled his hand free and continued up the stairs. "You might be right," he said, turning when he reached the top. "But I need more time to…process everything that's happened."

"I'm not goin' anywhere." Heydn stroked the banister. "Are you sure you don't want me to come up?"

"I'm good." Blue stretched and smiled down at Heydn. "I don't think I'll have any trouble falling asleep tonight."

"Happy to oblige." Heydn gave Blue a goofy salute and left the dorm. He made it down the front steps before he punched a fist into the air and exhaled a long "Yessssssssss!" There was hope.

"What are you so pumped about, Case?" Allerton King asked as he and Logan Newcombe stopped on the walkway.

"I've got nothin' to say to you," Heydn answered.

"We were just at your place," Allerton said. "Your roomie said you popped in and out like a bunny rabbit. Were you in a hurry to see your boyfriend?"

"As a matter of fact, I was."

"You really let the team down, Case."

"You got along just fine before I came to Acton."

"I hear you're in the Drama Club now," Logan sneered. "I always figured you for a fairy."

"What did you want to see me about?" Heydn asked.

"Nothing. We were there to invite Judson to a meeting."

"I'm sure he was thrilled." Heydn moved past the other two young men.

"Did Barclay suck you real good?" Logan said. "Bet he loves the taste of your cum."

Heydn spun and was chest to chest with Logan. "I'm already pissed at the two of you. Anytime you want to rock, I'm ready to roll."

"Logan," Allerton said sharply. "Quit screwing around. We need to see a couple more people."

Logan's eyes remained locked with Heydn's for another three tense seconds before Allerton called him to heel. Sullenly, Newcombe stood down and walked away with King.

"Assholes," Heydn said as he continued on his way.

Allerton and Logan stopped to talk to another member of the track team and then headed to their dorm. As they entered the front hall, Sloan Spalding rose from a chair in the lobby.

"Hey, Skip," Allerton said.

"You weren't at the play tonight, were you?" Sloan said.

"Hell no," Logan answered for his friend.

"I didn't think so. You're not going to believe what that fag Peyton Crane did."

"Come on upstairs," Allerton said, inviting Sloan to spill his news.

"Crane's dead," Logan said when Sloan stopped talking. "A walking dead man."

"I can't believe the little fairy had the balls," Allerton said, half-admiringly.

"He's not getting away with making me the laughing stock of Acton. Crane's a dead man."

"We get it, Logan," Allerton said. "Quiet down for a minute and let me talk to Skip."

"You seriously wouldn't believe this play," Sloan said. "I can't believe they're getting away with it. It's obvious who the characters are supposed to be. Crane's laughing in your face."

"When I'm through with him, he won't have a face," Logan said.

"Logan." The warning in Allerton's voice was plain and Newcombe subsided sullenly. "Thanks, Skip. I'll talk to some more people who saw the play and see what they say. If they tell me the same thing you did, then I'll decide what to do about it." Allerton walked Sloan to the door, slapping him on the back as he left. "Logan," he said softly. "We've talked about your impulse control problem before."

"I'm not out of control. And nobody heard me except Skip."

"This time.   You've got to learn to think before you speak. Seriously, man. You can't go off like that in a boardroom. No one will respect you. You have to act like nothing fazes you."

"Okay, okay. Just tell me Crane will pay."

"Crane will pay."

 # CHAPTER 17

BLUE opened his door and found Heydn on his mat. "It's five in the morning," he pointed out.

"Come running with me."

"Not on your life." Blue started to close the door, but Heydn stopped it with his foot.

"Alternate plan," he said. "It's Saturday. We're not doing the play until Mr. McIntyre gives the go-ahead. We have almost two whole days of freedom."

"Allegedly."

"That reminds me; how much do I owe you?"

"What?" Blue blinked owlishly and then sighed. "You might as well come in. I'm awake now."

Heydn happily entered the room behind Blue. "How much did it cost you to bail me out?"

"Forget it." Blue pulled on a pair of well-worn flannel pants.

"I won't. I may not be rich, but I pay my debts."

"You didn't ask me to do it. You don't owe me anything."

"That's not how it works, Cookie. Tell me how much."

"I don't remember."

"Don't make me tickle it out of you."

Blue's head swung toward Heydn. "That would be a bad idea."

"Scratch that. Why don't you finish getting dressed and go with me to Deerfield?"

"What's in Deerfield besides Godzilla Mall?"

Heydn smiled. "The Garden Villas Mall might be a blight on the landscape, but this weekend they're hosting the Transgalactic Millennial Con."

"How did I miss that?"

"You've been distracted. So, is it a plan?"

"No, it's spur of the moment in my case. How long have you known?"

"Heard it on the radio when I woke up."

"I don't know."

"Come on. We could be there by seven-thirty. All-day screenings of anime. The cast of Comet Chaser Thirteen. Five-dollar cups of ice with three ounces of soda poured over it. Chubby fan-girls dressed like punk metal samurai guys. Tables and tables of precious junk."

"It does sound like heaven."

"I could grab something from the cafeteria and meet you at the bus stop."

Blue chewed his lower lip. "I haven't been to a con since Halloween before last."

"Come with me."

"Arghhh, okay. Get me some breakfast and I'll be there as soon as I can."

Heydn trotted off and Blue shucked the flannel pants in favor of a pair made of a supple silk cotton blend of matte black. He pulled one of his old favorite T-shirts from the back of a drawer and pulled it over his head. The soft material stopped short of the waistband of the trousers and clung to the sleek lines of his coltish frame. Almost as an afterthought, he found the star sapphire stud he used to wear and put it in his ear, an ephemeral blue glow half-hidden in his dark hair. Slinging his backpack over his arm, he went to meet Heydn.

"Where are you going?" Peyton asked as they met just outside Blue's dorm.

"Deerfield."

"Godzilla Mall? For what?"

"Sci-fi convention."

"Do I want to go with you?"

Blue shook his head.

"Is Heydn going?"

"It was his idea."

"That cracker is a lot smarter than any of us gave him credit for."

"Speak for yourself."

"Oh, that's right. You always knew he had hidden depths." Peyton smiled. "I'd be bored out of my mind at one of those conventions anyway."

"What are you going to do today?"

"Find Mr. McIntyre and kiss his ass."

"Good plan. Good luck." Blue started to turn, but paused. "The play is really, really good, Peyn," he said. "I'm so proud of you."

It was a few moments before Peyton could trust his voice not to break. "Thanks. That means a lot to me. Now go play hooky with Huckleberry."

Blue gave Peyton a quick hug and walked away. Heydn was waiting at the bus stop, doing lunges with one foot up on the bench. Blue watched Heydn's thigh muscles flex under the worn denim and had the sudden intense wish that they'd stayed in his room. Heydn saw him and held up a bag.

"Bagels," he said, and pointed to two paper cups on the bench. "Coffee: two sugars, two creams."

"Thanks." Blue sat and sipped the coffee that was prepared just the way he liked it. "This is nice."

A two-hour bus ride ended at the sea of asphalt that was the mall's parking lot. As Heydn and Blue approached the south entrance, they entered the fringes of the convention, walking past people with multicolored hair and plastic swords, smoking alone and in themed clusters.

"Check it out," Heydn said. "The Lime Green Ninja on your right."

"With his arch-enemy Lady Fuschia. Nice wig."

"She'll never make it in the door without doing the limbo," Heydn said, eyeing the woman's purple platform boots and the towering spikes of her magenta hair.

"Doesn't matter if she bonks her noggin. Lime Green Ninja was played for laughs."

Heydn chuckled. "I remember. Just the idea of a ninja in bright green clothes is funny to me."

"Yeah. Hey, that chick has cotton candy. Let's go on in."

"It's barely eight o'clock. You'll be sugar-drunk by lunchtime."

"So I'll crash and be ready to binge again by early afternoon."

"You're such a fan-boy."

"I used to consider myself a real otaku, but this feels like a blast from the past. I didn't even know about the convention in time to plan to wear the Kat Kaoru costume or anything. Normally, my backpack would be full of energy bars and mini-cans of espresso shots along with my laptop and autograph book."

"One giant leap away from geekdom."

"Eat me," Blue said off-handedly. "What do you want to do first?"

"I like the suggestion you just made."

"Screw yourself."

"That doesn't sound like half as much fun. According to the event schedule, we can catch a sneak preview of the new *Hell Dwellers* movie in ten minutes."

Heydn and Blue strolled the broad main concourse of the mall to the convention center at the end of one arm. The enormous circular complex had a huge open space at the center with a dozen large conference rooms surrounding it. The entire featureless area had been transformed into a combination flea market and fantasy fashion show runway that almost made the young men late for the screening. They stayed for a second feature before wandering out to find food. After grazing at the food court, they dove into the displays and the vendor section. Blue got a black T-shirt printed with a circuit board in dull silver. Heydn tried on a wide leather cuff with metal accents that looked like something a Roman archer would wear to brace his wrist. The bracelet shouldn't have gone with the gray athletic department T-shirt and faded jeans, but somehow it did and Heydn found he was reluctant to take it off. After some indecision, he handed over the price of the cuff and wore it away from the table. He considered it worth every penny when Blue remarked several times how ultra-cool it was. They grabbed more snacks and took in a series of new Malaysian anime and Blue let Heydn hold his hand in the dark. When they came out, they noticed that the crowds had thinned. Blue looked at the time on his cell phone and rolled his eyes.

"It's ten-thirty," he said.

"That's not so late."

"The buses only run on the hour after eleven, remember?"

"We could always take a cab to the train and another cab to Acton."

"We'd be in transit for an extra hour at least."

"We could stay here."

"In the mall?"

"Ha-ha. There are several nice hotels around here."

"I'm beginning to be suspicious of just how spontaneous this trip was."

"If I'd planned it, I'd have reservations."

"If you planned it, I'd have reservations, too."

"Do you want to stay or run for the bus?"

"Well, I do have a fresh shirt."

"Come on. I have birthday money. Let's live a little."

"I'm not letting you pay. Get real. Let's catch a cab and find a Howland House hotel. The law firm that handles my trust fund has an account with them."

"You're the only person I know that could make a statement like that and not sound pretentious."

"Thank you," Blue said sincerely. "Let's go. There has to be a Howland around here somewhere."

Forty minutes later, Blue and Heydn were sprawled across a king-sized bed eating crab Florentine pizza in front of a huge plasma screen television watching *Extreme Hero Challenge* on satellite. Heydn lay on his stomach with his head toward the end of the bed, knees bent, bare feet crossed in the air. Blue was propped on a nest made of all available pillows, his legs stretched out in front of him. A promo for an upcoming show filled the screen and Heydn turned to look at Blue. Blue's T-shirt had ridden up, baring several inches of soft skin and his dimpled belly button. Heydn propped himself on one elbow and began decorating the area around Blue's navel with pesto sauce. Slowly, he licked it off while Blue squirmed and snickered.

"No fair," Blue said, clutching a fistful of Heydn's thick dark blond hair.

"You don't really think I'm goin' to play fair, do you?"

"I was planning on taking a shower after I ate."

"Then it won't matter if I do this." Heydn rubbed the last slice of pizza on Blue's belly and rubbed his face in it, licking and nibbling.

"I warned you about tickling me."

"Then let's go get in the shower."

"Together?"

"I'm sure it's big enough. Look at this place."

"Yeah. Okay," Blue said eagerly. "Let's do that."

The bathroom matched the scale of the rest of the suite. There was a tub and a walk-in shower walled in natural stone. Heydn turned the water on and grabbed some complimentary bottles of shampoo and liquid soap.

"Lean against the wall," he said.

Blue flattened his palms against the cool marble and let the hot spray soak him. Heydn poured shampoo in his hand and worked it into Blue's hair, massaging his scalp. After Blue's hair was rinsed, he tried to turn, but Heydn kept a hand on his nape.

"Don't I get to shampoo your hair?"

"No, you are mine to play with," Heydn said in a melodramatic voice.

"Who says?"

"I need no man's permission, juicy boy. You were born to serve my pleasure."

"That's from Tanaka Tetsuo's *Demon Overlord* series."

"So you are intelligent as well as beautiful." Heydn drizzled liquid soap down Blue's spine and began working up a rich lather. "Perhaps I will keep you for my harem."

Blue almost laughed and then he decided to give Heydn's role-playing game a chance. What did he have to lose? "I belong to no man," he said in the defiant tones of Demon Overlord's captive Monk Yuki.

"Thanks for bein' on the show," Heydn whispered, before raising his voice again. "Spread your legs wider."

Blue complied and was treated to a thorough, very stimulating wash. "What are you doing?" he moaned when Heydn eased a slippery fingertip into his ass.

"I must ready you for my manhood. Don't laugh."

"Sorry, but…manhood? Please don't tell me it's throbbing."

"I'm just trying to stay in character."

"Sorry."

Heydn worked his finger deeper and found Blue's prostate. Pressing firmly, he rubbed the springy bump as he reached around and took hold of Blue's hard cock. "I see that a man's touch pleases you."

Blue nodded.

"Answer when I ask a question. You would do well to show more respect."

"Sorry…my lord."

"That's better. Your captivity need not be…um…arduous. Please me, and you will be treated well."

Blue took a deep breath. "I have never been taken by a man," he said.

"Are you going to fight me, or will you let me show you the pleasures to be had in…with a man?"

"My honor demands that I fight and yet your touch persuades me not to." Blue gasped. "My lord!"

Heydn smiled as Blue's hard-on pulsed in his fist. "You were born to catch fire at a man's touch."

"Hey, that was pretty good," Blue said. "My lord."

"You stir the poet in me, boy." Heydn withdrew his finger and pressed his stiff cock in the valley of Blue's soapy buttocks. He placed his palms flat against Blue's upper thighs, his thumbs nestled in the crease between leg and torso, and snugged Blue's backside against his crotch. As the hot water bounced off their skin, Heydn flexed the muscles of his ass, sliding his hard length up and down the slippery cleft.

"God!" Blue gasped. "This is so damn hot!

Heydn sank his teeth into the curve of muscle where Blue's neck joined his shoulder, not hard enough to cause real pain, but with enough pressure to make Blue shiver and tighten his ass cheeks. "No other man shall touch you from this hour. Any who tries will die by my sword."

"Take me now," Blue said breathlessly.

"You are very demanding for a slave."

"Forgive me, my lord, but you have driven me mad with lust."

Heydn slid a hand up to Blue's chin and forced his head around until he could reach his lips. Covering Blue's mouth with his, Heydn let his tongue brag silently about what his cock would be doing soon. Blue joined the thrust and parry of tongues, moaning into Heydn's mouth when Heydn began stroking his arousal again. Everything was building nicely to a crescendo when Heydn let go of Blue and turned the water off.

"Come," he said gruffly.

"Why can't we do it in the shower?"

"Because soap makes a terrible lubricant," Heydn said. "And because it is my will that we do it over here."

Blue had just started drying off when Heydn picked him up and sat him on the counter. Scooping up his jeans, Heydn pulled a small bottle of lubricant from his front pocket.

"Where'd that come from?"

"A vending machine." Heydn smiled. "Or perhaps an itinerant shaman."

Blue smiled back. "Then anoint me with yon magic elixir."

"I thought I'd chow down for a while."

"Later. I'm really into this."

"Cool." Heydn poured a stream of thick clear liquid onto his cock and gave it a couple of strokes. Pulling Blue's ass to the edge of the counter, he squirted more lube down Blue's crack. Blue snagged a hand towel and slipped it between his butt and the cold marble. Setting the bottle aside, Heydn rubbed the slippery stuff around Blue's opening and pressed the end of his thumb inside. Blue mewled and let his head drop back against the foggy mirror as Heydn found his prostate again.

"Do not cum yet," Heydn ordered, taking hold of his dick. He seated the tip and leaned until it popped through the small port. Lifting Blue's legs on his forearms, he eased in a couple of more inches. "How does that feel, my beauty?"

"Good, my lord," Blue groaned.

Heydn withdrew and pushed back in, maintaining a depth of a few inches. Blue braced his feet against Heydn's chest, his toes curling against Heydn's chiseled pectorals as the curved cock dipped in and out of his sheath, tagging his prostate with each thrust. He began to moan helplessly each time Heydn entered him, savoring the stretch and the lancing bolt of dulcet lightning that galvanized his groin.

"Oh my God, Heydn," he groaned. "I can't believe what you're doing to me."

"Good?"

Blue reached for his cock, but Heydn got there first. He took Blue's shaft in his slippery fingers and pumped it to the same sweet beat at which he thrust into the tight channel. Blue whimpered and tried to lift his pelvis.

"I'm gonna cum."

"Show me how this pleases you," Heydn said, stroking faster.

Blue spurted with a strangled cry, his passage contracting strongly around Heydn's rod. Heydn continued to fondle Blue's cock as it dribbled another small load of cum. Leaning forward, he sank his full length into the clenched channel as he sought Blue's lips.

"Never have I known such pleasure, my lord," Blue sighed just before Heydn kissed him.

Sucking Blue's lower lip into his mouth, Heydn began to thrust slow and deep. When, he took Blue's mouth again, Blue responded hotly, melding their lips together as he plucked at Heydn's nipples.

Heydn moaned as he broke the kiss and leaned back, spreading Blue's legs wide, pinning his knees to the counter.

"Say you belong to me," he commanded.

"I am yours, my lord." Blue relaxed, leaning back on his elbows as Heydn plumbed his depths. "You have conquered me with your mighty sword."

Heydn looked into Blue's eyes and thrust harder, the strokes becoming erratic. "I love you," he groaned as he buried himself in the clutching quicksand of Blue's sheath.

Blue held Heydn's eyes as the other young man's release unfurled. Heydn put his arms around Blue and lifted him, hugging him tight. Blue wrapped his legs around Heydn and hugged him back. After a few moments, Heydn turned and carried Blue to the bed. Putting Blue down on his back, Heydn collapsed in the cradle of his thighs and let out a long satisfied breath.

"That was awesome."

"Aye...I mean yeah, it was. Still is, actually."

Heydn rocked gently from side to side, shifting his sated cock, and Blue made a small indeterminate noise. "Want me to pull out?" Heydn asked.

"No. I'm kind of curious about what it feels like to have you go soft inside me."

"That's not gonna happen," Heydn predicted.

"Fine. Let's just lay here for a while, okay?"

"Whatever you say." Heydn relaxed, nuzzling languidly at Blue's neck, trailing his fingers lightly over Blue's skin.

"This is nice," Blue said drowsily. "This is what I want."

"What?"

"Out of life," Blue clarified. "I don't care if I have a lot of money, or success, or fame, as long as I can have this with someone I love who loves me back."

Heydn kissed Blue then and the caress soon involved their entire bodies. Pushing Blue's legs farther apart with his knees, Heydn licked and sucked at the other young man's nipples. Blue twisted and turned, arching his back, his reactions moving Heydn's dick in his sheath. Tentatively, he lifted his pelvis, engulfing more of the hard length. Heydn groaned in sheer pleasure and bit down on one of Blue's nipples. Impulsively, Blue rolled until Heydn was under him. Bracing his hands on Heydn's chest, Blue rose up and sank down, tightening his sphincter, making love to Heydn's cock.

"Ah, shit, Blue!" Heydn panted. "That feels so damned good. I'm cumming." Grabbing Blue by the waist, Heydn thrust upward a couple of times and came powerfully. He froze with Blue astride him as his seed geysered out, his fingertips sinking into the soft flesh of Blue's flanks before he caved and his ass hit the bed. Blue grunted and grimaced as Heydn's cock was driven deep into his passage.

"Aw hell, I'm sorry," Heydn said breathlessly. "Let me just..." Gently, he withdrew and pulled Blue into his arms. "Damn. That was.... I've never felt anythin' like that."

Neither had Blue. The power he sensed once while making love with Astor had not been a fluke. He could give or withhold pleasure at his whim. It was another chance to make a choice that revealed his character, like his enjoyment of role-playing. Sex, after all, was no less complicated than anything else in life was, even though it was advertized as a primal function as natural as breathing.

"Hey." Heydn jostled Blue lightly. "You just let me know if you ever want to turn the tables."

"What?"

"Well, so far I got to be on top every time, with the notable exception of this last one."

"Are we supposed to switch off, or something?"

"We don't have to, but if you wanted to be the fucker instead of the fuckee..."

"I don't think of it that way. I think of us as doing each other. It doesn't matter to me whose dick goes where. Well…it kind of does. I like having you inside me."

"Mmm. I like bein' inside you," Heydn purred as he kissed Blue's shoulder. "But if you wanted to do it the other way 'round, I would."

"Sounds like you'd be making a big sacrifice for me."

"No, it's not like that."

"You sure?"

"Well, maybe a little. A guy put his cock in me once and I thought I was gonna tear right down the middle. But if you wanted it, I'd be glad to try it again."

"That's why you're so…" Blue's voice trailed off.

"What?"

"I wondered why you seemed so…grateful. It feels so good to me when you're moving in and out."

"Aw, damn. Now I'm gettin' hard again."

"That's okay. We know how to make the swelling go down."

Heydn shivered as Blue squeezed his shaft. "I was so surprised when you came that first time we did it. I just knew it meant we belonged together. Fuck. When I look back on it, I can't figure out how I could leave you. How could I fool myself into thinkin' that all we were doin' was playin' around?"

Blue leaned over and drew the flat of his tongue up the underside of Heydn's cock.

"Are you trying to change the subject?" Heydn raised his head to look down at his crotch.

Blue flashed him a wicked look from under his thick eyelashes as he wiggled the tip of his tongue in the slit at the end of Heydn's dick.

"This is my hell, isn't it? I pretended that all I wanted from you was sex, and now that's all I'm going to get. Is that right?"

With a sigh, Blue sat up and crossed his ankles in front of him. "I don't know," he said. "Would you hand me that bottle of water?"

Heydn watched Blue drink as he continued. "I know you're sick of hearing this, but all I want is you."

"Probably because you think you can't have me." Blue picked up the remote and hit the mute button.

"Ouch. Do you really think this is just about winning?"

"Well, you're a jock, and jocks are all about competition, right? You like trophies."

Heydn sat up too and swung his legs over the side of the bed. "I'm surprised that you of all people would reduce me to a cliché."

"You're right." Blue traced the pattern of the comforter with a forefinger. "I wasn't being fair."

Carefully, Heydn sat back down. "You mean just now, or did you mean something else?"

"I said I was over you and that I didn't blame you for doing what you did when you left me. The truth is that I never got over you and I never truly gave you the benefit of the doubt when you came back."

"If you needed revenge, you've got it. Every minute that I'm with you knowing that you're not mine is like hydrochloric acid in a razor cut."

Blue met Heydn's eyes. "Yeah. That's what it feels like. Approximately. But you left out how it's impossible to get warm."

"Yeah. That's right. And the hollowness in your stomach like you're hungry all the time."

"Love sucks."

"Not having it sure does blow."

"Come here," Blue said, opening his arms.

Heydn turned and lay on his belly, wrapping his arms around Blue's waist and resting his head in Blue's lap. Blue finger-combed Heydn's short hair and stroked the muscles of his back and shoulders as they rested in the companionable silence of people that share a bond. They roused again after a time and did to each other whatever things they thought would bring pleasure until exhaustion closed their eyes.

The new day began in the same way the old one ended: with a bang and more than one whimper. They barely got out of the room by checkout time and got into the elevator with hair wet from the last bout in the shower. To Heydn, Blue seemed an almost mythical creature as he lounged against the marble sheathing of the elevator walls, dark locks in disarray around pale features, his lips red from ardent kisses, eyes liquid with a passion recently quenched, a faun, an incubus, Ganymede.

"You have the goofiest look on your face," Blue said as the elevator chimed.

"Daydreaming," Heydn said as the doors slid open on the lobby. "And now, back to reality."

CHAPTER 18

THEY arrived at campus in time for dinner, but stayed away from the cafeteria. Without discussing it, Heydn followed Blue to Blue's room and came inside. As he hung his hoodie on the back of the door, he saw a piece of paper on the floor.

"Hey, Blue. I think this is a note for you," he said, holding it out.

Blue put down his backpack and took the paper. "What the eff?" he whispered as he read.

"What is it?"

"It's from Peyton." Blue pulled his phone from his pocket and turned it on. "Nine missed calls," he muttered. "Hang on."

Heydn scanned the note that simply directed Blue to check his damned messages. His eyes on the other young man, Heydn waited until Blue took the phone from his ear. "What?"

"Rolly's in the emergency room," Blue said, as he punched Peyton's number and put the phone back to his ear. "Yeah, I'm back," he said. "Where? Sure, come on over." Blue put the cell away. "He'll be here in a minute and tell us all about it. You want some water, or something?"

"You know what I want, but if Peyn's on his way over, we probably don't have time."

"I'm not sure I could even if we did have time. I'm just about sexed out."

Heydn put his arms around Blue from behind, crossing them under Blue's chin. Gently, he rubbed his jaw against Blue's cheek. "Don't mind me," he said. "We don't have to do it every five minutes."

Blue leaned against Heydn's solid chest. "You don't have to hang around, you know."

"I can handle Peyton in my present mood."

"It isn't necessary."

"I'd like to stay with you."

Blue flinched when Peyton knocked and called out simultaneously. Pulling away from Heydn, he opened the door and let his friend in. Peyton saw Heydn, nodded, and then ignored him.

"What happened?" Blue prompted.

"Rolly got bashed. He was hurt bad enough to go to the hospital. They broke his arm, some ribs, his nose and a few fingers. Rolly must have put up a hell of a fight. After they got him down, they kicked him for a while, called him names, told him they were going to kill him. Who knows? If Judson Lenoir hadn't come jogging down the path and scared them off, they might have killed him."

"Who were they?"

Peyton shrugged. "Rolly said they wore hoods made out of pillowcases. Can you believe that? We've got our own little Klan here at Acton."

"Rolly will be okay, right?"

"There could be internal stuff that hasn't shown up yet, but the bones will mend and..." Peyton's voice broke. "It's my fault."

"How is it your fault? Were they after you?"

"Rolly was my source for the newspaper articles about hypocritical homophobes at Acton. He kind of spied on some people for me and took photos. He told me the guys that attacked him started out by asking if he was that little fag that was always sneaking around."

"Then I guess it is your fault," Heydn said.

Blue gave Heydn a look of disbelief.

"No, he's right," Peyton said. "Thanks, Case. You're the only one that's had the balls to say it to my face. I did this and I have to own up to it."

"You didn't plan on Rolly getting hurt."

"Blue, please," Peyton sighed. "How many times did you warn me about messing with King and his pack of hyenas? I knew they could be dangerous if they turned on me, but I kept banging on the bars of their cages."

"That's what good journalists do."

"But Rolly's just a kid. We're all just kids, really."

"It still matters," Blue said.

"That's a bit cryptic," Peyton said. "What matters?"

"All of it." Heydn spoke up again. "Just ask yourself one question. Have you been true to yourself?"

"I thought so, but I might have lost sight of my idealism in the excitement of the play. The thought of sticking it to the preps right under everyone's noses was so seductive. I would've done anything to pull it off after they censored my newspaper article, and you know how Rolly is. He wanted to get me the best dirt and he took too many risks."

"He idolizes you," Blue said. "When can we visit?"

"I was there until five today. We could go in the morning if we skip classes."

Blue nodded.

"You're going to love this," Peyton said. "The attack happened on school property, right? The ambulance came from a private hospital. As far as I know, the police haven't been notified. I called Rolly's mom and she said Dean Whittaker had been in touch and she was making arrangements—her exact words. Meanwhile, the crime scene is open to anyone that cares to stroll through."

"So what?" Heydn said. "You know who it was."

"I have my suspicions."

"Suspicions? Would you like to hear mine? Allerton King might not care to skin his knuckles, but he's got friends willin' to do it for him. My money's on Logan Newcombe as the chief suspect."

"If no one saw their faces, there's not much that can be done," Blue said.

Heydn clenched his hands into fists. "A smack upside the head is what they need."

"You're such a knuckle-dragger," Peyton said. "Although, in this case, I understand your impulse toward violence."

"It's what they understand," Heydn said.

"Right. It's their tool," Blue said. "We don't have to be like that."

"Cookie, if one of those a-holes so much as sneezed on you, I'd make strawberry jelly out of him."

Peyton raised his eyebrows, but Blue spoke first. "No, you can't call me Cookie," he said.

"But Heydn gets to?"

"Not in public."

"I see. Well, I didn't tell you all the news," Peyton said. "Mr. McIntyre said we can keep doing the play as long as the offending scene is removed."

"He's quite a guy…for a teacher," Heydn said.

"Yeah." Peyton sat back in his chair. "He's kind of cute, too. In a Poindexter sort of way. The matching vests and bowties are meant to be playfully ironic, I think."

"Peyn!" Blue exclaimed. "Are you crushing on McIntyre?"

"Maybe just a wee bit. I can't do anything about until after graduation, so…"

"Man, I leave for thirty-six hours and look what happens," Blue sighed, falling back to lie on his bed with his feet on the floor.

"Tell me all about your adventure," Peyton said. "How was the con?"

"I got this shirt," Blue pulled the fabric away from his belly and looked at it. "I still like it."

Heydn held up his arm so Peyton could see the leather cuff. "We saw some pretty cool vids and costumes," he said.

"You stayed overnight. Nice hotel?"

"Howland House," Blue said.

"I love their room service menu, you lucky dogs." Peyton stood up. "It's late," he said. "You guys look tired. Call me when you wake up in the morning, okay?"

"Sure," Blue said, giving Peyton a quick hug.

"Hey, Peyn," Heydn said. "Thanks for being halfway nice to me."

"Was I? Guess I'm preoccupied. Good night."

Heydn closed the door behind Peyton and caught Blue watching him. "What? Do I have toilet paper stuck to my shoe?"

"No. I was just looking at you. You're really good-looking."

"Bullshit. I'm in pretty good shape, but my face is nothin' special."

"You look like a prince to me."

"Come on." Heydn turned away to hide his pleased smile.

"I'm not trying to embarrass you." Blue came to stand in front of Heydn. "Give me a kiss and say goodnight. I need to get some sleep."

"I can't stay?"

Blue shook his head.

"There are two beds."

"I can see that, but we both know you wouldn't stay in yours. And if you did, I wouldn't stay in mine."

Heydn interlaced his fingers at Blue's nape, cradling his head and gazing into his fathomless eyes. "We damn sure can't keep our hands off each other, can we?"

"It's not easy," Blue admitted, running his hands up and down Heydn's back. "Kiss me goodnight."

Heydn let one of his hands fall to the small of Blue's back and leaned in until their lips met. Blue took control of the kiss, tilting his head as he rose on tiptoe to hook one leg around Heydn's hip. Heydn made a purring noise that vibrated against Blue's lips and wrapped his arms around Blue's willowy frame in a crushing hug. Blue felt the unmistakable bulge of Heydn's reaction to the kiss and a warm glow of pride filled him that he could evoke such instant passion.

"Okay," Blue said breathlessly, as he broke the kiss. "Time for you to go."

Heydn groaned. "Come on. One more kiss…and let me jerk you off while we're kissing."

Blue shook his head. "When you touch me it stirs my brains like oatmeal, but I've got just enough sense left to push you out the door."

"I think we'd both be happier if I stayed, but all right; I'll go." Heydn stole a quick kiss at the door. "Lock up, okay?" He listened for the dull click of the lock engaging before he walked away.

The campus was deserted as Heydn jogged to his building. There were few lights in the windows. Heydn checked his watch as he entered his dorm and saw that it was barely midnight. He was not surprised to see his roommate awake and studying.

Judson Lenoir looked up as the door opened and closed, but quickly put his head back down over his book. "Hi, Heydn," he mumbled.

Heydn came to stand behind Judson's chair. "I hear there was some excitement while I was gone."

"Excitement?" Judson picked up a pen and fiddled with it.

"What? You forgot already? Peyton Crane says you're a hero."

"No, I…"

"Come on, Jud. You probably saved Rollins Morehouse's life. Aren't you proud of yourself?"

"I spent most of the day talking about it. You mind?"

"Yeah, Jud, I mind."

Judson glanced over his shoulder. "Could you not stand over me like that?"

Heydn grabbed the back of the other young man's chair and pushed down. Judson flailed, sending his pen flying as the chair tilted. Heydn looked down into Judson's eyes. "Is this better?"

"Why are you doing this?"

Heydn let go of the chair and the front legs hit the floor, jarring Judson. "Because I'm pretty sure you recognized the guys that beat Rolly up and because I owe a debt."

"What debt?" Judson turned to face Heydn.

"When I was in jail, two people that had no reason to be nice to me got me bailed out. One of them even got the owner of the car to tell the cops that the stolen vehicle report was a mistake. My record is clean because a couple of people who didn't owe me anything decided to do the right thing. That's what I'm trying to do now. All I want is a little justice for a chubby kid that didn't deserve to get his ass kicked by a gang of bigots."

"Man, he was a mess when I got there," Judson whispered.

"You were out training, right?"

"Yeah. Sometimes I run the lakeshore because…well, because you always used to and I wanted to be like you."

"I guess I really disappointed you, huh?"

Judson shrugged. "You're not what I thought you were, but that's not your fault."

"Why thank you, Jud. Now tell me the rest of it."

"I was just past the footbridge and rounding that curve where the leaves pile up and get real slippery and I heard weird noises. Swear to

God, it sounded like animals or something. Then I saw three guys with bags on their heads and they were all kicking at something on the ground. They were grunting and laughing and Rolly was just making this kind of gasping sound. I yelled something; damned if I can remember what. They ran and that's when I saw it was a person on the ground. One of his arms was twisted all wrong and there was blood all over his face." Judson looked up from the floor. "I had this weird kind of panic feeling. I almost turned around and ran. The thought of those guys doing the same thing to me scared the shit out of me."

"But you helped Rolly."

"Well, yeah. I couldn't leave him there. I mean…I had to leave him to go get help; I couldn't carry him, but I let him know help was coming. The whole time I was running back to campus all I could think was what if those guys came back while I was gone?"

"Those guys? What guys would those be?"

"They'll kill me."

"No they won't. They might have the guts to beat up a queer when it's three to one, but they won't go after one of their own like that. They'll count on intimidation to keep your mouth shut, and if that doesn't work, they'll most likely shun you."

"I can't go against them, Case. It's my future. My dad's a partner in Newcombe's dad's firm."

"So you do know who they are."

Judson put his head down again. "Yeah."

"Come on. We're gonna wake up Dean Whittaker and he's gonna call the cops."

"I won't do it. You can't make me."

"Then you're goin' with me to visit Rolly in the mornin'."

Judson's pink cheeks drained of color as he shook his head. "Hell no."

"I knew you had a conscience," Heydn put a hand on Judson's shoulder. "It'll drive you crazy if you don't do what's right."

"I'm not like you. I'm not a cowboy or anything."

"I'm not a cowboy either. I *am* from Texas and I've done a fair amount of ridin', but…"

"I just meant that I'm not brave," Judson interrupted. "I've got my life mapped out and something like this could change everything."

"I just learned that the best thing you can do is be true to yourself. I know I sound like a hippie, but I'm talkin' from experience. You'll be a lot happier and sleep a lot easier if you just do what you know is right. If you don't think you need to tell the dean who bashed Rolly, then don't."

"You won't beat me up?"

"I don't think Blue would let me."

Judson's expression changed so quickly that Heydn remarked on it.

"What's that look for?"

"Barclay's just a little too out-there for me. I know he's your friend and all, but he's weird."

"He's not boring, that's for sure."

"I just don't dig all that bizarre Japanese sci-fi stuff. I just don't get it."

Heydn blinked. "So his weirdness has nothing to do with bein' gay?"

"Barclay's gay? I've heard some talk, but I thought he was just a genderless computer nerd."

"I shouldn't a said that," Heydn said. "It's not my place to say if he's gay or not."

"I don't care," Judson said. "My older brother's gay. He just had a commitment ceremony with his friend Garry."

"No shit. You're pretty casual about it."

Judson shrugged. "Lee is sixteen years older than me. By the time I knew what sex was, he and Garry had been together forever. They met their first year in college and Garry was always around like a second big brother. When I was old enough to understand, Lee talked to me about it. I went through a few months where I felt all hurt and betrayed and whatnot, but I love Lee and Garry and I wouldn't want to have Christmas without them, you know?"

"That's pretty cool, man." Without thinking about it, Heydn reached out and tousled Judson's ash-blond hair. "Hope nothin' like what happened to Rolly ever happens to him."

"Look, I'll go talk to Whittaker first thing in the morning, okay?"

Heydn looked at his watch again. "All right. I think you'll sleep better than you did last night."

"I sure hope so." Judson rubbed his eyes. "I think I'll lay down now."

"I'm goin' down the hall. I'll try to keep the noise down when I get back."

"Thanks, man." Judson turned and began unbuttoning his shirt. "It was Logan and Skip Spalding and Copeland Graham. I could tell by the way they moved."

"Let's hope the dean believes you. If not, we might have to go to the police ourselves."

Judson got into bed. "In the morning," he said, closing his eyes.

Heydn flipped off the light as he left the room. At the urinal, he found that his persistent hard-on had subsided enough that he could bend it downward to piss. The trip to the convention had given him hope, but he was still in the purgatory of his making. He had denied his love for Blue and like the boy who cried wolf his word was now held in some doubt. Shaking off, Heydn washed his hands and went back to his room. Whether or not he won Blue's love again, he was going to listen to his heart from now on. With a glance at his sleeping roommate, Heydn lay down and closed his eyes. Tomorrow was going to be a stressful day.

CHAPTER 14

HEYDN said goodbye to Judson and watched the junior walk through the office door to face the dean. He jogged a circuit of the campus, passing close by the science building so he could see Blue through the window of lab 3. Blue was watching the instructor write on the overhead projector so Heydn ran on, using up his first-period study hall in a patrol of Acton. The last loop of the course took him through the area where Rolly had been attacked, and he paused to look at the faint marks in the snow. When he heard the faint ringing of the class bell, he moved on.

The Drama Club was excused from classes after lunch and met in the theater. Heydn arrived late, having showered and changed, and he was surprised to find the place almost empty. Spotting Blue at the side of the stage, he called out. "Where is everybody?"

"They went to visit Rolly. Me and Peyton went this morning really early."

"I would've gone."

"They only let a couple of people in at a time and after Mrs. Morehouse showed up, she kicked everyone out. Rolly looked really embarrassed."

"So he's doing okay?"

"He's doped up, so he's not in pain and he was glad to see us. He swears he has no idea who the guys were that attacked him."

"That's okay; I got Jud to tell me. He went to see Whittaker this mornin'."

Blue's eyes widened. "Are you kidding?"

"No."

"You talked him into going to the dean?"

"It didn't take much. Turns out his big brother is gay. When he started thinkin' about how he'd feel if his brother got bashed, he made up his own mind."

"Yeah, but without you there, he might have decided to keep quiet. You did a really good thing."

"So, Heydn the Barbarian isn't such a bad guy?"

"He shows promise."

Heydn leaned a little closer. "Methinks I deserve a reward."

Blue's gaze slid left and right. "I will never submit to you, savage," he said softly.

"We shall see, my captive beauty," Heydn smiled. "Once you are in my tent…"

"What are you babbling about, Case?" Astor said from behind Heydn.

"Just practicing some lines from another play," Blue said.

"Yeah. Right. Pretty cheesy dialogue."

"I like cheese," Heydn replied.

Astor ignored him. "So what's going on?" he asked Blue.

"We're just waiting for Peyton. He has a new scene to replace. You know, the one that was taken out."

"He's not here?"

"I haven't seen him."

"He told me he was coming over here right after French class."

"I still haven't seen him."

Astor's gaze slid toward Heydn before he spoke to Blue again. "Mom wants to know if you're still planning on coming to the lake for spring vacation. She needs to know how many horses to send up."

"You'd better tell her not to count on me."

"Why?"

"I don't think it would be a good idea."

"You don't think waterskiing and swimming and riding are a good idea?"

Heydn gave Blue a significant look, offering to leave or stay at Blue's request.

"I'll bet Peyton's up top getting high," Blue said. "I'm going to go check."

Astor's face bore a complicated expression as he watched Blue hurry away. "You're really enjoying this. Aren't you, Case?"

"What's that?"

"Watching me make a fool of myself."

"Actually, it's kinda painful. Reminds me we're in the same boat."

"How do you figure that?"

"We both want the same thing, and we can't have it."

"Is that right? Because I hear you're getting it."

Heydn put down the extension cord he'd just finishing coiling into a neat roll. "Do you really wanna get into this with me?"

"You think I'm scared of you?"

"Nope. I just think this is one rumor you don't want confirmed."

"You're fucking him," Astor accused.

Heydn clenched his fists and then slowly let his fingers unfurl. "I know you're trying to piss me off," he said. "But I really don't want to fight with you."

"Why not? Aren't I enough of a challenge for you?"

"Look, whatever you think is going on…"

"I think you're fucking Blue; that's what I think."

"You're right."

The short silence rang in their ears with the pulse of pounding blood.

"Asshole," Astor said at last, his voice choked with emotion. "You're just going to fuck him over again."

Heydn shook his head.

"Yes, you will. You'll fuck him until you get tired of him and you'll dump him again."

"That could never happen. Settle down, man. It's not even my decision."

"That's crap. You sucked him back in and when you're done with him, you'll throw him away."

"Do you really think Blue is that weak? Listen up; I might be sleeping with him, but that doesn't mean I have him. If anything, he's using *me*."

"You're so full of shit, Case."

"*I'm* full of shit?"

"Yeah. I would have loved Blue for his whole life. All you want is a piece of ass."

"I don't expect you to believe me, and I don't care, but you're wrong. I had to lose him to realize it, but I love Blue and I'm going to love him for the rest of my life whether we're together or not."

"Awwwww, that's beautiful," Rhodes said, as he came down the aisle toward the stage. "But you might want to lower your voices. I could practically hear you guys in the lobby."

Astor turned pale. "I'm going to look for Peyton around the dressing rooms," he said as he walked quickly away.

Rhodes raised an eyebrow at Heydn. "Was it something I said?"

Heydn smiled. "He's kinda sensitive."

"Are you guys really fighting over Blue Barclay?"

"No. I'm not anyway. Astor may have some issues to work out."

"Freaky," Rhodes pronounced. "Hey, I heard from Drex Ewing that Whittaker called Logan Newcombe to his office during third period and that Logan didn't look happy. In fact, he said Logan cussed in front of Mr. Olivet and stomped out of class even though Old Olive Oil was hollering at him to come back. His ass is gonna be grass for sure."

"Let me know if the blades on the lawnmower need sharpenin'."

Rhodes laughed. "Guess you guys aren't big buddies now that you're gay."

"It's more like I evolved and I don't hang with the apes anymore."

"You're a funny guy, Case."

"Yeah, it just sorta happened when I went gay." Heydn looked over his shoulder at the door to the stairwell. "Hey, Rhodes, would you mind havin' a look out back for Peyton? I'm goin' up and see what's takin' Blue so long."

"Sure. Just don't make out all day."

"You're obsessed with the idea of me and Blue kissin', aren't you?"

Rhodes rolled his eyes. "Isn't everyone?" he said archly as he sashayed off holding up a limp-wristed hand to wave bye-bye.

"That's hilarious, Vaughn," Heydn said sarcastically as he started up the stairs.

"No!" Blue yelled as Heydn opened the door to the roof. "Don't come out!"

It was too late. Heydn had seen Logan and the marks that Logan's fists had left on Blue. He charged out of the doorway and tripped over Peyton. The harsh surface of the roof abraded the heels of his hands as he tried to catch himself and then the toe of Logan's sneaker hammered the side of his head, flipping him onto his back. Blue threw a punch and cried out involuntarily as Logan seized his fist and twisted his arm behind his back.

"Stay the hell down, Case," Logan said. "Or I'll break your sweetie's wrist."

Heydn shook his head, seeing double when he tried to focus on Blue. "That would be a huge mistake," he said.

"I'm not screwing around. You just stay where you are until I figure out a couple of things, or I'll toss your boyfriend off the roof with the other faggot."

Blue kicked backward, catching Logan in the shin and making him yell. While Logan was distracted, Blue tried to pull free and succeeded in wrenching his shoulder from the socket. All the color drained from his face as the pain seized him in a fist of granite and crumpled him like an empty can. Logan yanked Blue up when he sagged, nearly making him pass out. Heydn saw the agony in Blue's pale, pinched features and started to get to his feet.

"I said stay down, Case!"

"There's somethin' wrong with him, man," Heydn said. "You're hurtin' him."

"I'll hurt him plenty if you don't get back on the ground right now! Take a look at Crane if you need a visual aid."

Heydn's gaze flicked to Peyton's prone form. Blood leaked slowly from Peyton's nose and the corner of his mouth, proof that he was merely unconscious and not dead.

"Logan," Blue gasped. "Let go of my arm. I think it's broken."

"Shut up, fag. Anybody that can take a dick up the ass can handle a little pain."

"I'm gonna kill you, Logan," Heydn said. "Just so you know."

"You're gonna do whatever I say as long as I've got your little butt boy."

"Looks like he got a couple a licks in on you." Heydn stared at Logan's bloody nose. "Not bad for a butt boy."

"He's tougher than he looks; I'll give you that. Now shut up and let me think."

"Yeah, go on; give thinkin' a try, you dumb shit. What happened, Logan? Why'd you snap? Did Whittaker tell you that you were gonna be expelled?"

"He said there was going to be an investigation," Logan spat. "My dad donated three mil to this school last year and they're gonna investigate my ass? Fuck that."

"So your plan was what? To beat the hell outta Peyton Crane? How'd you figure that would change Whittaker's mind? If you were gonna shut somebody up, it shoulda been Judson Lenoir."

"He's on my list; don't worry."

"Just tell me how in the hell you think you're gonna get away with this."

"My last name's Newcombe, in case you hadn't noticed," Logan said, sidling toward the door. "It'd be a shame if I didn't get to graduate from dear old dad's alma mater, but there are other schools. Some are even in other countries. I'm not worried."

"Then you're just plain crazy." Heydn had gradually gotten to a kneeling position and now prepared to launch himself at Logan.

"I'm sure you'd like to think so. Now get back on the ground or I'll make pussy boy gobble my hog. Go on; down on your belly."

Heydn's muscles tensed and he took one look at Blue's face for courage when the door opened again, hitting Logan in the back.

"What the hell?" Astor exclaimed, pushing harder. "Who's blocking the damned door?"

Logan lurched and Blue went down on one knee as Astor forced his way onto the roof. Heydn grabbed Blue's ankle and yanked him from Logan's grasp. Logan cursed as he scrambled to his feet, nearly tripping over Peyton. Seizing a fistful of the unconscious young man's jacket, Logan dragged him toward the low wall at the edge of the roof.

"What the hell?" Astor said again, as he divided his attention between Logan and Blue. "What's going on here?"

"Help Peyton," Blue groaned, as Heydn cradled his arm.

Logan had almost reached the edge when Astor caught up with him. Peyton's limp body fell from Logan's arms to the roof as Astor plowed into him. Logan regained his balance just in time to take a blow on the jaw that rocked him again. Taking an involuntary step backward, he gathered himself and leaped at Astor, wrapping him up in a bear hug. Astor's foot came down on Peyton's back and he pitched sideways. Logan held on, head-butting Astor as their legs struck the wall. Still locked in an inimical embrace, the two young men fell together, disappearing from sight.

Heydn ran to the edge and peered down. He saw Rhodes standing in shock over the two bodies splayed across the walkway and, for a moment, his mind refused to accept the reality. Blue took his hand and jarred him from his trance. "Call nine-one-one!" he yelled at Rhodes.

CHAPTER 20

HEYDN jumped out of his chair as soon as he saw Blue. "Are you okay?" he asked.

"The shoulder will be fine. The doctor said you did a good job putting it back in place. The police are done taking my statement, and I'm enjoying the effects of some very high-quality pharmaceuticals. How's Astor?"

Heydn quelled an absurd twinge of jealousy. "Fractured vertebrae. It's pretty serious, but from what they'd tell me, he's not going to be paralyzed. He's still in surgery, though."

"And Logan?"

"Not so lucky. Astor landed on top of him and he's got a lot of stuff ruptured inside. Couldn't happen to a nicer guy."

"Karma is a powerful thing."

"Sure is. He was spilling his guts to the cops at the top of his lungs while he was being taken to surgery. You'd a thought he was too busted up to do anything but moan in pain, but he was cussin' up a storm, sayin' he was gonna get everybody that fucked him."

"He needs serious help."

"Yeah, I think a few hundred years of therapy might do him some good. The police went to pick up Sloan Spalding and Copeland Graham. You know what's kinda funny?"

"What?"

"If Logan hadn't blown a fuse, I bet Rolly's attack would've been swept under the carpet."

"You're probably right. The board would've probably met with the parents and hushed it up. What a load of crap." Blue paused. "But at least everyone's going to be all right."

Heydn nodded. "I notice you don't ask about Peyton."

"Please. He was loaded on muscle relaxers when Logan jumped him and barely remembers getting hit. He was flirting with the EMTs as they loaded him into the ambulance."

"Yeah." Heydn snickered. "I think he actually got one guy's number. He said he did, anyway. His mom jetted in here pretty damn quick. She was nice about it, but she sure cleared the room in a hurry. Hey." He paused. "What about your folks?"

"Come on." Blue took Heydn's arm, ignoring the question. "Take me back to campus."

Using his injury as an excuse, Blue stuck close to Heydn on the journey back to Acton. He didn't talk much and Heydn didn't press him. Not until Blue closed the door of his room did he respond to Heydn's question. "My folks won't be coming," he said. "They've been dead since I was two."

"Shit, that's tough. Who raised you?"

"My dad's half-sister, until she died in a car wreck, and then a second cousin who was about a hundred years old already. I was out of family at about the point that I started school. Since all the schools I was enrolled in were boarding schools, Mr. Denison didn't see a problem. He's my dad's estate lawyer. Well, I guess he's really mine. He's my legal guardian and the executor of the estate too, but there's a board that oversees any activity."

"So how rich are you?"

Blue gave him a Mona Lisa smile. "Money isn't a worry," he said.

"Really? It's hard to tell with you. You don't act like the other rich pricks."

"I'm filthy with dough. Seriously, just my personal assets are over a hundred million."

Heydn looked stunned for a couple of seconds before he spoke. "Well, I wish I'd known that before I sold my bike to pay you back for bailing me out."

"You did what?"

"I don't ride it anyway. Is two hundred gonna be enough?"

"Not even close. It's going to take more than a measly two hundred dollars to satisfy me."

"What about your arm?"

"What?"

"Won't it hurt?"

"You've lost me."

"I just thought it might not be a good idea for us to get busy right now because of your shoulder."

"Who said anything about sex? Honestly, Heydn, you're such a guy."

"What did you mean then?"

"I meant that I want more than your money; more than sex even."

"You can have anything I've got."

"Good, because I want all of you. I want your body. I want your mind. I want your love. I can't promise how it'll turn out, but I'd like to give it another try."

"Gimme a second to catch my breath."

"I think it'll be better this time," Blue went on. "I really do. I feel like I've grown up a lot in a few months and that I can deal with you on a more or less equal basis."

"What's that mean?"

"It means I'm not that naïve little virgin I was when I met you."

"I never thought of you that way."

"Come on, Heydn. That was the attraction for you, wasn't it? That it was my first time for everything and you were teaching me?"

"First of all, all I was lookin' for was a friend when I met you, but things…sorta developed. I never set out to bust your cherry." Heydn made a frustrated noise when Blue still looked dubious. "You might not believe this, but I have just as much fun playing video games with you as having sex."

"I don't believe you."

"Okay, I was exaggerating a little, but I really do like just being with you. It hit me hard after I moved out. Sometimes I'd wake up and hear Jud snoring, but I'd imagine it was you. I jerked off under the covers a lot."

"Thanks for the mental image of your cum-crusted sheets. And I don't snore."

"Sure do. You rattle the windows."

"No I don't."

"How would you know? You're asleep," Heydn said triumphantly.

"Are you getting cocky on me already?" Blue paused, slapping his palm to his forehead. "I'm going to regret my choice of words," he predicted.

Heydn's smile was the definition of devilish. Lunging, he wrapped Blue in a careful hug, trapping his arms at his sides. Mindful of Blue's injury, he slowly walked his fingers up the dunes of Blue's ribs. Blue shook with laughter, tears running from the corners of his eyes, and the sight of him so happy was the strongest aphrodisiac Heydn knew of; Blue was his kryptonite and his saving grace and, wonder of wonders, Blue felt the same way about him.

"Stay right where you are, my beauty," Heydn said, mock-sternly, as he released Blue. "Do not resist me and I will be gentle with you." Tenderly, he removed Blue's clothing piece by piece, kissing each inch of skin as it was bared, interspersing his attentions with the long slow kisses Blue liked so much.

Blue did his best to reciprocate one-handed, but the sling hampered him considerably and Heydn's proximity made it difficult to remove by himself. "Help me," he said breathlessly, when Heydn left off sucking his right nipple for a second.

"I am helping you."

"No, help me get this off so I can participate."

Heydn's soft laugh was a fur mitten rubbing Blue's ears and going straight to his groin, stimulating him with nothing more than sound. "Okay, Cookie, but don't hurt yourself."

"You're the one cruising for a bruising. Stop treating me like I'll break if you breathe hard."

Heydn finished removing the sling and tossed it on the desk. "I already broke you once," he said. "It'd kill me if I hurt you again."

"I'm tougher now." Blue put his good hand on the back of Heydn's neck. "You didn't kill me, ergo…"

"I made you stronger?"

"Yeah, you did. Heydn, I don't want one mistake to become this big guilt trip, okay? I don't want you constantly second-guessing yourself. I'd rather forget that it ever happened."

"That *what* ever happened?" Heydn asked with a puzzled look.

Blue pulled Heydn closer and kissed him, surprised when Heydn slid from under the caress to skim down his body. Heydn settled on his knees and took Blue in his mouth in one motion. Wrapping his arms around Blue's thighs, Heydn engulfed him to the root. Blue groaned as Heydn slowly lifted his head while sucking hard. Heydn's scalp burned as Blue tugged at his hair, but he didn't falter in his adoring assault. As he bobbed his head, he kneaded Blue's butt cheeks, pulling them apart, rubbing his fingertips against the sensitive skin between Blue's balls and his hole.

"My knees are going weak," Blue gasped.

Heydn let Blue's shaft slide from his mouth and hugged him tight, his cheek pressed to Blue's flat lower belly. "I won't let you fall."

"Let me sit." Blue took a step back and plopped down on his bed. "Come up here," he said, coaxing Heydn to his feet.

Heydn's breath hissed in through his teeth as Blue took hold of his aching cock and kissed the drooling tip. With little kittenish laps of his tongue, Blue savored the liquid evidence of Heydn's desire for him.

"Eager, are we?" he teased, as he shuttled his fist up and down the hard rod of flesh.

"Are you kiddin'?" Heydn shuddered as Blue flicked his thumb over and around the head of his cock. "I've been rarin' to go since you said you wanted me."

"That's such a major turn-on," Blue purred as he nuzzled Heydn's tight sack. "Look at you; you're ready to pop, aren't you?"

"It's not like I can hide it."

"You want me to keep going or would you like to proceed directly to the beef injection?"

"You're killin' me," Heydn groaned. "Tell me what you want."

"I want you to put this inside me and make me cum." Blue gave Heydn's cock a squeeze.

"You are without a doubt the sexiest thing on the planet," Heydn replied, putting his hands on Blue's shoulders. "You know I love you, right? The real deal. Hearts and flowers and all that crap. It's not just about this." Heydn thrust once with his hips. "I'd marry you if I could."

Blue smiled even as his eyes prickled with incipient tears. Some turning point had been passed tonight and Blue hugged the glad news to his heart. He had visions of a day when he and Heydn walked together in the sun hand in hand with no worries about what anybody might think of them. It made him happy to know that when that day came, Heydn would be ready for it. "Just shut up and do me," he said, his voice tight with emotion.

Heydn kissed Blue's eyelids as he eased him to his back on the bed and reached under the mattress for the lubricant. Blue did his best to be still, but the thought of what was about to happen made him wriggle impatiently; whatever else he had learned about himself, he knew he had a healthy sexual appetite. Heydn put a hand on Blue's inner thigh and slathered his crack, pushing lube into the small opening, too eager to make a long production of it. With Blue's enthusiastic cooperation, he worked the head of his cock into the flexing port and forged ahead. Blue loudly expressed his approval of the penetration in case Heydn was still nervous about nailing an injured man, but he needn't have worried. Heydn was bent on giving Blue as much pleasure as he could handle, to show Blue that he wanted him with equal passion. Proceeding steadily, he sheathed his full length at a pace that had Blue bitching at him long before he slid home. He paused there, looming over the other young man, resting his hands on either side of Blue's strikingly beautiful face. Leisurely, he flexed his buttocks, shifting his shaft minutely in the tight passage, gradually stretching it.

"I didn't think I could love you more than I already did," Blue panted. "Don't laugh, but I feel so full of love right now that I might burst."

"I don't mind getting Blue all over me," Heydn said. "That's what showers are for."

"Can I...try something?"

"Please do."

"Just let me..." Blue looked down his body at the place where Heydn entered him and it was a moment before he continued. "I need your help," he said. "If you'll hold me up for a second?"

Heydn rose to a kneeling position, wrapped his hands around Blue's waist and lifted. Blue pressed one palm and the soles of his feet against the mattress and arched his back. A bit awkwardly, with his hurt arm lying across his chest, he began to rock on the last three inches of Heydn's hard shaft. Heydn urged him on with vulgar endearments, moving his left knee forward, tilting his pelvis to enter Blue at a new angle. His hand spidered across Blue's taut belly to take hold of Blue's lolling cock. Blue made a table of his body, the blunt tip of Heydn's arousal bumping his prostate with devastating effect. Heydn clenched his jaw, resisting the impulse to thrust as he pumped Blue's dick to a faster rhythm.

"Come on, lover," Heydn whispered fiercely. "Cum for me."

Two mores strokes of Heydn's hand, a pair of passes over Blue's trigger, and they both went off in the kind of fireworks-from-head-to-groin climax that leaves the body drained and yet full, needing for nothing while the afterglow lasts. They lay stuck together in their own humid atmosphere as the embers cooled. Not until Heydn softened and the drying cum on Blue's skin began to itch did either move. They separated briefly, settling back against the pillows, and then Blue took Heydn's hand and brought it to his chest.

"That was outstanding," Blue murmured.

Heydn kissed Blue's shoulder. "Then we'll have to do it again sometime."

Blue laughed softly. "I'm glad I opened the door when you knocked last summer, even if I didn't want to let you in."

"I'm awful glad you did."

"That makes two of us."

"Sure does," Heydn said, putting his head down on Blue's chest.

Blue clasped his hands over Heydn's heart and they drifted into dreams together.

CHAPTER 21

AT a shout from above, the members of the Drama Club looked up as one. Their upturned faces were the perfect target for Peyton's ammunition. With a gleeful laugh, he filled the air with shimmering color, dumping an avalanche of confetti and balloons on his colleagues. Laughter and good-natured threats rose from the inundated players and crew as Peyton was lowered to the stage on a rope. He landed lightly, shook his foot free of the loop, and took a bow in the center of the rainbow debris.

"My friends," he said expansively. "It's been quite a year." Peyton had to wait for the noise to die down before he continued. "Acton-Pierce Academy has seen quite a bit of drama this year, but we live for drama, right?" The ceiling of the old theater echoed with whistles and cheers of avid agreement. Peyton held up his hand and the small crowd obeyed their director by quieting instantly. "I'm glad I got the chance to work with all of you," he said. "Each one of you brought something special to the group that made this season the best this school has ever seen. This isn't like me, but I'd like to thank you all."

There was a brief moment of silence when everyone thought Peyton would continue and then applause broke out. Peyton took another bow and urged his cast, crew, and their guests to get back to partying. Susannah Morton Crane Scribner Valacci hugged her son, beaming proudly, her smile as bright as the many gems she wore. Peyton affected to be mortified, but his friends could see how pleased he was that his mother had made the effort to attend what he referred to as The Final Shindig. Only when Susannah went to join the other parents at the refreshment table did Peyton look around for Blue.

Blue nearly spilled his drink when Peyton grabbed him from behind in a bear hug. Heydn took the plastic cup from Blue's hand and took a step back as Peyton expressed his joy and affection. When Blue was released, he looked a little dazed and a lot disheveled. Heydn made a disapproving noise as he finger-combed Blue's hair and straightened his collar and tie.

"Now look what you've done, Crane. You've smudged the Blue."

Peyton smiled amiably at Heydn. "What are you going to do about it, stud?"

"Borrow your mirror?"

"Just don't crack it."

"You're the crack head." Heydn shot back, pretending to misunderstand.

"What's that, sonny? You want to give me crack head?" Peyton cupped a hand around his ear as if hard of hearing.

Heydn turned to Blue. "I give up. He's too quick for me."

"Sure he is, Deadeye." Blue took his drink back and toasted Peyton. "To a great director," he said.

"Thanks," Peyton said, without a trace of sarcasm. "Did you see my mom? I thought I was going to die."

"She's just proud of you," Heydn said. "I wish my mom was here to embarrass me. However, when she does come home, she'll be bringing an entire suitcase filled with manga books and DVDs. Since Blue won't take my money, I'm gonna repay him for my bail with anime."

"Nice," Peyton said, trying hard to sound like he meant it.

Blue chuckled. "I know you don't get the appeal, Peyn, but thanks for faking it."

"I'm an actor; it's what I do."

"Still planning on heading for Hollywood after graduation?"

Peyton did a broad double take. "Oh...my...God! If I'm at the Shindig that means...graduation is in three days!"

"Hence the timeliness of my question."

"I don't know." Peyton shrugged. "New York is looking very attractive to me right now. I'm an East Coast guy; maybe I should stay here and, you know, do theater instead of film."

"Who is he?" Blue asked.

"He who?" Peyton returned.

"The hottie who lives in New York."

"Oh, him. I'm afraid I can't divulge that name." Peyton paused. "All right, I'll tell you. Just stop badgering me, please."

"Go on," Heydn sighed. "You're clearly dyin' to tell us."

Peyton leaned toward the other two young men. "Alan, I mean, Mr. McIntyre, thinks that *Menagerie* is good enough for off-Broadway. He's tinkering with it to make it more universal, as he puts it, and we're changing the title, of course. He believes in it so much that he's going to take a sublet in the Village with some friends of his and shop the play around to some friends of theirs."

"And you're going with him," Blue said.

"Peyton, you dog," Heydn said. "I had no idea."

"Are you kidding?" Blue said. "I saw this coming months ago. I told you."

"Did you? I must not have been listening."

Blue punched Heydn before returning his attention to Peyton. "You're not being...inappropriate, are you?"

"I'm offended by the question."

Blue fixed his dark gaze on his friend and waited.

"Oh, all right," Peyton said. "We might have kissed a couple of times."

"Peyton! Don't you know how much trouble you could cause for him?"

"I'm eighteen, and besides, we haven't done anything yet. No touching below the waist."

"If you've kissed, you've done something."

Peyton's smirk evaporated. "Yeah, you're right."

"But graduation's in three days," Heydn reminded him.

"That's right. Then I can be as inappropriate as I want."

"It won't be inappropriate after graduation," Blue said.

"You take all the fun out of everything," Peyton complained. "But I'll miss you when we all go our separate ways."

"We'll be getting back together for Logan's trial," Heydn said. "Unless his lawyer bargains."

"But that would surely be seen as an admission of guilt, honey child," Peyton said in a florid Southern accent.

"I still say they'll send him to a cushy rehab center," Blue said.

Heydn sighed. "You're probably right, Cookie, but at least we faced up to him."

Peyton nodded. "Getting that kind of prejudice out in the open is the first step to ending it. Once most people see how ugly it is, they'll turn against the bigots."

Blue scrutinized Peyton. "Those don't sound like your words."

"Well, Alan, I mean, Mr. McIntyre, is a closet activist."

"You're kidding," Blue deadpanned.

Peyton smiled. "I know you're shocked that I could give up my dream of the glitz and glamor of Hollywood, but being famously famous and envied the world over isn't as important as it used to be. I'm more interested now in smashing some conventions that perpetuate the mistreatment of minorities."

"Boy howdy," Hedyn said. "He sure does talk fancy, don't he, Blue?"

"Yeah. I don't always know what he's saying, but I usually like the sound of it."

"Mom's waving me over," Peyton said. "Shit! She's talking to Alan!"

"You mean Mr. McIntyre," Heydn said.

"I cordially invite you to bite me," Peyton said as he walked away.

Blue laughed and then sobered again as a thought struck him. "I wish Rolly was here," he said.

"Poor guy," Heydn sympathized.

"You're kidding, right? I don't envy him the convalescence, but the idea of being home-schooled sounds like heaven to me."

"Well, there are always correspondence courses and—hi, Astor."

Astor dropped his inhaler in the pocket of his jacket as Blue turned toward him. "Hi, Heydn. Blue."

"Astor," Blue said warmly. "I'm glad you came to the party."

Astor shrugged. "Peyton sent a personal invitation."

"You've been missed."

"I have?"

"Of course. You're a great actor. Any of the plays we did after you left would have been better with you in them."

"I see. The Drama Club missed me."

"We all missed you," Heydn spoke up.

"Yeah, I'm sure."

"So am I." Heydn held out his hand. "I haven't had a chance to tell you, but what you did took real guts, man. You're a stand-up guy in my book."

Blue nodded. "If you hadn't taken Logan on, he would've thrown Peyton off that roof."

"Instead, I managed to throw myself off."

"Come on," Heydn said. "Own it, Aldrich. You kicked Logan Newcombe's ass and you saved Peyton's into the bargain. You did good."

Moving stiffly in his back brace, Astor gingerly took Heydn's hand. "Thanks." He glanced at Blue. "I see the two of you together and I know any chance I had is gone. I hope I don't have to elaborate, this being a party and all, but I'd like to say...bottom line: I just want you to be happy, Blue."

"I'm happy." Blue put his hand over Astor and Heydn's. "But thanks for saying that. It means a lot to me."

"I learned how to be gracious from my mom. Maybe if I had more of my dad's backbone, we'd still be together. Anyway, I'll never forget you. You made me feel like the world wasn't such a bad place after all."

"It's not," Blue said. "Unless we make it bad."

"I suppose. All I know is that my dad is thrilled that I'm majoring in engineering and mom is in seventh heaven over the promise ring I gave Cecelia. I've made my parents happy and proud. That's not so bad, is it?"

"No," Heydn answered. "But you deserve some happy too."

"Right now, I'm concentrating on the rehab for the back surgery. The rest of it is happening almost by itself, just falling into place like clockwork. Once my mom and Cece got together, it was out of my hands. With any luck, I can use the back injury as a get-out-of-sex card. I should thank Logan."

"That's a terrible thing to say," Blue told him.

"It's just a joke. Listen, I'm taking off in the morning to go to Cece's graduation, and I won't be back until ours, so try not to burn the place down while I'm gone."

"No guarantees," Blue said.

"You stole my line," Heydn complained.

"You're lucky," Astor said. "He stole my heart. See you in a couple of days."

Heydn and Blue said goodbye and Astor waded across the floor rubbing elbows with the crowd, but none of the joy stuck to him. As he disappeared from view, Rhodes Vaughn and his dance partner gravitated over to Heydn and Blue.

"Hello, lovebirds," Rhodes said. "You're not worthy, but I'm going to introduce you to my girl anyway. Brooke Barclay and Heydn Case, I have the honor of presenting Miss Elizabeth Claire Brandeis."

"Hi, I'm Betsy," said the petite brunette girl. "I've wanted to meet you since Rhodes first started talking about you." She leaned forward and confided charmingly to Blue. "I've always wanted to be called Rosie. I use it as my pen name and I'm ramblinrosie on the 'Net."

"Betsy's impressed that you chose a name and made it stick," Rhodes told Blue.

"It's surprisingly easy when no one talks to you anyway," Blue said.

Betsy giggled. "Sorry to interview you, but where are you going to college?"

"I've been enrolled at Harvard since before I was born, but I'm not sure I'm going."

Heydn shrugged. "I'm living dangerously; playing it by ear."

"Go ahead," Rhodes said to Betsy. "They won't be offended."

"I'm putting together a group," Betsy told the other two young men. "I should have started by saying that I'm an aspiring set designer, but the group would be a workshop where creative types could get together and sharpen themselves on each other, if that makes sense."

"I'm in, obviously," Rhodes said. "What Bets would really like is…"

"What I'd really like," Betsy took over, "is to establish an artists' colony, but that's a dream, of course."

"I like it," Heydn said.

"Me too," Blue said. "I'd love to live in a community like that."

"There you are, Bets," Rhodes said. "Two more citizens for Fantasy Island."

"I asked you to stop calling it that. It's not funny to me."

"Sorry. What should we call it?"

"You think all my ideas are too girly."

Heydn laughed. "What does he expect? You're a girl. Sometimes I wonder about Rhodes."

"What would you call the colony?" Betsy asked him as Rhodes and Blue groaned.

Heydn threw them a look of wounded reproach. "Have a little faith. You act like I'm goin' to suggest somethin' vulgar or childish."

"Only because we know you," Rhodes said.

"Hey, I'm not a penis-brained jerk twenty-four hours a day. I have to sleep sometime, you know."

"Okay, what's your idea then?"

"Well, I know it's overused, but I like the name Pegasus and what it represents."

"I love it!" Betsy said. "To keep it from being cliché, we can call it Pterippus."

"Huh?"

"It's the generic name for winged horses," Blue said. "Good call, Betsy."

"See, we're already working great together," she answered. "I'm serious about this and Rhodes is impressed with both of you."

"I'm touched," Heydn said.

"Where will the colony be?" Blue asked.

"Ideally, it would be itinerant," Betsy said. "Different parts of the country have a different feel, you know? Mountains affect your creativity in a different way from the beach."

Blue nodded. "The seasons have completely different energies," he said.

"Yes! We'd have to hold our workshops at different times of the year," Betsy said. "I'm really starting to feel like this could happen."

"I'll host the first one," Blue said. "At the end of summer. I own a big-ass house on Lake Huron, complete with cottages and servants' quarters. This will be a good reason to open it up. There's a town nearby that doesn't allow any motorized traffic within city limits; at least it didn't when I was five. And when autumn comes the trees are so beautiful."

"That sounds perfect," Betsy said.

"Great. Now let's go talk to Peyton," Rhodes said.

"Just a minute." Betsy smiled at Blue and Heydn. "I hope you don't mind, but Rhodes told me that you two are a couple, openly. I thought you were awesome before I even met you, but now I think you're…"

"Fabulous?" Heydn suggested and Blue punched him again. "Ow!"

"E-mail me at blue at bluesmeanies dot com," Blue told Betsy. "We can set up the Pterippus in cyberspace while the house is being aired out. I'm totally serious."

"Oh. Well, if you're *totally* serious, I'll come, too," Heydn said.

Blue gave him a strange look. "You'll be there already."

"I will? Oh, yeah. Of course, I will."

"I'm so excited," Betsy said. "I'll talk to you soon."

"Harvard, huh?" Heydn said, as Betsy and Rhodes left to talk to Peyton.

"Forget Harvard. Unless you want to go."

"I'd love to go to Harvard, but it's a little out of my league. I'm more bush than ivy."

"Heydn."

"What is it, Cookie?"

"I'm serious. If you want to go to Harvard, we'll go."

"I can't let you pay for my education."

"Why not?"

"I don't know. I just…"

"Look, buckaroo, I'm not letting you out of my sight again. Wherever we go, we go together."

"I wouldn't have it any other way." Heydn put an arm around Blue's waist and whisked him behind a piece of scenery. "I love you, Blue," he said.

"I love you too." Blue pulled Heydn closer and brought their lips together. He felt the spark of the same sweet fire that had melted him the first time he'd kissed Heydn. Now it was attended by the glow of embers that Blue was certain would burn for all time.

Heydn returned the kiss with equal ardor and relinquished Blue's lips with great reluctance. "You are spared for now, my beauty," he growled. "But when this feast has ended, you will be mine."

"Yes, I will," Blue answered.

EPILOGUE

"WILL you please put down the damned joystick and get dressed?" Blue Barclay, half of the design team of Hey Blue Hippogriff, put his hands on his slim hips and regarded the other half.

Heydn Case didn't look away from the screen until the eerily realistic swordsman he controlled cut the last head off the guardian of the necromancer's tomb. "Yes!" he exulted, bouncing out of his custom-built captain's chair with built-in speakers among its other conveniences. "This rocks immensely."

"That's what you were mumbling when you finally dozed off around four this morning."

"No it wasn't." Heydn stopped in front of Blue. "The last thing I remember saying was something along the lines of 'oh God, Blue, oh, God, that feels so good, oh, oh, oh, I'm cumming, snore.'"

Blue chuckled, putting his palms against Heydn's bare chest over the heart with wings tattooed there. Heydn put his arms around Blue and rested his hands on the tattoo's mate just above the declivity of Blue's butt cheeks.

"I stand corrected," Blue said. "And it is a brilliant game, isn't it? The graphics are just as good as the movie. I realize we did the special effects for the movie, but still…"

"We're both good designers on our own, but when we work together…critical mass achieved!"

"Just like the sex."

"I can't help noticin' that you aren't dressed either," Heydn told his naked lover.

"Your grasp of the obvious never ceases to astound me."

"What about my grasp of this?" Heyden squeezed Blue's ass.

"Still gets me hotter than summer on Mercury in about zero point zero seconds. However…"

Heydn groaned as he pressed his crotch against Blue's. "That's about how quick I'll be. Just touch me once."

"No. We're already going to be late."

"Like it matters. No one's going to send us to bed without supper if we get there a little late."

"Aren't you looking forward to this as much as I am? We haven't seen most of them in a year."

"I guess. It's kind a different for me, Blue. As long as I have you, the rest of it is…not inconsequential, but…I could do without it if I had to, you know?"

"I feel the same, but I love our friends and I miss them. And since the Pterippus is at Peyton's this time, we have to fly."

Heydn rubbed his nose against Blue's and kissed his forehead. "I'll get dressed," he said. "What am I wearing?"

"It's on the bed, as always."

"Thanks, as always."

Blue watched Heydn pad away, admiring the sculpted muscles rippling under smooth tanned skin. "I'll be right there," he called and went to get his phone from the kitchen counter. The acid green cell phone was on the oak butcher block where he'd left it when Heydn got home last night. As he picked it up, he smiled at the photo displayed on the tiny screen: a high-resolution shot of Heydn's arousal with the Blue Heaven tattoo prominently featured. He went immediately to the computer to move the pictures to his private photo file and opened his mail while he waited. Typing a quick message, he clicked send, picked up his phone, and went to the bedroom.

Heydn was nearly dressed in the wide-wale wheat-colored corduroy trousers and a chocolate brown long sleeved silk T-shirt Blue had chosen. He looked up from pulling his boots on and saw Blue in the doorway. "Thought we were in a huge-ass hurry," he said.

"Just finish getting dressed. You look good, by the way." Blue quickly donned a pair of black slim-cut trousers and a white linen shirt with French cuffs. He put on the large onyx cuff links Heydn had given him a couple of birthdays ago and tied a bright red scarf around his neck. "Done," he said, turning to see Heydn watching him.

"You look like a movie star," Heydn said. "Or a particularly sweet vampire."

"Thank you," Blue said as he picked up his overnight bag. "Let's go. You know Andrew doesn't like to wait once he's filed a flight plan."

Heydn snatched his bag off an antique sea chest and held it up. "All set."

A short ride in the Land Rover over country roads lined with snow-frosted trees brought them to the small airport where they kept the smallest of their corporate jets. They drove into the hangar, parked, and crossed the cavernous space to the shiny Sabreliner with the bright blue hippogriff emblem on its sleek flank. Andrew glanced at his watch, nodded to his copilot, and took his seat. Blue and Heydn strapped themselves in for takeoff and the jet taxied out to the runway. They were cleared by the tower and left the earth of Vermont for California, the waters of Lake Champlain glittering behind them.

"WELCOME, my friends," Peyton said, bowing in the doorway of his Topanga Canyon mansion. "Welcome to the commencement party of the tenth season of Pterippus."

"Thanks." Blue hugged Peyton and continued through the three-story foyer to the left wing.

"Hi, stud," Peyton greeted Heydn.

"Great to see you, Peyn," Heydn said, embracing Peyton warmly. "How's show biz?"

"Did you see *Orders of March*?"

"Yeah. Blue loved it. He took a bunch of people to see it when it played Burlington."

"What did you think?" Peyton asked, as he escorted Heydn to the back of the house.

"I liked it."

Peyton held open the door to the long enclosed back porch and the smell of chlorine teased Heydn's nostrils. "What did you like about it?" he said, over the sounds of splashing, laughter, and bright music.

"Well, the fantasy element appealed to me, but…" Heydn paused as he waved to Rollins Morehouse. "But honestly, I thought the message was a little heavy-handed."

"It probably was for you, but I think some people need things spelled out, and I wouldn't want to shortchange them."

"Since when, you big snob?"

"Whoa, watch it," Peyton said as Betsy and Rhodes' two children charged past on their way to the pool.

"Damn," Hcydn said. "Azure and Orlando are growing fast!"

"Well, they are eight and nine this year."

"Kinda makes you want a rug rat, doesn't it?"

"Ew." Peyton grimaced. "Absolutely not. These two are adorable, naturally, but a few hours with them are all I can manage."

Heydn laughed. "I remember the year Betsy asked if you wouldn't mind babysitting and you said of course you wouldn't if she didn't mind coming home to find all of you sedated. I nearly pissed my pants. Remember?"

"Well, I do have a reputation to maintain as a master of quips and dampener of pants. What would you like to drink?"

Heydn spotted Blue sitting on the side of the pool with his feet in the water talking to Betsy Brandeis-Vaughn. "Let's start with beer. What's your current boutique brew of choice?"

Peyton lifted the lid on the large cooler and the light came on, sparkling on an array of bottled beers. "Take your pick," he said. "Rolly's good about reminding me that people like a choice."

"So… are you two… you know?"

"Are we going steady?" Peyton rolled his eyes. "What grade are you in? But the answer is yes, as you already knew, because I e-mailed Blue about it months ago."

"Just makin' small talk, dude."

"Don't dude me. I have directed three films and starred in countless others as an openly gay man and I'm only twenty-seven years old."

"Countless others?"

"I did a lot of movies in a short period of time. Oh, why am I bothering?" Peyton opened Heydn's beer for him. "Here. How's that taste? Pretty crisp, right? Yeah it is. Anyway, I'm getting out of the industry soon. Rolly's convinced me that I can make more progress in politics."

"For what it's worth, I'd vote for you."

"I'll count on that…if we ever live in the same state."

"I meant for President."

"Oh…. Okay, that's cool."

"What's cool?" Blue said, leaning against Heydn's back. "Hey, cocktails! I want one."

"The usual?" Peyton asked, not even waiting for Blue's nod before he got out the cranberry juice.

"Peyton's going into politics," Heydn said.

Blue thought about that for a minute. "It could work," he said at last.

Peyton handed Blue his Cosmopolitan. "Wow, curb your enthusiasm, babe," he said.

"I'm just feeling sorry for the movie industry," Blue said, taking a sip of his drink. "Yummy."

"I'm sure Hollywood will manage without me, and you know I've always had an interest in civil rights."

"An interest," Blue exchanged a look with Heydn. "That's what he calls it?"

"It's time," Peyton said. "I've been basically drifting for the seven years since I broke up with Alan and it's time I got hold of the reins again."

"You call your brilliant film career drifting?" Blue said.

"More or less. The movies were something I allowed to happen, if that makes sense to you. I'm not saying I didn't work hard, but in a way, making movies was easy for me. Fighting for the rights of minorities will be more of a challenge, I think."

"And that's what you want?" Heydn said.

"Yeah. I'm not sure I'm equal to it, but I'm going to give it a shot. Maybe my relationship with Alan didn't last, but his ideas sure stuck with me. You had an influence, too. Do you remember telling me that all I really needed to do was be true to myself?"

"I actually spouted somethin' that self-righteous?"

"Yes, you did, and I took it to heart. Eventually."

"Let us know what we can do to help with the campaign when the time comes," Blue said.

"I will; believe me. Rolly's going to be my campaign manager. After four years with the senior statesman from Massachusetts, he feels ready."

"I'm excited for you," Blue said. "And now I'm going to take my drink and go for a swim."

"He still makes me want to put my arms around him and shield him from the world," Peyton said when Blue was out of earshot. "Even though he doesn't need a protector."

"I feel the same way. It annoys him sometimes, but mostly it amuses him."

Peyton smiled, but it faded. "Listen, I got some bad news while you were in the air. I wanted to tell you first so you could tell Blue if you want to. Astor Aldrich was found dead in the lake behind his parents' house. Apparently, he took a Windsurfer out and drowned."

"Jesus," Heydn said under his breath.

"Yeah. He was twenty-nine. Never even saw thirty, poor miserable bastard. I doubt his butterfly wife will miss him, but I feel sorry for his daughter."

Heydn nodded. "These things are always hardest on the innocent."

"Astor named her Brooke, you know. I wonder what his mom thought of that?"

"I'd say Astor had his own ways of venting his resentment at the life he chose. This is sure gonna throw some gloom over Blue's weekend."

"I can tell him, if you want."

Heydn shook his head. "I'll do it. The sooner the better." He lifted his beer bottle as he moved away. "To Astor," he said.

"Goodnight, sweet prince," Peyton said and took a drink.

Blue looked puzzled by Heydn's request, but he rose and followed the other man outside. Heydn leaned on the rail of the deck that jutted out over the canyon and took another long drink of his beer. "I have to tell you some sad news," he said.

"What?"

Heydn took a deep breath. "Astor Aldrich is dead. He drowned sometime yesterday."

"He...Astor drowned?"

"Apparently. He was found in the lake at his folks' place."

"That's...hard to believe. He's such a good swimmer. He loves that lake. He knows it like..."

"You told me," Heydn interrupted. "I'm really sorry, Cookie." He put his arms around Blue.

Blue didn't move for a few seconds, and then he returned the hug. "It's just so weird. I can't quite believe it yet."

"What was it you said about the last time you saw him?"

"He looked haunted. That was almost three years ago at the Acton alumni barbecue that you refused to attend with me. I walked in on him and Allerton King in the locker room toilet. Drunk as hell and groping each other in one of the stalls. It made me so sad."

"I know." Heydn held Blue close and held his peace about the long-ago incident with Allerton King on the beach. It wouldn't make Blue feel any better and was of little consequence after all. "Poor guy."

"I feel so sorry for his little girl."

"I know." Heydn kissed Blue's forehead. "She'll miss her daddy."

"When Cece was pregnant, Astor asked me to be godfather. I told him it would be better if he chose someone in his family."

"Nothin' wrong with that. You were as good a friend to him as he let you be. It's not your fault he couldn't let go of his obsession with you."

"I think I reminded him of someone he lost a long time ago when he was a kid. So many sad things happened to him."

"That's somethin' you had in common." Heydn raised Blue's chin on his palm. "You managed to rise above the shit that life threw at you."

"I could've given him more of my time."

"Blue, you didn't cause Astor's death. You told me yourself that he was self-destructing. I honestly think you're a saint for having lunch with him now and then."

"Or was I torturing him?"

"No. The fact that you'd even ask convinces me you meant him nothin' but good. He made a choice, Blue. You couldn't make it for him."

Blue made a frustrated noise. "I don't believe people go to hell after they die," he said. "There's enough hell right here on Earth."

"You got that right, Cookie…and you got me."

Blue tightened his arms around Heydn. "Thank you," he whispered.

"I love you," Heydn replied, as though answering a question.

"I love you, too."

"Hey, I've been savin' some good news. Maybe now is the right time to tell you."

"It couldn't hurt."

"Okay. I didn't tell you I'd been keepin' tabs on some of our old classmates because I know you live in the present and, for a Goth, you're not very big on vengeance."

"I'm not a Goth. Who have you been following?"

"Logan Newcombe, Sloan Spalding, and Copeland Graham."

"I should've guessed. Do I want to hear this?"

"I think so, but I'll save the best for last. Logan underwent extensive counseling after the judge found him unfit to stand trial. For once, it appears his dad's money didn't do him any good. Judge Persons turned out to be honest and he took a special interest in Logan's case. It didn't change Logan, except to make him meaner, but it kept him off the streets for a couple of years. He never went to college and he didn't go to work for his dad either. He appears to have been an embarrassment and was given a title at some company owned by a friend of his dad's. He lost that job and every other job his family got him. He padded expense accounts. He had a poor attendance record. He embezzled, though he has never been formally charged. He's been married three times in eight years, no children. His good buddy Allerton King never lifted a finger to help him out. In the last report I got, wife number three left him and the real estate company he started had filed for bankruptcy. He drinks too much and he takes long drives at night, getting into shouting matches with other drivers."

Blue shivered. "That's enough about him."

"Okay. Sloan Spalding turned out exactly like you'd expect. He's a corporate lawyer in his dad's firm and belongs to the country club, married a deb, two kids and a pedigreed dog in a McMansion with a staff of underpaid illegals. Movin' right along, we have Copeland Graham, dull of wit with the character of a sheep, but…his story has a happier ending. The community service that he and Sloan were sentenced to had more of an effect on Cope than it did on Skip. Copeland went ahead and got a law degree, too, but it seems he didn't quite have what it took in the corporate world. So guess what he did? He became a civil rights attorney and he specializes in cases where gay men have been victimized."

"Really?"

"Yep."

"That actually makes me feel better."

"Good. Do you want to go in and have lunch with everyone, or would you like to stay out here for a while?"

"Let's go in. We haven't even said hello to everyone yet." Blue paused at the sliding glass door. "Heydn, I understand why you wanted to know what happened to Logan Newcombe, but I don't like you keeping secrets from me. Not even the ones you think will hurt me."

"I knew you'd be mad at me if you knew. I also knew I shouldn't be doing it. Won't happen again."

"Thanks."

"Hey." Heydn put a hand on Blue's shoulder and craned his neck to kiss Blue's cheek. "It'll be all right," he said.

Blue smiled, as Heydn had hoped, and slid open the door. They went in and sat at Peyton's table, made from the door of a deconsecrated church. The heavily carved and inlaid slab of wood was covered with brightly glazed dishes that resembled various fruits and vegetables and the centerpiece was a towering palm tree sculpture made of leaf rakes and shredded rubber. Peyton sat at the head and as soon as Blue and Heydn were seated, he proposed a toast. The tribute included everyone present as well as absent friends in a roll call of some of the best in their fields, recounting triumphs and the occasional disaster in a capsule history of the floating artists' colony that had become justly famous for the output of its members. The odd term *pterippus* had become a household word and the number of applicants grew each year until a full-time staff had to be hired to help Betsy handle the requests. The Pterippi, or Trippies, as they were dubbed by less-serious reporters, were responsible for some of the most innovative examples of film, poetry, music, sculpture, and almost every other art in the past decade. As Peyton reminded the core group in attendance, they had a lot to be proud of.

Dinner began with carrot ginger gazpacho that set the tone for the dishes that followed: arugula, dried cherry and walnut salad with poppy seed dressing, lacquered salmon and crab paté, grilled eggplant and red pepper, rosemary rib roast, sweet potato sticks with cinnamon butter, honey-cheese pie with preserved strawberries, chocolate gateau with dark chocolate ganache, sliced pears and bleu cheese, each served with a wine chosen from Peyton's cellar. The mood was convivial as old friends ate, drank, and discussed the doings of their lives while they'd been apart. Congratulations, commiserations, and affectionate teasing passed back and forth with a lot of laughter and a few tears. Amid groans and protests of fullness, Peyton announced that coffee and liqueurs would be served in his small but complete theater. In no great hurry, the guests broke into groups, continuing conversations begun at the table.

Blue listened to Sig Herzog talk about his latest project, a video game based on Wagner's Ring Cycle. Sig wanted Blue's opinion on his idea for a computer-generated dragon and was happy to describe it at length. Blue gave Sig his ear, but his eyes strayed often to Heydn on the floor playing with Azure, Orlando, Annabelle, and Sarah. It was clear that he had the little ladies charmed, and nine-year-old Orlando had adopted Heydn's habit of winking broadly. The children of other members were attracted to the group and joined the game of adding a rhyme to the silly song they were making up. Sig finally noticed Blue's preoccupation and bluntly pointed it out. Blue apologized and took Sig's elbow, walking him over to Betsy and Rhodes. Briefly explaining Sig's dragon to Academy Award-winning set designer Betsy, Blue excused himself and headed toward the kitchen.

Peyton started the introduction to his short film tribute to Pterippus and it was a little while before Heydn missed Blue. When he didn't see him in the audience, he got up and left. A short search of the first floor and inquiries made of everyone he ran into yielded no clues. Heydn looked out on the deck and then went back inside to look upstairs. After checking the bedrooms and bathrooms, he opened the secret door in Peyton's walk-in closet. A set of rungs led upward and Heydn climbed to the crows' nest, seeing Blue's feet before he emerged through the floor of the tiny widow's walk. Blue smiled over his shoulder and went back to gazing out over the spectacular view. The breeze was raw up here and carried the tang of salt from the ocean. Maybe that's why Blue's eyes were watering.

"You wanna be alone?"

"Never." Blue's voice sounded strained.

Heydn put an arm around his lover's shoulders. "I'm not going anywhere."

"I was watching you with the kids."

"They're great, aren't they?"

"Yeah. So much energy in those little bodies. It's a wonder they don't self-combust."

"That's quite a mental image."

Blue rested his cheek on Heydn's shoulder and slipped an arm around his trim waist. "You know what I mean." He paused. "Do you want children?"

"I thought we decided a while back that neither one of us was dad material and that the obstacles were many and forbidding."

"That was a while back. What do you want now?"

"Do I have to decide right now?"

"Of course not. I just want a gut reaction."

"Okay then. I'd like a kid someday; just not today. Maybe after our friends' kids grow up."

"Good enough. I know that adopting, or hiring a surrogate, won't be easy, but I don't want you to miss out on being a father, if that's what you want."

"It's about what *we* want, not what I want."

"I know you mean that, but I don't want us to end up in some absurd version of *Gift of the Magi* where we each make sacrifices and inadvertently deprive each other of what we want most."

"I have what I want most." Heydn squeezed Blue. "The rest is gravy."

Blue smiled. "I like to think of it as icing."

"That's because you're my Sugar Cookie."

Blue turned so that he and Heydn were face to face. Demurely, he lowered his eyes, long lashes brushing his cheekbones. "You find me sweet, my lord?"

"Aye," Heydn growled. "And I shall taste your sweetness ere long." Sliding an arm down to the small of Blue's back, Heydn dipped him and swooped on his mouth. Blue braced his right foot against the rail on the opposite side of the tiny turret and responded eagerly to the passionate kiss. Heydn pressed his lover against the rail behind Blue's back and worked a hand between their bodies.

"You go too far, barbarian!" Blue gasped as Heydn fondled his rising shaft.

"Goddess help me!" Peyton exclaimed as his head appeared through the hatch. "Are you two still playing that lame Barbarian and the Slave Boy game?"

"Yes, yes we are," Heydn said. "Or we were, until you interrupted."

"The film is starting."

"You came all the way up here to tell us that?"

"Well, I beg your pardon," Peyton started back down. "I thought you'd like to be included, that's all. Forgive me for intruding in my own house."

Blue laughed and Peyton looked up at him from the bottom of the ladder, gladdened by the sound of his friend's laughter. "Come on," Peyton said. "You can canoodle later."

"Hollywood has ruined your vocabulary," Blue said, as he started down. "Canoodle? Really? I don't believe I've ever canoodled and it doesn't sound like something I'd like to try."

"What an accomplished liar you've become," Peyton replied. "You should've stuck with acting."

Blue shook his head as he watched Heydn descend. "Two experiences with the film-making machinery in front of the camera were enough for me. It's much more fun making pixel monsters and heroes."

"Well, it seems to suit the both of you and Heydn still has an excellent bubble butt."

Heydn stuck his ass out before he stepped off the ladder. "It's what's kept us together," he said. "Blue just can't get enough of that bubble stuff."

"It's true," Blue shrugged. "I'm his sexual slave."

"Yeah, I can see how you're suffering by that cloying aura of lovey-doveyness that surrounds you. And I'm jealous as hell, of course."

"I don't know," Heydn said. "I think I see a little light in your eyes when you and Rolly connect across the room."

Blue gave Peyton a hug. "Me too."

"I don't want to jinx it by hoping too hard, but I feel the same way." Peyton led the way back down the stairs. "Rolly's so different now. He takes charge, you know?"

Heydn raised an eyebrow as he glanced at Blue.

"Oh, stop it," Peyton said without looking over his shoulder. "Come and watch my tribute and try to be decent in public, will you? Just because the lights are off doesn't mean you're obligated to canoodle."

"Good one," Heydn smirked as they joined the rest of the group.

Blue groaned. "Great. Now I'm going to have to hear this ridiculous word in all its permutations."

"You love it when Heydn teases you." Peyton kissed Blue's cheek and went to the projector.

Heydn found a seat and patted his knee.

"You don't think I'm going to sit on your lap, do you?"

"Please?"

Blue settled himself across Heydn's thighs with an arm around Heydn's neck. Heydn supported Blue's back with one arm and draped the other across Blue's legs. Despite Blue's protest, he was happy to sit so close to Heydn and he didn't feel self-conscious about it among his friends. He snuggled in and Heydn automatically held him a little tighter, turning his head to kiss Blue just below the jawline as the lights dimmed. Caught in the spell of Peyton's talent and the fellowship of the group, Blue and Heydn felt a resurgence, a reaffirmation of the love that had never faltered in ten years together.

"Thanks for taking me back," Heydn whispered in Blue's ear.

"Thanks for never making me regret it." Blue's eyes glimmered in the scant light as he turned to look at Heydn.

"Want to make it official and legally binding?"

"You're such a romantic."

"Shhhhhhh," Peyton shushed them.

Blue stifled a snicker. "Okay," he said, his breath warm on Heydn's ear.

"You're not shittin' me?" Heydn said loudly.

"Come on!" Peyton yelled.

"Sorry, but I think Blue just accepted my long-standing proposal to make him an honest man."

"I did," Blue managed to say before Heydn swept him into his arms.

To the applause and cheers of their friends, Heydn and Blue made a vow with their kiss. It was the same promise they made to each other each time they kissed, but this time, it included the people they loved most in the world. When their lips finally parted, little Annabelle informed Blue that he should stop kissing Heydn because she was going to marry him. Her pout became more pronounced when the grown-ups laughed. Heydn picked her up and gave her a kiss and a wink before her mommy took her to the kitchen for the instantly accepted husband substitute of chocolate ice cream. Glasses were filled, toasts were made, and Blue and Heydn basked in the golden nimbus of camaraderie.

And when the evening drew to a close, they pledged their love with their bodies once more and fell asleep in a joyous tangle. The moon shone in their window, a silver sentinel keeping watch through the night, reviewing an army of stars, until the sun returned to duty with the dawn.

Life was good, and there was still so much of it left to be lived.

Connie Bailey

I was born on an Air Force base and I've been in flight ever since. My father took the family with him wherever he was stationed; Spain, Morocco, Turkey, and Alaska were among his postings. While studying commercial arts, I married a musician who turned out to be a pilot in disguise. Having no burning ambition of my own at the time, I devoted myself to his dream. His job as aircraft designer and competition pilot has taken us all over the world. I have now set foot on almost every continent (a personal life ambition), but I don't hold out much hope for Antarctica anymore.

I have always loved to read. Since I was four, reading has been my favorite diversion and books my best friends. A few years ago, with my husband's support, I set out to become a writer. I wrote every day and posted what I wrote at various Internet groups and later on LiveJournal. I cannot recommend this school of writing highly enough. The candid feedback I received was invaluable to my development. I kept working at it, and one day I received the most exciting e-mail ever. A publisher wanted to talk to me.

That's pretty much it so far. There are a few fun facts like: my only child is a rescued Greyhound named Lizard, I live at a small grass airfield with a hang gliding school, I have what's commonly referred to as a "photographic memory", I collect words as a hobby, and my only nickname is "The Judge".

www.ingramcontent.com/pod-product-compliance
Lightning Source LLC
Chambersburg PA
CBHW051628260626
47170CB00004B/1087